KUDOS for *Stranger on the Tonto*

Stranger on the Tonto by Ramona Forrest is an historical romance with a twist. It is about a young woman in 1893 Arizona, left on her own to not only run, but fight for, her ranch. Dealing with having her cattle rustled and her father murdered, our heroine Cherry doesn't know who she can trust...I thoroughly enjoyed the story. There are plenty of twists and turns in the plot and Forrest's characters are totally believable. She really seems to know her Arizona history. The book is definitely worth taking the time to read. – *Taylor, reviewer*

The story was filled with details that made me feel as if I were experiencing some of the scenes firsthand. For example, when Cherry's father is murdered, Cherry finds him in the barn, bleeding to death. She gets help to carry him into the house and sends someone for the doctor. Of course, the closest doctor is in the village miles away, and Cherry knows, even as she sends for him, that there is no way he will get there in time. Even if he is not out on a call, by the time the rider gets to town and locates him and then they ride back to the ranch, it will be several hours. Not that there is much that could be done for gunshot wounds in those days anyway. – *Regan, reviewer*

It had seemed like such a good idea last night, but in the cold light of morning, she was horrified by what she'd done.

Cherry opened her eyes and looked about at the rustic interior of the shack, trying to remember where she was. When she turned her head and saw John lying on his side, looking her in the eye, she gasped, "Oh God! I remember it all!" Thinking of all that had happened between them during the stormy night shook her with guilt and shame. Yet, her body retained the soft fulfilling glow of all the things she had known in this man's arms. It took her some time to set things in focus, but she did at last.

Her cheeks burned with the heat of a furious blush as she tried to turn away from that smiling face and the heated memories of what they had done in the dark of night. She struggled against the wiry encircling arm that held her. "How did this happen?"

"We were caught out in the rain, if you remember." She saw him trying not to grin. "You were kind enough to help me stay warm last night, my dearest Cherry—I truly believe you saved my life."

"How well I remember. And I'm not your dearest anything! I believe you took advantage of me when I was terrified of the lightning and at my very weakest." She tried to move from under his arm, but the bed was so narrow she had no place to go.

"There's nothing weak about you, my dear, I'll have to say that."

"Would you please get out of this bed?" She realized how ridiculous her situation was and that it was far too late to save any vestige of virtue. She faced up to it, as the edges of fear seeped into her mind. *What have I done?*

STRANGER ON THE TONTO

by

Ramona Forrest

A BLACK OPAL BOOKS PUBLICATION

Acknowledgements

I wish to thank Mark A. Forrest for contributing his knowledge of mining and minerals to this work, and forever and always my gratitude goes out to my author friend, Pinkie Paranya, for her constant help in my writing career.

CHAPTER 1

Cherry Bender, her face tight with anger, rode at break-neck speed into the ranch yard, looking for her father. She flung herself off Checky, her foam speckled Appaloosa, tossed the reins over the hitching rail, and turned away to search for her father, the tears nearly blinding her. *I've got to let Dad know about this latest and most disgusting loss of livestock.*

The fringes of her doeskin split riding skirt, lashed against the tops of her trail-worn boots as she ran to each of the outbuildings that ringed the expanse between the house and the corrals. Finding none of those areas occupied, she threw out her hands in frustration.

Their ranch had suffered frequent acts of vandalism and cattle theft, over the past two years, but what she'd found out there today had been more than sickening. She wanted to cry but had no time for it. She glanced frantically about, but saw no one, not even the Mexican boy, Manny. Scratching her head in puzzlement, she wondered where everyone had gone to. The ranch yard, usually such a busy area, seemed unnaturally silent and desolate for this time of the day, almost ghostly, in fact.

Cherry looked about the familiar place, seeing how softly the late afternoon sun gleamed off the rust-colored tile roofing of the house and the way the leaves of the gnarled old oak tree shook and trembled in the soft breeze. Over the years that tree had grown and spread its protecting branches over the house. She dearly loved the comforting look of it. Such small things, normal and usual to her, offered little comfort to her after the grisly things she'd just seen.

Over the past two years, their ranch had suffered numerous acts of evil intent. It had happened repeatedly and today, she'd discovered the heartbreaking sight of two mother cows missing. Their two very young calves lay dead—shot and left to rot in the sun.

Tears filled her eyes at the sickening waste of life and her stomach churned. The heat of anger burned her cheeks while her mind asked the questions. *Why those? Why not a decent beef animal, for heaven's sake? Was it really rustlers?* Her father had questioned that more than once. But it was 1893, and he'd said rustling was a thing of the past in Arizona. But Cherry, a twenty year old rancher's daughter, had her doubts. She couldn't see it that way anymore, not on the Bender Ranch.

She left the yard and ran into the ranch house to find Margarita, their Mexican cook and housekeeper, standing white-faced in the kitchen, wringing her hands. At the sight of her ashen face, Cherry asked the woman. "What's happened around here? You look scared to death."

"*Senorita*, I hear gun shooting outside." Her face, though browned, was ashen-hued, her eyes were wide with terror as she clutched and twisted her apron into knots. Her hands clenched and unclenched as she uttered in a trembling voice, "I much afraid, *senorita*! I think something go bad out there."

Manny, a young boy of twelve, hurried from a back room to stand beside Margarita and grab her hand. Cherry noticed his sun-browned face had whitened, and he bore the same wide-eyed look of alarm as Margarita. Manny did odd chores and helped out on the ranch. He was alone in the world, and the ranch had become his home.

"I need to find my father," Cherry said. "Have either of you seen him lately?"

"Not since we eat this morning, missy. We look for you when we hear man yelling out there, loud noise—hear shooting." Her eyes brimmed with tears and Manny stood beside Margarita, sweating and fearful. He stroked her hand in his boyish attempt to calm her.

"I need to find him—must be out there somewhere." She turned and left them standing there. She returned to the yard, searching the outbuildings, and calling his name. Passing near the open barn door, she caught the faint sounds of garbled moaning. The ghastly sounds of distress emanated eerily from somewhere in the dimness of the horse stalls.

Her heart hammering frantically, Cherry listened carefully as she moved quickly towards the sounds that meant trouble for someone—sounds that didn't belong here. She knew the barn should be empty right now. It always stood unused in the warmer months, unless newborn calves or injured animals required housing for extra care.

She entered the familiar barn and looked upward. Shimmering bits of sunlight shafted through upper open areas. Visible dust motes floated gently about. At any other time, she would have thought it a magical sight, but in searching for her father, she ignored that mundane bit of normalcy.

Her horse had a stall in the barn, but the sturdy little Appaloosa gelding stood tied at the hitching rail, sweating, blowing from her mad ride, and switching flies off his nicely spotted rump.

Approaching Checky's empty stall, the sounds grew louder. Icy apprehension shot through her as she cautiously approached the moaning sounds. Reaching the source of the noise, she felt shock waves run through her at the sight of the poor soul laying there, sprawled on his back amidst scattered straw and half-dried horse dung.

Instantly, in spite of the man's swollen, bloodied face, she knew she'd found her father. She'd seen that familiar old shirt many times, and his well-used old boots only hours ago, and right now, those things were all she could identify, along with the familiar long, gaunt form lying in the soiled bedding, bleeding, limp, and helpless.

Falling on her knees at his side, she cried out, "Daddy—Dad! What happened—who did this to you?" Tugging at his flaccid form, she tried to arouse him. His arms moved a little when she pulled at him and he made a soft moan, but did not open his battered and swollen eyes.

His head, discolored and misshapen, was barely recognizable in the dimness of the stall.

Desperate to help him, she glanced frantically about, deciding what to do first. Then, looking downward, she gulped for air and clenched her jaw, seeing the bright red blood oozing into the fabric of his frayed old shirt. Horrified, she watched it creep slowly, insidiously, soaking the garment across his chest, and on down into the soiled straw beneath.

She pulled the shirt apart to find a round bluish hole. "Oh Dad, you've been shot!" Though she was young, she was a rancher's daughter and recognized a bullet wound when she saw one. Sick with fear for him, she balled up what she could reach of his shirt, pressing it into the wound. "My God, Dad, you're bleeding to death!"

She tugged gently to arouse him, but he made no sound and his battered eyes remained closed. Her efforts made him moan once again, but he did not awaken until a short time later, when he moved his head a bit. He opened his eyelids enough that she could see part of his eyes through the bloodied slits.

"Cherry?" He mumbled her name through swollen lips and tried to raise himself, but unable, fell back into the stained straw bedding beneath. His lips opened, and he tried to speak. His weakened voice uttered a few garbled words, "What's going on here—Link?"

It seemed to her that he didn't really see who was at his side, but had only responded to her voice. "Dad, what are you trying to say? Tell me, please." Worried he was delirious or confused from the blows to his head and face, she nearly screamed when his head rolled back and he responded no further.

Knowing she had to find help for him, she pulled his shirt closed, leaped up and ran out of the barn, calling out, "Help, Manny—Margarita—Dad's been shot!" Her words echoed against the emptiness of the open spaces of the ranch yard. The boy must have stayed in the house with Margarita.

Her jaw clenched tight in anger at her own sense of helplessness and the savage treatment of her father. "I've got to get some help here." Desperation gave her strength, and fear for her father filled her with added resolve.

Heading for the house, she cried out, "Help someone—anyone—Dad's been hurt!" Her voice died away. She was alone in her crisis, since neither Manny nor Margarita had heard her desperate cries for help.

Her head snapped up as she heard the rapid clip of horse's hooves. A surge of hope ran through her. The ranch foreman rode in at a mad gallop. Link was a steady, reliable man—a faithful hand who'd always stayed on when so many others had drifted away.

Utterly grateful to see his solid presence, she yelled out to him, "Link, oh thank God you're here! Come quick, something's happened to Dad!"

At her words, the big cowboy leapt off his panting, heaving mount, tossed his reins to the ground, and rushed toward her. "What's wrong, Miss Cherry? You're lookin' all churned up."

"Someone's hurt Dad. He's been shot and someone has beaten him so severely, I hardly knew it was him! He's bleeding! He's terribly hurt, Link. I can't believe someone could be this rotten mean." She let out a sob. "He needs help right now. He needs the doctor!"

While she raced ahead of the heavy-set cowboy, she questioned in the back of her mind why he'd returned to the ranch so early in the day. But that didn't matter right now. She needed him and was happy to see him. Any other concerns could wait.

Entering the barn with Link close behind, she was glad to hear her father softly moaning. With a rush of relief, she knew he still clung to life. "Look what they've done to him."

She knelt at her father's side. The terrible rasping sounds of his breath, and occasional deep moaning, filled her with fear for his survival. "Thank God, he's still with us." Her throat hurt so much, tears came to her eyes, but there was no time for crying, not now.

"Goddamn!" Link exclaimed, kneeling on the other side. He made a quick assessment of the man's condition and turned to her, his face pale, "Miss Cherry, go to the house, fix up a bed for him. I'll take care of things here and bring him in." He was emphatic, "and send that Manny out here if you can find him. He can ride for the doc. Go on, girl. Get things ready, this ain't no place for you, right now."

Cherry hesitated, fearing to leave her father, yet things had to be done and she was grateful for the man's help. "Thanks, I'll get things ready. Bring him quick as you can, and Link...please, be careful." Before turning away, she asked, "Were you looking for him? You're not usually back this early."

He looked up at her, "I wanted to report the loss of more cows from the red herd. Them rustlers have been at it again."

"I see," was all she could think to say. She already knew about this latest loss. With a heavy heart, she ran to the house. *What was happening? Who'd want her father dead? Rustlers? Why?* Fear and anger dogged her every step and her heart pounded with apprehension as she raced to find Margarita. Something had been terribly wrong on this ranch for a long time, and things had come to a head today, in a terrible, deadly way.

Entering the wide oaken door of her home, she called out, "Margarita, quickly, Dad's been hurt, and we must make a bed for him. We need to pad it good. Link's bringing him in. He's lying in an awful mess out there."

"Miss Cherry, *Dios mio*! *Nada mas*?" Margarita twisted her hands together as tears flowed down her dusky cheeks. Her speech sounded more broken that usual. Manny stood there, saying nothing, his face white.

The questions in the woman's eyes went unanswered until Cherry found her voice again. "Someone's hurt my father, and he's real bad. Uncle Omar's gone to town and not returned yet, either." She fought a losing battle against her bitter tears as she turned to the boy. "Manny, go to the barn. Link needs you to go for the doctor." She sobbed the words, tears streaming down her face.

"*Si*, I go." The boy, his face tight, rushed out most likely glad to see action—and to help, she guessed.

Cherry got herself in hand. A multitude of things needed doing. She ordered, "Margarita, boil some water, tear up some rags. We've got to do what we can to help my father until the doctor gets out here." She already knew that would be many long hours as Perkins Grove was five long miles away. Sick at heart, she worried that he'd be too late.

The Mexican woman paused from trying to comfort her young charge and sprang into action. She got the supplies she needed, shoved more wood into the stove and put a large pot of water on to heat. Together, she and Cherry made up a folding bed in the front room to receive Cherry's father when the foreman brought him to the house. Outside, they heard the sound of a horse moving rapidly away, and Cherry guessed Link had sent Manny for the doctor.

Cherry's mother had died when she was thirteen. Margarita, in many ways, had become a soft, comforting entity in her life. She'd kept the home, cooked the meals and filled the empty places in her life many times, and she was ready to help her now as well.

Taking a moment, Margarita folded Cherry into her ample arms. "*Hija*, who do this thing to your father?"

Cherry had long since grown used to Margarita's heavily accented voice and to the fact that she called her, her "child." She seldom noticed the familiarity anymore, needing and appreciating the warm, loving presence in her life.

"I don't know, oh God, I don't Margarita!" Cherry snuggled close to the woman's ample bosom, desperately needing the comfort of the warmth she found there.

Hearing the sound of thumping boots outside the door, Cherry flung it open to a red-faced Link, puffing his way across the wide wooden porch with her father's heavy limp form, as he carried the big man into the house.

"Put him right here, Link." She indicated the bed they'd hastily prepared.

"He hasn't done any moanin' for a while," Link offered, his brow dripping with sweat. Together they knelt beside the bed and pulled away the bloodied shirt to see the fearful way her father's life force still seeped from the blue-ringed hole in his chest. Cherry was relieved it was above his heart or he'd be gone by now.

"He's lost a lot of blood, Miss Cherry," Link said, panting from his efforts.

Fearing to guess how much, she got the scissors to cut his bloody clothes away. Link helped her. They worked together to place a large dressing over the wound. Her father was flaccid and heavy, but with Margarita helping, they removed his soiled clothing, except the lower under things, and washed his body. With satisfaction, Cherry finally saw her father lying in a clean bed.

"Dad?" she called softly as they re-dressed his wound and bound it tightly as possible. She soothed his forehead trying to bring him around, hoping he could tell them who'd tried to kill him. She clenched her teeth, remembering the numerous dark, bruised, and swollen areas where he'd been beaten.

"My God, Link, who could have done this?"

"Don't know, Miss Cherry. Some low-down, rotten bastard, that's for damned sure." He flushed, "pardon my cussin', I sent Manny for the sheriff and doc right away." His worried expression dampened any hopes for her father's chances.

"He looks so bad, Link." She could barely get the words out, looking at her father's face—not only pale, but slowly and insidiously taking on the waxy shades of death. Cherry knew the signs. She'd seen people die before.

She had no answers to the questions that flooded her worried mind, but most of all, she feared her father wouldn't hold out until the doctor to came. It was so far into Parson's Grove. And what if he were out on a case?

The fine bubbles of blood oozing from her father's nose and mouth were additional signs that added to her heartbreak. It meant his lungs had been hit. Over the years she'd seen enough injuries to be sure of that.

"Looks like the bleedin's stopped some," Link offered, trying to sound hopeful. He kept his eyes on the floor.

Cherry knew he sought to ease her worries, but she wasn't fool enough to have false hopes.

"Looks like the dressing over his chest hasn't gotten any darker with his blood," he added.

She tried to find hope in Link's words, but her father's fingers had already taken on the pale, yellowish pallor of death. The blood from his nose and mouth still came at a slow seep, and his rasping breath brought a pinkish froth from his nostrils. She changed his dressings, bathed his face with cooling cloths, and stroked his ashen brow, knowing no other way to help him.

It had long since grown dark, and while she waited for the doctor, she stayed beside her father, hour after hour.

Gently, she smoothed his hair and stroked his face. Worried the doctor wouldn't come until near morning, she murmured, "Even if he isn't tending some woman in childbirth way out somewhere, it'll still be a long time before he gets here." Sick with dread, she faced the fact he'd never come in time.

Her father stirred for a bit while Link had gone for fresh water. His eyes were completely swollen shut, his lips barely moving. She knelt close to hear his words. "Daughter—love you—Link—bewa—" With those few words, his head rolled back and he ceased breathing.

Cherry let out a loud, choking sob and held back a scream. "Oh no, oh God—Margarita, he's gone! He's gone, Margarita, he's left us." She couldn't stop her deep sobbing nor did she try.

Margarita sobbed right along beside her. "I so sorry, *hija*, what we do now, he gone? He was good man."

Though the woman cried quietly, the deep sobbing sounds caused Cherry to realize the woman's sorrow was real and very deep, equaling that of a loving spouse. Often in the past Cherry had seen a few instances—a soft touch, a knowing smile—and wondered. In her youthful innocence, she had often considered that Margarita might have been more than just a servant, but she wasn't sure what that meant.

Link re-entered the room to find the women clinging to each other in their sorrow. He directed his look at Cherry, as she'd had just become his new boss, and offered, "I'm sure sorry, Miss. Don't you worry your head about things around the ranch, here. I'll take care of everything."

Cherry noticed how his broad chest puffed out and, along with his words of comfort and reassurance. His stride, as he crossed the room, had already taken on an important swagger.

Link's words relieved a burden from her young shoulders and right now, that feeling was welcome indeed. Lost and bereft, she heard only the note of caring in his words and, in her sorrow, was glad to hear them. She'd never given thought to running a ranch, and now it loomed as the next step in her life. Uncle Omar had never been much help to her father, and she didn't figure he'd help her that much now, but he was a kind and generous uncle, and she loved him.

Looking long and lovingly at her father, she finally reached out and patted the battered face that had once been so warm and wise. Tears fell as she kissed his forehead and slowly pulled the sheet over his head. In her mind, her father's last whispered words came to her. *What had he meant when he said, Link?*

"Link will stay and help me, Dad. Did you mean to give him some last orders?" Her brow furrowed as she sat beside him. "You don't have to worry. I'll be fine."

CHAPTER 2

Remembering the housekeeper's question, Cherry went to the weeping woman. "Don't worry, Margarita, we'll be all right. We'll have to hire help again, though, can't seem to get men to stay on here."

She sniffed back extra tears that might be a release as she felt the burden of ownership thrust upon her. The weight of her situation descended upon her. Everything lay on her slim shoulders from here on out. But first, she resolved to make things right for her father's sake. Clenching her fists into a hard knot, she vowed, "Margarita, I'll run this ranch, and I'll find who did this evil thing to my father. I will, I swear it."

Cherry's words brought a wave of fresh weeping from the gentle Mexican woman. But Father lay dead, and nothing could change that. Continuing trouble loomed ahead for their ranch. The reality of it overwhelmed her thoughts, threatening to swamp her.

She squared her shoulders. She wanted vengeance and she had to know what lay behind the insidious things that had been happening on the ranch. Seeking comfort, she looked about her home, hoping to find something to give her encouragement. She saw it all, and knew that everything in this house now belonged to her, yet nothing meant anything in her deep sorrow.

She studied the adobe walls, plastered smooth, with *ristras* hanging here and there for color, pictures collected over the years, and the many comfortable chairs and rugs that looked so familiar. Yet, in looking at these things, she realized nothing was the same to her, not any more.

She still had her father's brother, Omar, but could she rely on the man? He'd never amounted to much in any case. This very day, he'd been sent to town for supplies—a job they always sent him to do, hoping he'd handle it better this time than the last. He hadn't returned by this late hour, and she figured he was probably off gambling again.

She shrugged, remembering her years with her errant uncle. *Useless he may be, but he's a good man and I need him now more than ever.* She'd always enjoyed his fantastic tall tales of his years at sea, and the strange places he'd seen. Yet he was so completely different from her father that she'd wondered many times if they'd really had the same parents.

Fighting an overwhelming sense of unreality, Cherry settled in a comfortable chair to sip the cup of hot tea Margarita had brought to her while she waited for the doctor and Sheriff Delavan. The sheriff had never been any help with the rustling and vandalism, and she expected that it would be no different now. For the doctor, it was too late. Death had already happened. Would that get some action from the lawman? She snorted at the thought, feeling utterly alone.

Cherry sat thinking about the past few years. Behind her father's back, cattle had been stolen, fences torn down, and horses lost. Cattle were only a small part of their losses as the incidents multiplied. Strange things occurred repeatedly on their ranch and it had everyone on edge.

Cherry knew little of the world outside of their ranching community, except for books she'd been exposed to during her younger years. She wondered if she could find the courage and strength to run the ranch. Did she have what it took?

She had noticed Link's eyes on her more than once over the past several years, and though she had little experience with men, his frequent glances had told her of his interest.

"She is a lovely black haired girl." She'd heard that comment enough times to believe it, yet young men never stayed around long enough for her to find one she could care about.

In daydreams, she fancied herself being held in a pair of strong arms, going to dances in town, getting married, and maybe having a child or two. She could easily handle a ranch like this, if she had the right man beside her, but as a picture of the heavyset Link entered her mind, she shook her head at the very thought of it.

She frowned, trying to sort out her future. They had a determined enemy, one who remained unseen, yet his work was plain as day with rustled cattle, brush fires so like lightning strikes, and even going so far as throwing salt licks into the deepest parts of the swift flowing Tonto River that watered the ranch.

What she didn't know, however, was who wanted them gone, and why? It lay more heavily on her mind, now, but her father had been worried for some time. She'd known it, although he'd tried to shield her from hearing the worst of it. Most of his concern regarded the safety of his daughter and, finding the local sheriff totally inadequate, he'd written to the territorial governor a few months ago. But to her knowledge, he had heard nothing back.

Cherry had long, softly curling, hair, and wide, deep, blue-violet eyes. She'd seen her small waist, full breasts, and long-legged image in her bedroom mirror often enough. She was considered beautiful, but none of that meant anything to her when men never called on her or took any interest in seeing her socially. Because of the lack of suitable male suitors, she had no real confidence in her beauty and often wondered if she was desirable at all. She had traveled little beyond the small town of Parson's Grove, and aside from the small rural school she'd attended for her early grades, her mother had done almost all of her educating.

Cherry often had the eerie feeling that someone unknown to her or her father, some hidden person, had insidiously and quietly staked a claim on this ranch, and maybe on her, too. If so, whoever it was hadn't the courage to declare his interest, and that thought infuriated and frightened her.

With no mother to confide her thoughts to, expressing such ideas to her father got her exactly nowhere. He never gave credence to her ideas. He'd been a loving and good father, but he'd often said her claims that someone was out to ruin them were merely a young girl's nonsense.

Had he said that to allay her fears? She didn't know. But if she ever found out who was behind these things, they'd regret it deeply. She swore it.

In early evening, Cherry heard the long awaited sounds of hoof beats entering the ranch yard and ran towards the door to greet the sheriff and doctor. She was sorely disappointed. It was only some of the ranch hands riding in for the night, later than usual. She barely knew these men as they were mainly the ones who'd never looked her way.

Watching Link stride out of the barn and go up to them, she knew he was informing them of her father's death. The men sat their mounts in shocked silence until one of them shook a fist in the air. She didn't try to move closer as she knew their muffled comments were not intended for her. They'd be mighty embarrassed if she overheard the words they were using.

The men washed up before coming to the house. She greeted Larry Price, an ungainly young man with poor teeth and unkempt hair; Monte Blue, older and stiff-legged; Booker, the cook; Waddie, a young man with thick unruly white-blond hair; and Lee Heckel, older and very short of stature. After a few quiet words to Cherry, they filed one-by-one past her father's still form. After paying their respects and whispering comments of support for her, they sat around in silence, except for a few muttered comments among themselves.

Margarita had been busy in the kitchen. Knowing that food was always helpful, she'd made a generous meal.

Everyone got a plateful along with *tortillas* and lots of hot coffee. If the woman sought relief from her sorrows in work, Cherry was glad to let her.

Keeping busy also helped allay Cherry's worries as she'd begun to feel the onus of ownership. At this time in Arizona, a woman might be thought unable to manage a ranch, especially one so young, but what other option did she have? Theirs was a large ranch, well situated between two mountain ranges, and abundantly watered by the constantly-flowing river. Several cold water streams served to keep some areas greener than others with verdant grasses during the warmer months. Those areas also provided hay for some of the winter months, and it was usually needed.

She knew the road ahead would be difficult, but laying her father to rest was all her mind could encompass at present. She'd worry about running the ranch later, and after all, she had Link. He'd handled things for her father over the years and she felt confidant she could rely on him. She held out hope that Uncle Omar would be some help, too.

❧❧❧

The smoke filled, fuggy atmosphere of Pete's Place was full up and humming with business when John Carmona entered through the swinging, slatted doors. His spurs made a small jingling sound as he sidled up to the bar and ordered, "I'll have a whiskey."

"You bet, stranger." The heavy set barkeep reached down, puffing with the effort, and pulled a bottle of deep gold liquid from beneath the massive, scar laden, wooden bar. He dragged a poorly washed shot glass over and sloshed the whiskey into it, splashing several drops on the scummy bar surface. "Here you go." He shoved it forward while giving John an intensive once over. "New in these parts, mister?"

John smiled inwardly. The man hadn't seen him around Parson's Grove before, and apparently he couldn't restrain his curiosity. John imagined that although things were changing in this hidden-away, rustic part of the Arizona Territory, few strangers happened along in these parts. The barkeep, being a nosey sort, no doubt made it a habit to keep abreast of things so he could generously spread what news he heard. Things like that made life more interesting and might give him a bit of added importance.

"Passing through, if it's any concern of yours," John replied. He turned away from the man, leaned against the bar, and surveyed the crowd as he slowly sipped his drink. He'd scouted this area all day and was tired and thirsty from taking care of business.

His horse was bedded down at the town stables. He'd taken a room for the night, but he sought certain localized information. Spotting three card players at a table with an empty chair, he sauntered over. A bit of action in a friendly little card game might be relaxing and, with luck, informative. After a bit, he planned to turn in at the Rose Hotel across the street and enjoy a good night's rest between a set of clean sheets.

"You gents mind if I sit in?" he asked.

A smaller man with a dirty, checked shirt and a twisted, string tie around his scrawny neck, raised his head and eyed him. "We got room, mister. Set yourself in." He extended a hand. "I'm Harvey Bent."

The avarice and greed gleaming from the man's narrow, beady eyes faintly amused John. He reached across the table and shook hands with a smartly dressed, narrow-eyed gambler, who introduced himself as Jeems. The gent had slicked back hair, a shiny floral vest, and looked like a man to keep in mind. After meeting an older gent named Omar Bender, John pulled up a battered chair and settled in.

Looking around at each of the men sitting there, he introduced himself. "I'm John Carmona. "What're we playin' then?"

The slick-looking gambler said, "Five card draw, five dollar ante."

The stack of silver beside him and the confident smile across his clean-shaven face spoke volumes and John took note. *This dandy never soils his hands with honest work. Makes his living off the ignorance of others.*

"Ante's a mite steep for these parts to my way of thinkin'," John commented.

"Door's right over there, mister," Jeems replied.

John had been answered. Nothing more was said, the cards shuffled and dealt.

Harvey Bent, the non-descript sort with the scrawny neck and weathered skin of a man who worked out in the elements, had a sour scowl across his face. John figured him for a man suffering deep losses.

Omar's frown indicated his hand wasn't worth the five dollar anti. "Hell of a deal," he muttered, a tight look of worry across his aging, wrinkled features.

Harvey growled at the older man. "Shut the hell up, Omar. Pay and play, or git the hell out."

Omar flushed red at the comment but held his retort. He still had a small pile of silver at his side. He passed and took two cards.

John checked his hand, felt a rise in his pulse, but betrayed nothing as he tossed in a few silvers. "I'll stay."

The slick gent tossed in two fives. "I'll see—and raise." Omar passed again, but he had a gleam in his eye that was new.

Bent tossed out a few more bills. "See and raise you."

John stayed and played, waiting to see which way things were headed.

The game went on until, exasperated, the older man, Omar, tossed out a handful of bills. "I'm callin'." He laid out the last of his money, three silver coins and two five dollar silver certificates.

The slick gent laid out four kings, a triumphant smile on his face. He looked Omar in the eye. "How's that?"

Omar laid out his hand, a heart flush, king high. "So, where'n hell did you get all them kings, mister?" He rose from his chair, face red with fury. "What the hell you pullin' here?"

"You sayin' I'm a cheat, you scrawny little bastard!" The fancy-vested man reached inside his jacket for a small gold plated gun with a pearl handle, and Omar Bender, suddenly fearful, hurriedly scratched leather for his own gun.

Two shots rang out and the older man slumped to the floor.

"Call me a cheat, you damned low-life skunk!" the fancy-dude gambler snarled at the crumpled form lying on the floor. The smoke from his fancy, little, double-barreled Derringer spiraled upward to drift away in the shocked silence. Omar's bullet had missed him clean.

John got up and stood back, waiting, and taking in the action. It was so quiet, you could hear a pin drop except for the muffled sobbing of one of the bar girls.

The sheriff happened to walk through the swinging doors right then. "I heard shootin' in here. What's going on?" He eyed the bleeding carcass on the floor. "Who's that?"

The barkeep finally found his breath and rushed up, wiping his hands, and wheezing with the effort. "That's Omar Bender layin' there. Got all riled up over a poker hand and Jeems here had to defend himself. I seen the whole thing, sheriff." His paunch swelled with his delivery of the information.

The slightly grizzled sheriff took in the scene. "Anybody else got anything to say about this?" He looked at the rest of the players, his blue eyes questioning. An older man, he tended toward fat around his girth. The buttons of his shirt had pulled apart, showing a spot of dirty white underwear.

"Ol' Omar was a drawin' his gun, sheriff, I seen 'im." The weather-beaten little man moved forward. "I'm Harvey

Bent, in from the Slash Nine. I was playin' along here and saw the whole thing. The man appeared eager to be noticed and have a say.

John said nothing, merely watched and listened.

ᘓᘏᘓᘏ

The sheriff spoke to Jeems for a few moments, then turned to the stranger and looked him over. *Now, who's this?* he wondered. Aside from wide shoulders clad in a good quality dark shirt, plain leather vest, and a thin neck piece of braided leather, the man had a chiseled jaw, hawk-like nose, and piercing gray eyes. The sheriff knew instantly, this was a man he'd not want to cross. "How about you, mister?" he asked. "Who are you and what've you got to say?"

"Who's asking," the man wanted to know.

"I'm Monte Delavan, sheriff here and I like to keep things peaceable." It wasn't often a stranger came through Parson's Grove, and a few questions rose in his mind.

The stranger replied, "I'm John Carmona, just traveling through, heading for parts east of here." He extended a hand, shook, and went on. "Seems it happened about like these folks said, except—funny thing, Sheriff Delavan, I had a king in my hand, too." He laid out his hand, a royal flush in spades, pretty as a picture, black ace high.

"Whoa, here! Jeems, you got somethin' to say about this?" Delavan put his hand on his gun, ready as he faced the shifty-eyed gambler.

"He's a lying son-of-a-bitch, sheriff!" Jeems turned pale and instantly took on a glossy sheen of sweat. "I swear

The last thing she needs is another man she can't afford to trust...

When Cherry Bender discovers her father's been fatally wounded, she vows to find his killer and stop the constant trouble on her ranch. Very short-handed, but unsure who to believe, she reluctantly hires a tall, gray-eyed stranger who comes to the ranch with the news that her uncle has also been murdered.

He only wanted information...until he met her.

John Carmona didn't come to the Bender ranch looking for work, but to find out who was illegally mining a rare mineral from the nearby hills. But one look at Cherry and John's plans change drastically. Determined to save her ranch from the forces working against her, he must fight not only Cherry's suspicions of him, but also the evil assassin sent to kill them both. Can John win Cherry's trust in time or will he die trying to save her life?

to God, I never cheated any man. These are the cards I got dealt to me!" He indicated John. "You gonna believe some passin'-through stranger over one of your own, here?"

"Reckon I do, Jeems. This ain't the first hassle I've had with you, and you damned well know it. Looks like I'll be takin' you in for murder."

Delavan, feeling a moment of regret, pulled out a pair of handcuffs and moved toward the slick-vested dude gambler.

"Like hell you will!" Ignoring the sheriff, the gambler whipped out his deadly little Derringer once again from within his fancy frock coat and aimed it towards the stranger.

But John was faster. He sent a bullet into Jeems chest before the sheriff could clear leather with his own gun.

As the gambler hit the floor, Delavan felt a shock run through his body. "Hells bells, man," he exclaimed. "I never even saw you draw that thing! Shore enough he had it comin', but where'n hell'd you learn to pull leather like that?"

"Nothing special, sheriff. He was just a mite too slow, is all," John said over the mumbling in the background.

"A damned gun-hand, that's what he is."

John didn't seek out the source of the comment as long as the sheriff stood there, but he'd obviously better be watching his back from now on. Jeems had apparently had a few friends around the place.

The sheriff picked the small pistol from Jeems's limp hand and frowned as he examined it. "Hell, didn't know they'd made a double barreled Derringer, but looks like they have."

He indicated the first dead man. "Anyone know this man?"

"He's from a ranch way out along the Tonto, sheriff." Harvey Bent said. "Name's Omar Bender, neighbor of mine. We run cattle along the same river." He uttered a soft snigger. "Wasn't much at playin' cards, never was. S'posed to be haulin' supplies, that's what."

Lonnie Helms, owner of the general store—a small, nicely dressed man—came forth with his bit of input. "He was in earlier and bought a wagon load of supplies. Never came back for 'em."

"Thanks for the information, Lonnie," Delavan said.

"Think nothin' of it, sheriff. Old Omar comes into the store of a month, to buy a big order for the ranch." Lonnie informed him. "Well, if that's all you need of me, sheriff, I'd best get back to the store afore the wife hears of this shootin'. Woman's a worrier." The man took his leave, stepping out through the swinging doors.

"We'll need to get word to his kin about this." He looked about for a deputy and asked a youngster who stood staring at the two dead men, "Call Akins, if you will." He added, "Better call the undertaker, too, if he ain't out buyin' coffins somewhere."

The kid took off like a shot out of the swinging doors as a voice from the back said, "I'm not out doing anything of the kind, sheriff. I'm right here tryin' to have a nice quiet evenin'." He coughed. "Now looks like I've got work to do."

A titter of laughter came from somewhere in the crowd.

The doctor, Ben Coogan, edged his way through the throng and took a quick assessment of the two men lying on the floor. "They're dead all right."

Delavan reached inside the Jeems's vest and withdrew a partial deck of cards. He spread them out and took a look. "Well, what do you know? Guess we know where all them extra kings came from. Cheatin' bastard."

In a short while, Bill Akins, a slim young man wearing a badge, pushed through the swinging doors. "Needin' me, are you, Delavan?" He cast a glance at the dead men and waited. "What's happened here?"

The sheriff gave a short synopsis along with his orders, and then turned to John saying, "You're free to go. There won't be any charges. This little dust-up sure as hell spoilt one of the nicest hands I've seen lately." He motioned for John to help himself to the winnings. "Looks like you had the hand to beat, so it's all yours unless Harvey there's got anything against it," he said, pointing to the big loser.

Bent, pale and nervous at the events that had taken place, quickly said, "It ain't mine, sheriff." He huffed. "This sure as hell wasn't my lucky night!" He looked down at the fancy dressed gambler. Blood still oozed from his chest wound onto the silky patterned vest he'd worn, but his face had already taken on the waxen pallor of death. "No wonder I never won anything. Looks like that bastard, Jeems, was cheatin' us all along."

✦✦✦

John didn't want the winnings, but he swept them off the grimy table, knowing where they ought to go. He needed information and hadn't found what he hoped for. But with these winnings he had something that would lead him in the right direction. Deciding a night at his room in the Rose Hotel wasn't in the cards, he walked across the street, removed his pack, and left.

As he walked towards the stables, he saw a young Mexican boy on a sweating, blowing horse, hightailing it toward the sheriff's office. Though curious, it was not John's business, and he ignored the excitement. He had his own agenda.

At the stables, he roused up the old man who fed the stock and cleaned the stalls. His gray hair standing on end, the man brushed the sleep from his eyes and came shuffling from a small room at the end of the box stalls. "Howdy, stranger. Needin' some help, are you?"

"Just wonderin' if you'd be familiar with things around these parts?"

"Been here near all my life. Name's T. J. Miller."

John heard the note of pride in the answer.

A team of light draft horses were among the animals stabled in the facility. "Know who these horses belongs to?" John looked at the brand on the animals flank. "Humm, interesting. Know what the lazy 'B' stands for?" He couched his words carefully, not wanting to alarm the old fellow.

"Belongs to Omar Bender. Got a wagon outside there, too. S'pect he's here for supplies, like usual." T. J. warmed to the subject and John quickly sized him up for the kind who enjoyed talking, maybe a good bit too much. "That's lazy 'B' for the Bender outfit. Omar ain't a man I'd send for goods. Likes his liquor and cards too much."

"Know where their place is? I hear its right good country out there."

"I hope to tell you it is. Good ranch. Runs along both sides of the Tonto for quite a stretch. Never want for water out there. Them cattle don't. No siree. Used to work out there, but I got too damned old and the foreman fired me a few years back." John noted the distaste in the man's voice as he added, "They's somethin' funny goin' on out there these days, too, so they say."

John was ready to ride and, cutting off the old man's gossiping discourse, he asked, "If I needed to see Bender, how'd I find the place?"

T. J. walked to the barn door and pointed towards the east slope of the nearest mountain range, barely visible in the night sky. "The lower mountains over there are the start of the Blue River Range. The ranch sits between them and the higher ones to the other side." He sighed. "Easy enough to find. Road's right good, now a days, so I hear. Takes left off the road south of here, out of town a mile or so."

John's big butter-hided buckskin, Muley, was well rested and needed a steady hand. John kept a strong grip on the reins and kept watch out for trouble from any friends of Jeems. But he saw no signs of it. By the faint sliver of moonlight, he found the trail he sought. His introduction to this area had been violent, but he'd found a way to turn it to his benefit.

He nudged the buckskin and moved down the rock-strewn, rutted trail. After a few miles, he pulled off the wagon road. He needed to get the lay of the land around the home ranch before encountering the inhabitants. *Best head on out and see what's going on. Won't be a happy place when they find out about losing their kin.*

CHAPTER 3

Finally, nearly into morning, Cherry heard sounds of horses entering the ranch yard. Link was quick to go out to meet them. She heard parts of a muffled conversation before Sheriff Monte Delavan entered the house, along with a couple of deputies and Dr. Coogan.

After seeing the victim and hearing the doctor's opinion, the sheriff took what information Cherry had to offer. "Sorry for what happened here, Miss Cherry. We'll do our best to find the bunch who done this. Don't you worry your pretty little head about that."

Finding his words shamefully empty and definitely patronizing, she fumed inwardly. In her absolute disgust, she decided the sheriff was very lucky he hadn't tried to pat her on the head.

Sickened further with the feelings of hopelessness, Cherry replied, "Thanks Sheriff Delavan, I'm sure you will." If her words and tightened lips betrayed her feelings in the matter, she didn't care. This particular sheriff had never done anything to solve their problems—not even once.

Dr. Coogan examined her father's remains with one of the deputy's aid then drew her aside. In a low voice, he said, "Miss, I'm very sorry for your loss. Someone certainly wanted your father dead. This was just plain murder, if I had my say."

Surprised at this statement of the obvious, she welcomed the man's earnest concern and saw him, at the very least, as somewhat trustworthy.

"Don't you have a say, Dr. Coogan?" Incredulous, she realized this good man's voice didn't count for much with this sheriff.

He shrugged and said nothing further. Her frustration with the inadequacies of the local law mounted into additional anger at the terrible waste of her father's life.

Sheriff Delavan approached her with another matter, his face drawn into a serious cast. "Miss Cherry, is Omar Bender is your kin?"

"Why, yes, he's Dad's brother." Her face went tight, Uncle Omar should have returned last evening but hadn't. She'd been too upset and worried to give much thought to her missing uncle, but with the sheriff's question, her heart began to race. "Why do you ask, Sheriff Delavan?"

"Well, uh, Miss Cherry, sorry to have to tell you this, but he got himself shot during a hand of cards just last evening. I'm afraid he's dead, too. Sorry for another loss, but I had to let you know."

"Oh no, that can't be! He went in to Parson's Grove for supplies just yesterday. He was gambling?" Her shoulders slumped and tears sprang to her eyes as she shook her head at the sorry actions of her useless uncle, and one more devastating loss. The gentle, unassuming older man had been family. Now even he was gone. She was more alone than ever. She nodded. "Of course he was gambling again." Her shoulders slumped as she fought back more tears, her voice wavering. "How'd it happen that he was shot?"

The sheriff told her about an incident during a card game that involved a card-slick and a quick-drawing stranger.

Cherry figured he gave as little information as he dared. She understood, knowing her uncle's weakness for cards, but felt there was more to the incident than the sheriff had said. Broken hearted, she couldn't bear to hear any more. She'd shed many tears for her father, and managed a few more for her uncle.

She dried her eyes and turned to her foreman who stood nearby. "Please, Link, could you go get Uncle Omar in the morning, if the undertaker has taken care of him? He had the wagon and team. Perhaps you could bring back the supplies along with him," she added. "And would you ask the minister to come see me? I'm sorry to ask—you've been up all night helping out."

With those words, the mantle of ownership and management of a large ranch had passed firmly into her control. The enormity of it overwhelmed her, adding to the weight and sorrow of her father's passing, and now, the loss of Uncle Omar.

"I'll get it done, Miss Cherry. I'll take care of everything." Link's big chest swelled with importance at this first charge from her. "I'll take one of the boys an' maybe catch a few winks on the ride in."

As the sheriff, doctor, and deputies left the ranch, the sun rose—a fiery ball in the eastern sky. It'd been a long night for those men, but after seeing the sheriff in close conversation with her foreman, she'd developed a very unsettled feeling, one she could not name.

This knowledge increased the overwhelming sense she had—everything was wrong. She didn't have a handle on it, nor did she know what to do about it—yet.

ᏗᏔᏗ

In a small room at the top of the stairs above the Rose Hotel Lobby, Harry Bourdain and Wilmer Mains sat contemplating the evening's events at Pete's Place. "Hate to lose a good man like Jeems, kept me in ready cash if nothing else. Tell me, how are things out at the ranch comin'? Gittin' closer, are we?" Bourdain asked, looking across the room to Mains.

"Movin' right along, from what Links says." He coughed and took another drag on his cigar. "Takin' too damned long, to my way of thinking." The smoke spiraled upward, drifting throughout the room. "Ever seen that young woman out there?" Wilmer added, with a snigger that disgusted Bourdain.

"You bet I have. Ain't nobody stayed workin' there long enough to get next to her with Link around." Harry laughed. "He wouldn't be much of a problem if I set my mind on courtin'. Hell, I'm a decent lookin' fella'. With one of her men-folks down, she might be lookin' for some help one of these fine days, and I'm just the man to step in and help her out."

"Yeah, too bad about her uncle, eh?"

"And that ain't all, partner. That ain't all," Harry returned. Wilmer's knowing look told Harry all he needed to know.

CHAPTER 4

Two days later, in the company of numerous townspeople and all the local ranchers, Cherry stood woodenly and red-eyed, listening to the solemn words of the minister from Parson's Grove. He repeated all the proper portions of scripture to lay her father and uncle to rest beside her mother in the little cemetery west of the ranch house.

The family burial plot lay in the protecting embrace of a small grove of stately Ponderosas, trees she especially loved for their grandeur. Their orange-tinged bark gave her an inner feeling of warmth and seemed to protect and shelter the area with their lofty limbs. That comforted her in some small way.

Harvey Bent and his son, Martin, came up to her. "Sure sorry for what happened, Miss Cherry. Thought the world of your father, your uncle Omar, too." Harvey shook her hand. His son, Martin, blushing red, finally found his tongue. "If there's anything I could do to help you out, Miss Cherry, just you give a holler. I'd be proud to help you in any way I could." Tall and gangly for his youthful age,

Cherry saw the light of more than friendship in his pale blue eyes and somehow that basic touch of male interest helped her to understand that life goes on, for herself as well as everyone else.

"Why thank you, Martin. I surely will call on you if I have the need." She squeezed his hands in hers before she turned to speak with several others who had come to help her lay her loved ones in their graves.

Another neighbor, Hettie Jamison, provided especially solid support and comfort. She was a young widow and Cherry's closest friend and was no stranger to the sorrows of life. Many others offered what comfort they could, until Cherry's mind blurred with their words of sympathy. They'd all, in one way or another, known the sorrow of lost loved ones, yet, the pain of laying her father and his errant brother in the cold earth was seemingly hers alone.

Cherry feared she wasn't being the best of hostesses. She had tried as best she could, but her actions had become wooden and automatic with the confusion surrounding her father's death. Her senses numb, she tightened her jaw and swallowed hard as she fought the tears the many offers of sympathy prompted. She had repeated, "I'll be all right, in time. I will—I know I will," more times than she could remember.

Hettie came close and hugged her. "Cherry, I don't know what to say or how to help, but call on me anytime. I do know how it is, but oh God, I wish I didn't."

Cherry nodded, understanding Hettie's feelings. She had already faced the sudden loss of a beloved husband to become a woman alone, with a ranch to run. That sad fact made the bond between them that much closer.

"Thanks, Hettie. So much has happened, and it came so fast." She smiled at the tall, dark-blonde woman who stood there wanting to help. Despite knowing the young widow had a multitude of her own problems, she asked, "How are things at your place?"

"I'm makin' out just fine," Hettie lied straight out.

Cherry knew it, but now was not the time to discuss those things. Her friend promised, "I can't stay too long today, dear, but I'll come for a good visit in a week or two."

Hettie hugged her warmly and went on to chat with several other neighbors. Later in the day, Cherry watched her friend ride away and felt the loss as soon as Hettie passed out of sight beneath the trees.

After the close neighbors and most of the cowboys, with Link among them, had paid their respects, they heard the ringing of the dinner bell. Margarita, with Manny's help, laid out an ample meal to feed the remaining guests and the hungry bunch took full advantage of her fine cooking.

Cherry felt the exhaustion of futility creeping over her. Tomorrow she must face the daunting task of running her father's spread. Right now, worn out with weeping, worrying over insurmountable odds, and the heavy burden of everything she faced, Cherry wanted to scream, or fly away on Checky's back and let the wind blow across her face as he pounded down the trail. *These terrible losses are too much. I'm too young to run a ranch. I don't know where to start!*

৩৩৩

John rode his big buckskin, Muley, over what he believed to be the final ridge before actually sighting the Lazy B Ranch. He'd spent several days looking over the general area before coming in for a closer look at his ultimate goal, the Bender place.

He topped the overgrown and brushy ridge and gazed down to see a nicely situated home-ranch layout. The cluster of buildings lay nested in a small valley surrounded on the upper slopes by groves of magnificent Ponderosas and slender, willowy Aspens, blending their shaded greens together as they spread up into the hills.

The ranch yard looked to be wide open and clean of clutter. Numerous buildings were situated, according to their use, about the outer edges of the wide space in front of the rugged, sprawling, stonework and adobe ranch house. The entire setting looked solid enough. A shiny gray patina of weathering had mellowed the look of the outbuildings, giving them a solid sense of permanence. Farther off, fenced pastures held grazing horses and cattle that looked to be young stock, needing to be close in for observation.

Tonto Creek meandered gently towards the southeast on the far side of the buildings. The rancher had damned up a smaller stream that fed into the Tonto, creating a blue-surfaced lake of about two acres or more. The ranch house was only partially visible under two huge trees that spread dappled shading over the tiled roof. "Nice enough place for a ranch, damned nice, in fact," he murmured aloud.

Frowning, he shaded his eyes against the fading sunlight, noting how a few random clouds created a mottled pattern over the entire landscape. That ranch sitting serenely below made him feel like he was coming home, although he'd never seen the place before today. Heaving a sigh, John nudged his horse and started down.

୧ଽ୧ଽ

It was late afternoon when Cherry decided to walk behind the house to the forlorn looking little graveyard. The funerals were over, but she frequently went to sit on a rustic bench put there years before. She usually sat for long moments looking at the newly turned earth that held all of her loved ones, quiet and deep, in its dark embrace.

Cool and clear today, the pine-laden scent of those towering Ponderosas filled the air as she entered the small fenced area. Restless and at odds with herself, she had visited the graves again and again. She had no real reason for it, but it helped somehow.

Her dress of thin, printed dimity was generously sprigged with tiny lavender flowers that, according to her friend Hettie, echoed the color of her eyes. She'd also said those shades of lavender changed her eyes into purple and gave her an exotic look. Cherry, not too sure what Hettie meant, had easily laughed away the fancies of her friend.

The chattering of birds flitting about in the softness of a lovely day helped to lessen the depths of pain she suffered. She missed her father, longed to hear his familiar, comforting voice once again and, to a lesser degree, that of his brother Omar. Both men, taken away by savagery and violence, had left her alone to fight the bitterness that seeped into her heart.

The family cemetery had been started years earlier when her baby brother Chad had died from diphtheria. He'd been the first. Cherry hadn't been very old, but she'd had it also and lived. Through accidents and illness, there were more than ten graves in all, comprising family, cowhands, and a few poor wandering souls who had no place to call home. It gave her a peaceful feeling to walk among the markers, seeing the faded names and remembering some who'd passed so long ago. She paused at her mother's grave. A stone marker, worn a bit from time and the weather, brought warm, loving memories of that sweet woman who'd been her friend, teacher, and mentor. A lost one who never left her deeper thoughts.

Life had been serene and predictable before her mother had fallen ill and lost her battle for life. Cherry had been fourteen. The sight of those graves made her throat go hard and tight, and she held back the tears that were eager to flow once again. She had' cried enough.

Her father and uncle Omar had crude wooden crosses for now since there hadn't been time for a proper marker. Vowing to avenge her father's death, her anguish at his loss crept over her once more and her fists tightened into hard knots. Uncle Omar had gotten himself shot over a stupid card game, but she'd loved him. She accepted his death, smiled, and understood, forgiving his weaknesses.

At the snapping sound of a horse stepping on a dry branch, Cherry tensed. Looking toward the sound, she saw a tall rider on a large, muscular buckskin horse emerge from the trees. Puzzled at this intrusion, she squared her shoulders and lifted her chin, ready for the encounter. *Who on earth would be riding in the back way like this, for heaven's sake?* she wondered as she waited.

The man drew his horse to a halt as he reached where she stood, doffed his hat, and said, "Howdy, ma'am. This the Bender place?" He replaced his hat on his head, pushed it back, and waited for her answer, taking in the newly formed graves.

Cherry looked into the man's steel-gray eyes and for some strange reason, the sight of them sent her mind reeling, completely off center. After some length of time, she regained her senses and replied, "Uh—yes, this is the Bender Ranch. I'm Cherry Bender. Why do you ask?"

Fuming for feeling such strange unsettled sensations from merely looking into this man's eyes, she mentally upbraided herself over her inane conduct. *How difficult could it be to tell the man where he'd come?* A heated flush of embarrassment crawled slowly upward over her face and neck. Cherry hated the feeling of it.

Something about this man made her senses swirl with uncertainty. She didn't like that strange, unsettled feeling. Was it the length of him, the spread of his shoulders, or his solid, fine features? She didn't know, but she'd never before laid eyes on a man quite like this one. Her pulse racing, she watched him dismount from his big, solid looking buckskin, and move toward her with the sinuous grace of a mountain cat.

"I'm just passing through, and I'd like to sit a spell, ma'am, if I might." He moved a bit closer, "I've something to say to you." His voice had a deep, soft resonance about it that struck her as comforting and strong, yet something in its tone made Cherry tremble inside. Disgusted with herself, she had trouble being civil and fought for control against the strange, unusual sensations this man so easily aroused within her.

As an inward unsteadiness settled over her, she wondered, *Who is this man who makes me act like a complete ninny? And what business could this stranger possibly have with me?*

Getting herself under control, she answered, "Certainly sir, follow me and we'll go to the house." She left the raw, newly turned earth of the graves, the quiet, fenced graveyard, and turned toward the ranch house. At this moment, walking before this stranger, she easily suppressed her recent sorrows and nearly forgot them. She didn't understand it or know why, but her heart raced madly in her chest. She hoped she could manage to be a gracious hostess.

Cherry walked on ahead of him, worried over his reason for coming here. *What could this man possibly have to say to me?*

John led his buckskin and followed behind the tall, slim, black-haired young woman who walked before him, completely unaware of the enticing picture she presented. He observed her every move and liked what he saw, every lovely inch of her. He stayed back far enough to feast his lonely eyes on the sight of the woman's gentle, undulating walk. How graciously her long, glossy, slightly curling black hair tumbled down her back. Did he imagine the scent of flowers in the air? *I must be going damned loco.* Feeling light-headed, he nearly tripped over a small branch. *I never imagined* running *into something like this.* He couldn't take his eyes off the beautiful young woman to the point he wasn't sure his feet hit the ground as he followed her.

After laying the reins of his horse over the peeled-pole hitching rail in front of the house where she'd indicated he might tie his mount, he followed her across the wide porch into the ranch house.

He took in the gracious surroundings of the huge sitting room and the numerous chairs and couches covered with Indian rugs or leather depending on the make. The walls were adorned with *ristras* of drying chilies, colorful Navajo rugs, old family tintypes of long dead ancestors, and a few colorful paintings made by some artist or family member. He also noticed a large bookcase filled with books and an upright piano sitting idle, the lid closed over the keys.

He thought he saw a trace of fear cross her lovely features as she asked him to take a seat, sat down herself, and turned to face him. "You had something to tell me?"

"Yes, ma'am, I see those fresh graves out there and I know this is a bad time for you, but you might want to know what happened." John hesitated a moment. "I believe you might like to know that I was a part of the poker game where your uncle met his death."

She met his gaze full on. "You were there?" Hot tears started, but she held them with all the strength she could muster. "I'm sorry, mister, you didn't say your name." She studied the black haired man with gray, piercing eyes—eyes that almost held her in a trance and sent strange thrills rushing through her body.

"Sorry for not thinking, ma'am," he replied. "I'm John Carmona. I was passing through this part of the Territory when I stopped for a night in that little town over yonder and happened onto that card game. A man called Jeems did some dirty dealing and your uncle called him on it."

Her eyes roamed over those big, fine hands that held his hat and his hair, black as night, and dampened with sweat from where the hat had been.

Cherry tried not to stare at him, but found it hard to do. He was big and rugged yet polished and refined in some way, too. He certainly didn't fit the picture of an ordinary cowhand. She wondered who he was, what he was, and why he'd come here.

"Uncle Omar was in town for supplies, not card playing." She shrugged and smiled helplessly at the vagaries of her weak-willed uncle. "He wasn't much of a hand or much of a card player either, but we'll miss him. We're short of help these days as it is and now we'll need a few more men to work the roundup that's coming up."

Cherry felt 'she'd laid out too much information to a total stranger, but it had just come out and the burn of another flush went stealing upwards over her neck and cheeks, adding further to her feeling off-center and flustered because of this stranger.

Noting the rose-hued flush that had crept upwards to steal across those lovely dimpled cheeks, John fastened his eyes directly on her. "Well, I could speak to your foreman, if you have one. I'm in no hurry to get where I'm going and might be able to lend a hand."

He glad for the opening she'd just handed him. He wasn't ready to leave the Bender ranch just yet, and after meeting this lovely girl, he nearly forgot what he'd come for. He found his voice and said, "Ma'am, the reason for this visit is to leave your uncle's winnings with you."

The surprise and disbelief on her face regarding Uncle Omar's prowess as a gambler was obvious. "He actually won something?" She raised her chin and frowned. "Huh. He usually lost everything."

At her small, escaping laugh, John heard lilting sounds that sent streaks of liquid fire right through him. Unbelievably, he found he was totally captivated by this lovely girl and hoped the hot flush he felt creeping up his own neck went unnoticed.

He reached inside his jacket." I believe it should rightly be yours." He brought out a small buckskin bag and handed it over. "This was in his pile. Not so bad for an evening's play."

Cherry took the small buckskin bag, and as her fingers brushed against his, a flash of lightning shot through her at the brief touch. She barely managed a murmured, "Thank you, Mr. Carmona." It was all she could say at the moment with her pulse racing the crazy way it was. It angered her that this man affected her like he did.

Trying to calm her racing heart, she looked into the bag of money, mostly bills with a few coins, but did not count it. Suspicion reared its ugly head and her brow wrinkled with conflicting thoughts: *Could this man have had a hand in my uncle's death? If so, would he still have the gall to come here like this?*

CHAPTER 5

Cherry frowned, reconsidering, then set her jaw set firmly, and lifted her chin. "I don't want this money, sir. This is dirty money as far as I'm concerned. I realize I don't really know everything about Uncle Omar's death, but I do know he's never won anything in a card game. Never."

"You're wrong about that, miss. Aside from being consistently cheated by that card slick, Jeems, no one can lose every hand, no matter how poorly they play."

Cherry heard his words, but to accept the money her uncle had won was another matter. Wanting no part of it, she handed it back to him. "I can believe what I want, sir. My father has just been murdered and now my uncle has been shot dead by a crooked gambler. Someone is out to ruin us on this ranch, and it might be you. How would I know? How can I possibly trust some strange man who rides in here after all the trouble we've had?"

Cherry's voice rose with her temper. She knew she was being unreasonable. She had no proof, but somehow this man had managed to throw her completely off-kilter. She was upset and didn't care what he thought.

He'd known of the uncle's death, but not of her father's. Shocked, John offered his condolences. "Ma'am, I'm mighty sorry to hear of your father's death. I had no idea."

He further realized how vulnerable this young woman must be, faced with such devastating losses, left to run a ranch on her own, and at a very young age. Seeing how alone and defenseless she was, his heart went out to her. She faced a very difficult situation for one so young. He sat across from her, patiently biding his time, waiting to see what followed.

Margarita came into the room, interrupting the tenseness that had developed between them. "Miss Cherry, this man, he stay for supper?"

She studied the big man sitting across from her young charge, and Cherry wondered if Margarita had heard her angry outburst.

Ashamed of being uncivil to a stranger, one who did not appear to be some uncouth wanderer off the trail, or some conniving thief who sought to toss her off her own place, she regretted her hasty words. Accusing a man who only sought to bring her something from her uncle seemed unfriendly and made her rethink her words. She managed to stammer, "Why y—yes, if you'd care to eat with us, you're welcome, Mr. Carmona."

"Why thanks, ma'am. I'd like that. I can't remember when I've had a good home-cooked meal; I look forward to the pleasure."

She nodded the information to Margarita and the woman left the room. Cherry noted the Mexican woman's obvious curiosity regarding the stranger. Well, she had plenty of her own. This man, John Carmona, had proven to be a completely new entity in her life, one whose presence on her ranch filled her mind with questions: *Has some unknown fate sent this man my way to be of help or could he be behind all the evil deeds done on this place?*

Conflicted, Cherry did her best to be a gracious hostess. Managing a semblance of a smile, she watched him place the small bag back in his pocket and nod to her as he glanced out the windows. "I believe I'll step outside and have a look around if it's just as well with you."

With a sigh of relief, she watched the big man take his leave. *I've got to be careful of strangers from now on.* Nodding her head, she also decided, *If he's behind these terrible things, I need to know about it. It might be best to keep him around for a while.* Aside from her suspicions that this man might be one of those who sought her ruin, she knew she didn't want him to leave. Unable to take her eyes off of him, she watched him through the window.

Remembering how his deep gray eyes had mesmerized her and that low soothing voice, she cried out, "Oh God, what's wrong with me?" Yet, she couldn't stop watching his fine swinging gait as he sauntered about the ranch yard.

"Who that man?" Margarita came quietly into the room. Her deep, dark, questioning eyes betrayed more than a passing interest in the stranger. Cherry had the feeling the woman looked upon this man as someone sent to them. Why, and for what reason, she didn't know, but that thought had entered her mind, too. He couldn't know of their problems, being a total stranger. But, then again, he could, if he was a part of them, couldn't he?

"I don't know, Margarita," Cherry answered. "He's no tramp cowboy, I know that much. He wants to stay around and work a while, and we do need more help with Dad gone. Even Uncle Omar did some work around the ranch." She puzzled over this new event in her life, but found no ready answer. She'd have to be on her guard with this stranger while she sorted out who he was. *A well-dressed, well-spoken man like that couldn't be the devil who seeks our ruin—or could he?*

∽∾∽∾

Outside, John surveyed the ranch yard. Seeing activity around the barn, he decided to take care of his horse and have a word with some of the men. After Cherry's comments, and what the man at the stable in town had implied, he was very certain that something was off-kilter on the place. The ranch had a fine location and should be profitable if handled well.

Possibilities grew within his mind. He needed to stay around long enough to find answers regarding his own personal mission. If he found work on this ranch, some things might be closer to completion. Beyond that incentive, the slim, black haired young woman with deep, lavender-hued eyes was heavily on his mind. He was very taken with her and that fact, on its own, had him nonplussed. A thing like that had never happened to him before and he didn't know what to make of it. The mad stirring in his loins had taken hold of him like nothing he'd ever known.

After taking his horse to water, he unsaddled the big buckskin, found an empty corral to hold him, and shoved an armload of hay in for his feed. The horse cared for, he walked about looking into some of the outbuildings. The place boasted a nice blacksmithing set-up, a large barn, and several corrals. Hay fields lay farther out, but fenced pastures for livestock were close in. Shortly, he came face to face with one of the ranch hands.

"Howdy mister, can I help you? Lookin' for someone are you?"

The distinct coldness in his voice put John on alert. He knew instinctively that this heavy, solid-appearing man saw him as an adversary.

"Just might be looking for the foreman of this outfit."

"That'd be me. Name's Link. Can't say as I've ever met up with you, Mr..."

"John Carmona. I came out to see the owner on a personal matter." He paused after that bit of explanation, gazing across the surrounding hills, taking in the sweep of the mountains and how well set up this ranch looked to be, nestled in a wide, flat valley as it was. "I'd like to stay a spell and put in some time on the ranch here if you'd be needing help. The little lady inside thought you might be short-handed with her father and uncle gone and the roundup coming up."

"Naw, we're real well fixed for help. I've got some new boys hired on and they'll be ridin' in right soon."

The man was lying through his teeth, which set John to wondering. The shifty squint in Link's eyes and the way his hand hovered near his six-shooter raised a few hairs on the back of John's neck. For now, he didn't see this man as much of a challenge, but he did see him as trouble ahead.

"Wonder what made Miss Bender say that to me. She seemed of the opinion you were more than a little short-handed. Keeping her in the dark, or not so well informed— that it?" He gave Link a frowning sort of look that said, *What's really going on around here?*

Link's hand strayed towards his gun. He stayed his action, but warned, "You'd best mind your own damned business and get the hell out of here. We got enough riders, no worries there."

He stuck his generous chest and stomach out to emphasis his words. He was a good-sized man, but John knew instinctively the man wouldn't brace him any further on the subject, not face to face, at any rate.

"Well, since I'm invited for supper, I'll let you know later about my leaving." John walked into the barn and checked things out, not looking for anything in particular, but refusing to concede any territory to Link.

He'd taken a distinct dislike to this man, Link, and believed him overly territorial about the running of this ranch. Cherry Bender might place her trust in the man, but he doubted she knew her foreman as well as she ought to. She had said riders never stayed very long in their employ, and John figured Link had a hand in that. *Why wouldn't a man with secretive plans of his own want to keep young cowboys away from that lovely young woman?*

After another hour of nosing around various out buildings and the barn, he heard the dinner bell ring and headed toward the house. Link walked that way as well and stopped at a washstand to wash some of the crust off his hands before dinner. John followed suit since he had plenty of his own trail dust to wash off. With his black hair slicked down and his face and arms still damp from washing, he entered the ranch house along with Link for dinner.

Cherry looked up to see them heading toward the dining table. "Welcome, I hope you're hungry...both of you." She was wearing a soft cream-shaded dress with a blue sash about her slender waist and looked like an angel to John. She indicated their seats and sat down with them to have dinner.

Margarita hurried in with bowls of *albondigas* soup to start the meal and they set to with gusto. John tore small pieces of tortilla to stir into the fragrant, spicy delight and conversation remained light during this time as they dug into Margarita's fine cuisine.

John, more than hungry, hadn't enjoyed fare like this for far too long. With a touch of jealousy, he figured Link enjoyed it every day if he was handy. The big chair at the head of the table sat empty. He surmised it was her father's seat, a chair that would remain empty unless the pretty little miss took on a husband. With a sense of relief, he didn't get the feeling Cherry entertained any thoughts towards Link in that way. None at all.

It did strike him that he felt some jealousy regarding Link's assumption of power over the affairs of the ranch with the boss dead and in his grave, especially the familiar way Link said, "Say, this here's mighty good chuck, Miss Cherry," as he dug into the large juicy steak, hissing and sizzling from her kitchen, that Margarita had just set on their plates.

The woman quickly loaded the table with potatoes, peas, and corn, all of it John assumed to be bounty of the ranch. Margarita obviously enjoyed the chance to feed two big hungry males and literally beamed as she piled on the fluffy Mexican *boletas* she had made with her own hands. The yeasty smell made him reach for them in anticipation.

Link, adopting an air of command regarding ranching affairs, commented, "I believe we ought to move all the mother cows and yearlin's down to the lower sections, bringin' the stock in closer, getting' ready for the roundup. Thought to get at it tomorrow."

"Oh, that's a good idea, Link. Dad had mentioned something about that a few days ago. He'd want you to go ahead and do that."

John saw she fought fresh tears as she handled the renewed pain of losing her father. His heart soared when she cleared her throat and added, "Link, I've asked Mr. Carmona to stay and work with you boys for a time. I know how short we are with roundup coming and all." She turned to John. "You did say you'd stay and work for a spell, didn't you?"

"Sure did, ma'am. I'm in no hurry to get where I was goin'."

The foreman swelled up like a toad at her words, apparently angered by his acceptance of a position on the ranch. John smiled. Link couldn't bluster about it in front of Cherry. She was, after all, the new owner since her father's death and she'd hired him on her own.

The man had lied to Carmona about needing help, but it didn't seem to bother his conscience. The man had no shame, and in Link, he knew he had an enemy. For some reason, he felt Link would be a dangerous one. He would need to watch his back from now on.

He also decided the man was about as proprietary as he could get away with. After watching the interplay between Cherry and the foreman, however, she appeared completely oblivious of the man's attempt to establish some sort of claim to her, above that of ranch foreman. With an inner feel of exhilaration, John saw she had formed no discernible attachment to the man.

He'd needed an "in" to this ranch and now he had it. He relaxed and, along with a very fine dinner, enjoyed the silent fury he observed on Link's face, who made no further comment regarding his employment.

Margarita brought in a couple of fruit pies and several dishes of *flan*, a Mexican custard John especially enjoyed. She set a large pot of scalding black coffee on the table to accompany any further dining they wished.

Cherry said little during the meal. He'd felt her curiosity about him, wanting to know where he was from and where he was headed, but she refrained from discussing it before Link. After the man rose from the table, tossed his soiled napkin down, and stalked out the door, she turned her eyes towards him.

"Mr. Carmona, how do you happen to be passing through this country? It's rather isolated. We see few travelers of any kind." Her eyes had grown darker with only lamplight for illumination, which brought out the purple depths that much better. The sight of her mesmerized him to the point he could barely answer her question.

He hitched about in his chair. The seat had grown hard as hell, but he didn't want to end his conversation with this lovely girl just yet. "I have something ahead of me, but nothing I can't delay. My line of work is more in keeping with mining and minerals and, at times, seeking out claims of certain rare metals. These are found just about anywhere and, though not so valuable as gold or silver, they will soon be used in manufacturing back in the east."

"How interesting! I didn't *think* you looked much like a cowhand, but I'm sure Link will be glad to have another rider."

She rattled away, but beneath her attempt at being a good hostess, he saw and felt the lack of trust and barely concealed suspicion. It lay in the narrowing of those marvelous eyes as she looked at him.

John rose from his chair. "Miss Cherry, I'm no cowboy, but I can ride a horse and chase a cow, and I'll do my best for you. I appreciate the chance to work here." He placed his hat back on his head and nodded. "I'd best turn in, might have a big day tomorrow. I'll say good night, miss, and thanks for a very fine meal."

He tipped his hat to her and headed to the bunkhouse. He found that facility well furnished, with solidly constructed bedsteads and thick mattresses for sleeping. It boasted a stove, cupboards, a table with chairs, and washing facilities as well. Link gave him a quick introduction to the cook, Booker, and two cowboys who had ridden in earlier, Monte Blue and Waddie Barnes. With muffled replies of, "Howdy" and "Pleased to meet you," they all turned in.

For John sleep was elusive. Awake, on rough bedding, he thought of black hair, violet eyes, and a slender form of willowy, feminine grace.

CHAPTER 6

The next morning John rose early. Along with the other two men, he ate what Booker put in front of them, bacon, flapjacks, eggs, and coffee that could take the hide clean off an elephant. He sat across from Monte and Waddie. In the light of day, both appeared scruffy and run down, certainly the kind Cherry wouldn't find attractive. His idea that Link manipulated the men who came and went on his ranch gained added fuel after running into these two.

"Nice meetin' you, boys," he said. "I'll be ridin' along with you for a spell. Any more out there besides you two?" He knew Link overheard the questioning, but the disgruntled man offered no comment.

"Why shore, there's six of us all together, but we could use another hand or two right about now." Waddie was young and stringy in build but looked strong enough to get the job done. His shock of straw-like yellow hair stood straight up this morning. "Maybe you'd like to ride along with me today. We got a lot of cows with calves runnin' up in Box Canyon. We'll be needin' to drive the lot of 'em toward the roundup valley."

"That'd be fine with me...Waddie, is it?" He looked over toward Link. "If that's okay with the boss, here."

"Fine by me, John. Waddie can take you wherever he's a mind to." His voice, smooth as silk this morning, bore no trace of animosity and John took this as a subtle warning to be on the lookout for trouble. He had an enemy, or at the very least, competition here at the Bender Ranch.

They saddled up and set off. "Say, that's a mighty fine horse you're ridin'," Waddie offered as they rode out from the ranch. He cast a speculative eye on John's big buckskin gelding, Muley, "Steps out right fine, he does."

"Thanks, he's been a good one. Can last all day and then some," John replied. "How's things been around here? Miss Cherry told me you've lost some stock over the past year and no one seems to know the how or why of it." He added, his tone off-hand, "Sounds like she don't seem to think much of your sheriff here-a-bouts, either."

"Well, that's true enough all right. He ain't been much help. Never gets to the bottom of anything. But Link, he don't seem real worried, long as he keeps his job." John detected Waddie's note of dissatisfaction with the foreman, as he continued. "I just ride along and get my work done. Glad to have this job. This ranch's been a good place for me."

"Pretty rough on the owners, seems like. Anybody figure out what happened to Bender?"

"Naw, never have so far. Shame about him—real good man and damned good to work for, too," Waddie rambled on. "Happened the day I's way off in them far mountains with most of the boys." He indicated a blue line of mountains lying far to the west. "Cattle got out and we found 'em way on up there." He shook his head. "Couldn't believe he'd been shot that way when we heard of it. Knocked about real bad, too, by the way his face looked."

"Well, someone must have wanted the man dead, damned hard to figure a thing like that." John decided to hold off on any more information gathering. No need to arouse suspicion from the other hands. But he had to ask, "Anybody ever take a shot at you?"

"No, but a man who worked here for a spell had somebody aimin' for him. Took a bullet. It just grazed him—left here after that."

"Who hired the man?"

"He was one the boss hired on. Good enough hand, but Link didn't cotton to him too much. Too bad." Then Waddie pointed off to the right. "Look over there. Looks like it's a decent sized bunch. We'll need to bring 'em over towards that big roundup valley." Indicating off to the left, he pulled on his reins and headed out at a slow lope.

They worked the cattle, bringing them together from where they had been, spread out all through hills and gullies, into a manageable herd. John wasn't a cowboy, but he knew what had to be done. He found a lot to admire in Waddie. The young man knew his work.

Pointing out a few red spotted cows, Waddie said, "These are part of the red bunch and ain't supposed to be up here, neither. They're some that disappeared from the herd over in Carter Canyon." Waddie shook his head in puzzlement. "Somethin' damn funny's goin' on around here, that's for damned sure."

John didn't know those places, but the information about underhanded activity slowly added up. In silence, but for the necessary virulent cussing required when working cattle, they assembled the bawling cows and calves. At Waddie's direction, they herded the cattle over a high ridge and on toward another wide valley that lay a few miles beyond.

When the sun got high and hunger set in, Waddie pointed off to a grove of trees. "They's a line shack off that way, might go see if we can rustle us up some grub."

John felt his hunger taking hold. They left the cattle to graze in a wide, grassy area, rode into the grove of trees, and tied their horses outside a rustic yet snug-looking shack.

Waddie pushed open the door and went in. "We keep a few vittles around in these places. Too hard to haul stuff when you're workin' stock."

John followed him inside and noted a small cooking stove that doubled for warmth in foul weather. The shack also boasted a chair and low bunk with a few ratty blankets folded in a pile. "Looks like you boys stay out here sometimes. Maybe why I only met a few of you."

"Yeah, we don't mind it too much. Beat's runnin' afoul of the boss when he's got his tail in a twist." Waddie grabbed some fine bits of wood from a half-stocked wood box near the door and got a fire started in the cast iron stove. It was flat on top for cooking, but gave off a nice heat as well. He pulled out a can of peaches and some dried jerky he put out to soak. He mixed up some biscuits, put on a pot for coffee and, in time, he produced a decent meal of jerky gravy over biscuits, with peaches to top it off.

The coffee tasted dead awful, but John was glad to have a cup. "Hey kid, great chuck you've made. You'll do just about anywhere won't you?" He had developed a good bit of admiration for this young, hard-working cowboy. The young man knew cattle and did his job full out.

Waddie shrugged, grinned, but said nothing.

John smiled in return. "You mentioned the boss getting in an uproar. What about? You sure seem to know your work."

Waddie laughed. "Aw, he don't give a damn about this place, never has. Mostly worries if anyone gets too close to Miss Cherry." He shook his head, "If they do, things happen, and they drift away. She don't seem to notice it, but that's how come we're runnin' so short of help all the damned time."

"Got ideas about marrying her, does he?"

"Looks like he does. He'd never own up to it, but it's either that or something else going on around here. Wonder if maybe Bender found out about whatever it is. I don't want to say anythin' out of turn, but I've seen some strange men ridin' around the place most of the past year, like they're lookin' for somethin', and it sure as hell ain't cattle, no siree." He'd become extra garrulous in his talk with a meal and the warmth of the line shack.

Waddie proved to be a goldmine of information, and John said nothing except to add a few encouraging grunts.

They fed their horses a feed bag of oats before moving out again. After several sweaty hours under the blazing sun and breathing dust from the cattle-torn earth, the two riders noted how the sun had sunk low in the horizon. The cattle were well settled across a wide valley where the roundup was scheduled to occur.

"We can make it to the ranch before sundown," Waddie said. "These cows oughta stick around here. There's graze enough down there to keep 'em happy."

John had already come to like the Bender Ranch and hoped that black-haired goddess would let him stay long enough to become friends—if not a whole lot more. His mind was a buzz with ways to get next to her. She'd already gotten under his skin, and deep as hell.

He'd used muscles long dormant and it felt damned good. He smiled with satisfaction after a hard day's work as they headed out for the home ranch. He looked forward to a full belly and maybe, if he was very lucky, another good dinner in the ranch house. Being in the presence of the beautiful girl that owned the place wouldn't hurt anything either. He kept his thoughts to himself, but visions of Cherry Bender haunted him constantly since he'd laid eyes on her.

They rode in silence. Waddie had unwittingly filled him in on a multitude of events taking place against the ranch and the unsuspecting Cherry. Passing a small body of water that lay just off the trail, John said, "We got time for a wash-up in this pond?"

"Yeah, fine idea. I could sure do with some cleanin'." Waddie laughed as they headed their horses toward the water, dismounted, and dropped the reins to ground-hitch both horses.

After divesting themselves of their clothes, they threw themselves into the cool water. "Not bad for a cow tank, is it?" Waddie offered. "We make 'em in several places so when it rains we catch the run off. Makes better grazin' if the stock don't need to go so far to water and this'n is bigger than most. Got deeper sides"

John wondered at the proffered information and mused, *Waddie must see me as a real greenie if he thinks I've never seen a cow tank before.* But he agreed. The water was decently clean despite the cow droppings around the side. The day's dust and sweat washed off, John stood naked at the edge of the tank and pulled a clean shirt from his saddle bags. "Sure feels better with some of that dirt off me."

The skinny, rangily-built Waddie donned his dirty shirt and pants. His yellow hair was several shades lighter, however, as the kid slicked it down with his hands. "Wish I'd thought of a clean shirt—" He laughed. "Well, if I had one, leastways."

Across the wide reaches of the ranch, soft, purple shades of night encroached as the sun sank behind the western mountains. They rode into the ranch yard as long shadows deepened along the sides of the out-buildings. The grandeur of the surrounding landscape faded from his mind when John stepped into the bunk house and met Link face to face.

"Seems you're invited to the house for supper again." The scowl across his face relayed his deepening dislike, smoldering anger, and without a doubt, a raging jealousy over the beautiful Cherry.

"Thanks, Link, for letting me know." John wanted to laugh in his joy, but held his features steady in a noncommittal pose. In fact, he added an expression of puzzlement to his face, "Wonder what's going on?"

Link looked like a man ready to chew nails—big ones. "Better get on up there, you interferin' son-of-a-bitch!"

"Whoo-ee, guess, I'd better." John slicked his damp hair the best he could without hunting for a comb and headed to the ranch house.

Cherry must have seen him coming. She opened the door before he knocked. "Come in, Mr. Carmona."

Pleased to hear the soft way she said his name, he felt a small buzz zip through him. He liked the way it sounded on her lips. She stood before him dressed in a long floral print dress caught at her waist with a narrow purple belt. The color of it enhanced her wonderful eyes and to boot, she'd let her hair hang long and glossy. It hung in loose waves and curled a bit at the ends. She was radiant tonight and a delight to his eyes. *She may not trust me or like me much, but she sure as hell dresses up for me.* He saw that as a sign. *Maybe she's softened some in her thinking about me.*

As they sat together at the dining table, she raised her eyes to him, and to his surprise, they were brimming with tears as she asked, "Who are you really? I know you're no cowboy. But why come to this ranch? And what exactly are you looking for?" Her voice, barely more than a whisper, told him she was dead serious.

He understood the animosity, tinged with the fear, and replied, "You've no need to worry over my showing up here. You're right about it though, I do have a purpose in coming through this country." He took a few bites of food and sat back, "The area around here looks possible for a few things the government needs." He leisurely buttered a biscuit, taking longer than needed, seeing that it drove her wild, waiting for his next words.

"Like what?" she prompted, her eyes snapping with exasperation. "What could we possibly have on this ranch of interest or use to the government?"

"Well, not especially this place, but this general area of the Arizona Territory looks to have a few needed minerals our government is interested in."

"Oh, I thought by your words that we had something of value on our ranch. If we do, I think someone is trying to take it from us."

She stopped talking, her brow furrowed, and she began again. "My father was murdered. But who would want to kill him? And why?" She lowered her voice again. "He came awake for a little bit, enough to try and warn me, J– John." She hesitated at the intimacy of using his given name.

"What did he say?"

"I couldn't quite figure it out but it sounded like he said to watch out for someone close to me or words to that effect. I'm not sure."

"You say things have happened around here. He must have discovered something, but who'd know if he did and be close enough to take his life like that?" John leaned toward her with that question and saw her pale.

"What are you thinking, ma'am?" he queried. "Is there someone you'd be suspicious of?"

"No, not really, but I'm trying to remember who was here that day and it seems no one was here but Link. I heard he'd left way before noon but I never heard where he was going."

She frowned and to John even that looked utterly charming on her.

"Link came riding back in time to help me take care of Dad." Tears filled her eyes as she remembered. "I was so glad to see him that day—he handled everything right when I needed him."

Wiping tears from her eyes, she glared at John as if he had said something derogatory about her foreman. John had his own thoughts, but made no reply. They continued to eat in silence.

Dinner was finished and he was so torn between gazing into those dark purple eyes and thinking about his work that he wasn't sure what they had eaten. The mystery of the place only deepened and John felt divided between the young woman before him and his reason for being here.

Cherry was confused. She had asked about his work and he'd answered, but she still had questions. *How could the reason he came here relate to what happened to my father? And why would he just happen to be in the same card game as Uncle Omar? Why did he come here after Dad's death? Is there any way I can trust this stranger at all?*

Was it John Carmona she wanted to know better or did she only care about why he'd come here? In any case, she didn't to want him to leave so soon.

CHAPTER 7

Rising from the table, Cherry moved toward the patio. "Let's walk out into the orchard. It relaxes me and I'm tired from thinking over and over about everything that's happened. I miss my father terribly. He always knew what to do—well, until this past year. Then, I guess he had too much stress from worry. Everything seemed to wear him down."

The slump of her shoulders made John want to comfort her—if only he dared.

She proffered her feelings as much to the air as she did to him while they moved across the patio and out under the fragrant trees that were laden with ripening fruit. "It always smells good out here," she said while sniffing the night air. She reached a bench beneath an old apple tree and sat down, leaving room for him.

John sat beside her and edged closer. "It sure does, miss, and if you don't mind my saying, so do you."

Cherry felt his nearness acutely. Catching the intensely masculine scent of the big man who sat so near, hearing him breathe, aware of his size and his closeness made her heart race with wild imaginings. Whether from fear or what, she didn't know, but she felt dizzy for some reason and clung to the edge of the bench to keep from falling. She didn't completely trust this man. And she didn't trust this feeling of strangeness that had taken over her mind and body.

He turned toward her in the moonlight and, seeing her stricken face and clamped lips, reached for her hand. "You all right?"

Cherry jumped at his touch. "Of course, I'm not all right!" She pulled her hand away and clasped her arms around her body as if to protect herself from him. "Everything has been turned upside down in my life." Slowly shaking her head, she gritted her teeth. "I wonder if things will ever be right again!"

Hearing the tears in her voice, John reached out to place a hand of comfort and solace on her shoulder. "Things will be all right again. You've suffered terrible losses and a thing like that takes time to get past. Try not to worry too much about it." He took the liberty of patting her on the shoulder while his voice took on a crooning tone. "Cherry, I imagine you feel very alone after the loss of your father and uncle. I know from experience how hard it is to recover from something like this, but you will."

He'd softly called her by name in an intimate way and she didn't call him on it. He wanted very much to pull her across his lap and into his arms, but only reached a bit farther to lay an arm across her shoulders.

She stiffened, her head came up, and she pulled away. "You shouldn't take hold of me like that!" Regretting how easily she'd let this stranger know her inner feelings, she turned away from him. Then, remembering a deep sadness in his voice, Cherry turned back. "I'm sorry I said anything about our troubles. It seems you've had your share too. Please, you'd best go now. You'll need to get to the bunkhouse and rest. Link might have a big day ahead for you in the morning."

She thought that sounded inept. If so, it was because in this man's presence, she had unusual feelings that kept her off balance and incredibly tense. Her heart raced so rapidly in her chest, she was afraid it might burst.

"I'm sorry you're hurting, miss. I'd like to help if I could."

Cherry made no further comment. He then added with a shrug. "Well, I'll be going, but before I do I have to say I think your foreman, Link, may be running off your ranch hands." He hesitated for a moment, "Just an idea that came to mind, miss." He rose from the bench and turned away. "I'll just say thanks for the supper and good night."

"Good night, Mr. Carmona." Tight lipped, Cherry managed to say only that much.

He'd boldly taken liberties with her feelings, put his hand on her, and even offered a few small words of comfort. After all, she wasn't completely sure who he was or why he was here, and the crazy things he did to her emotions upset her. She'd never felt like this before. Having little experience with men, she didn't understand it and was disgusted with herself. She hadn't protested, instead she had allowed his touch, not wanting to appear rude.

A mass of confusion, she took the time to watch his tall form fade into the darkness. The touch of his hands lingered to burn through her clothing and into her skin to the point she could scarcely catch her breath. A flush rose, burning and hot over her face. *Why does he make me feel that way?*

Many questions lingered in her mind as she entered the house. Her feelings, still heightened from her encounter with John in the garden, burned within her. The man-woman thing she'd seen between Margarita and her father came to mind. She'd seen the two of them together at odd times, finding stolen moments when they believed her asleep or outside the house. In her mind, she had become more aware, and somehow she now understood. She imagined what might have happened between the two of them and wondered, *Is something like that happening to me?*

She blushed and burned in the cover of darkness with her guilty secret, while looking out the window to catch one last glimpse of the tall man who'd just left her, but he'd disappeared into the darkness.

Cherry considered his warning about Link, and although a completely new idea to her, she couldn't dismiss it. The foreman had been her rock after her father's murder, and it hurt to cast suspicion on that small bit of refuge. In defense of Link, she asked herself, *Who is some stranger off the trail to say a thing like that?*

After John left Cherry, he spotted a dim figure slinking away and faced the cold reality of knowing he had an enemy on this ranch, maybe more than one. He walked about in the ranch yard, cooling his temper, before entering the bunkhouse. Link was lying on his bunk, blankets drawn over him, but John was certain he wasn't sleeping. Sure it had been him in the shadows, John said nothing and turned in. Surrounded by snoring men, he lay awake a long time sorting things out in his mind.

☙☙

The next morning Link sent John out with Waddie to Horner Canyon. Waddie told him it was a whole day ride up and a whole day back again. A rather distant area of the ranch for them to locate the livestock and drive them to the roundup area. *Getting the competition out of the way, are you Link?*

John didn't mind the distance since it gave him a chance for some needed exploration and he had further information to gather.

Waddie was bright and chatty as they headed out, "Old Link sure had his tail in a twist last night. Don't know what the hell came over him, just crawled into his bunk and lay there, wouldn't set for a hand of cards 'er nothin'."

"Can't imagine what'd be his idea," John offered. "Maybe the roundup's got him buggered." He figured this bit of nothing should cover his suspicion of Link's night time activities.

"Aw when he gets like that, somebody's gonna get fired. I've seen it before an' we're short-handed enough as it is."

They rode past noon and finally stopped by a spreading oak tree that edged against a small, bright stream. They dismounted.

"This is a good stoppin' spot," Waddie told him. "A good drink for the horses, and a bite for us."

John checked the lay of the land, his mind occupied with several things besides cattle. He carried a small leathern pack behind his saddle at all times that contained certain supplies unneeded for the care of cattle. "How much farther do we need to go?"

"It'll take most of the day to reach the canyon and another day to chase 'em out where we can gather a herd big enough to drive back. Ol' Link won't be satisfied if we leave any up there, either."

Waddie watered his horse and put some oats in his feedbag. John did the same for his horse and then watched as the young cowboy hauled out a thin pack of dried biscuits and handed a couple to him. "Here, chew on one of these. Ain't much but they's a line shack up there, too, and we can fix us somethin' for supper."

"Hey, this is not too bad—when it's all you've got." John laughed and Waddie joined him. As they relaxed beneath the spreading trees, John's thoughts went back to the ranch, the black-haired girl, and those mesmerizing violet eyes.

☙❧☙

"Cherry, what you do about this man? He stay this rancho, he work?"

Margarita's dark eyes probed for more than the answer to that question. It was mid-morning by the time Cherry had gotten up from her bed despite how invitingly the sun shone outside.

"Yes Margarita, I've asked him to stay and work for us. He isn't really a cowboy, he told me that. What he is, I'm not sure, although he did mentioned mining. We need the extra hand with Dad gone," she said, unable to keep the defensiveness out of her voice.

"He one fine looking man, no?" Margarita's black eyes sparkled and Cherry saw a knowing smile form over the woman's broad face.

"I suppose so," Cherry replied.

She ached with the need to ask this gentle woman so many things that puzzled her, yet she couldn't broach her conflicted feelings. Something momentous had happened, but what?

Margarita came close and folded Cherry in her arms. "*Pobrecita*, the big man, he watch you all time, I see him. He follow you always with his eyes." She smiled down at Cherry with a mischievous grin. "And your eyes—they follow him same way, eh?"

"I do like many things about him. He seems to be a fine man and well educated, but I don't know his people or anything about him. Could he be the one behind all the bad things that have happened here and now he's come to deliver the final blow? I can't help worrying about it. He was in that card game where Uncle Omar was killed. Do I dare to trust him? How do I know he didn't have something to do with that?"

"Maybe he's no good man, I don't know, but he's strong. He very much man, *mi hija*—very much man." She held Cherry a moment longer and then asked, "What you do about him?" She deepened her tone and said with added meaning, "But I think he good man, Cherry, I know this."

"Margarita! How do you know and why must I do anything?"

The Mexican woman chuckled in her knowing way. "I think one day you will know what to do about him. He show you—everything." She suppressed a smile and gave Cherry a good hug.

Cherry flushed wildly and the heat of it flashed and burned across her face. She ran into her bedroom, trying to blot out the knowing look on Margarita's broad face and how she'd smiled in a way that said so much.

Cherry was about to throw herself on the bed but changed her mind. "Oh God! I can't stand to be cooped up in here anymore. I'm going for a ride. I need to get outside in the cool, clean air." She dug out her split-leather riding skirt, added boots, spurs, a warm blouse, and a vest. She strode out to the corral for her small spotted Appaloosa. She no longer kept him in his stall in the barn—she never failed to remember her father in that befouled stall and stayed away.

She called to him, "Checky. Come see me."

The horse put his head down and moved toward her. Coming up to her, he put his head against her chest. A dollop of slime from his wide mouth dripped down onto her riding skirt.

She loved the look of him with his white rump, heavily dotted with rusty roan-shaded spots that matched the color of his body, head, and legs,

"Hey, boy, miss me?" She caught him under his chin and pulled him along to the barn. She got her tack, soon had him saddled, and turned his head down the trail toward the high mountains on the east side of the ranch.

Cherry had a favorite spot in the lower foothills she called her Eden. It held a thick grove of Pinóns, a small sun-lit grassy area, and a couple of Ponderosas, all fed by a tiny, running brook. She'd spent many happy hours out there, thinking and daydreaming. Today, she especially longed for the feeling of peace she'd sought desperately but not known lately. Things had built inside her since enduring the lasting pain of her father's terrible death and the newer onus of the responsibility of managing a huge sprawling ranch. For a little while, she sought relief from all of it.

That someone had deliberately and cruelly killed her father never left her mind for long, and she vowed again to find that devil and make him pay.

And then there was Carmona, a man who lingered in her mind as a man of mystery in too many ways. Yet, unsure of him as she was, she found it hard to believe he wasn't being on the level with her. If he'd come to the ranch with evil intentions, she certainly had no proof of it. She needed to keep an eye on the man, and for that, she felt a deep happiness.

The sun was high and when she let Checky have his head, he leaped out in a mad gallop. She reveled in the speed of flying hooves as the wind burned her cheeks. "Oh, how good it feels!"

After a decent run, she pulled him into a steady soft jog-trot, about half walk, and half trot. The air was warm, birds wheeled against the soft blue sky, and she let the horse lead the way. Her eyes closed, she rode her mount in a momentary state of peaceful, healing bliss.

Her quiet reverie was rudely interrupted at the sound of a man's voice booming out. "Well, howdy there, Miss Cherry, what'er you doing a way out here all alone like this?"

She opened her eyes to see Link sitting his big bay gelding and positioned squarely across her trail.

"Just taking a ride, Link. How about you? Looking for cattle out this way?" Seeing the bold way he'd placed his horse across her trail, she remembered Carmona's words. Link, by his present actions, reinforced what the big man had said about Link keeping her for himself. "Mind moving your horse so I may pass?"

"Goin' out to your nice little hideaway, are you?"

Link's voice had turned arrogant and commanding, using ugly tones she didn't like or understand. That he'd obviously spied on her in her most private moments sent her anger to a high pitch. *How does Link know about my special Eden? Has he followed me before when I visited my favorite spot?*

Disgusted at his display of arrogant behavior, Cherry was convinced Carmona was right in saying the man had most likely run off potential suitors over the years. As far as she was concerned, he'd just proven it with his boorish and possessive behavior.

"Link, will you please move your horse out of my way?" Her furrowed brow and angry look should have been enough to make him move. After all, she was his boss. But he sat his horse, smugly leering at her, a wide grin spreading across his fleshy face.

"No need gettin' mad, missy. I'd like a bit of time for a friendly chat with you. You can't spend all your time makin' eyes at that damned stranger dude." The firm set to his jaw and the cold look in his eyes left her in no doubt as to his opinion of Carmona. "My God, girl, he just rode in. You don't even know the man!"

Her jaw was set just as firmly as Link's and her temper had reached the boiling point. "Never mind about my personal business. I can choose my friends as I see fit and talk to whomever I want."

"Your daddy didn't see it that way. He left me in charge of the place, and I aim to see his orders carried out. That Carmona feller won't be around long enough for you to take a big shine to him, anyway." A smug look crossed his face and his chin jutted out. "I hear tell he's ready to light out of here any day now."

Cherry hid her feelings of disappointment. *John might be leaving*! Had she played the fool, getting close to him only to have the man up and disappear, just like all the others that came to work on the ranch? Remembering his words about Link, she replied, "I don't believe you, Link. He would have told me if he was leaving."

"You mean while you was out there in that orchard cozying up to him last night?"

She hated the sneer that played across his face. Furious at the thought of Link spying on her, she declared, "What I do is none of your business. Not ever!" Shaking with anger, she continued. "I don't believe my father gave you leave to talk to me like this. He would never have!"

Though furious at him, she'd suddenly become fearful of the bulky foreman. The ugly scowl across his face was something she had never seen on his face before. It struck her as unsettling and even more as threatening.

Going to her Eden was out of the question now. She pulled Checky around to head for home, but Link rode close and grabbed her reins.

"Hold on there, girl! No need getting all riled up. I'm just tryin' to protect you like your daddy said." He pulled Checky close to his horse and was about to lay his hand on her when she grabbed her quirt and lashed out blindly at him.

"Ouch, goddammit, Cherry!" He clutched his face, feeling at the welts rising quickly across his nose and cheeks. "What'd you do that for, girl?" Enraged, he grabbed her quirt and screamed at her, his damaged face flushed red. He raised his hand, the quirt held high, ready to strike her. "Want some of your own medicine?"

Cherry sat tight in her saddle, burning with anger. "If I had my gun on me right now, I'd shoot you, you monster!" His upraised arm settled back and she added, "You'd better stay out of my personal business or else. And don't call me girl!"

She didn't like him using her name or being familiar in any other way either. She jerked the reins from his hands, turned her horse on the trail back to the ranch, and let Checky loose. He took off like a shot and she clung low in the saddle. Tears streamed from her eyes as she rode and the burning wind seared her face. She should have fired the man on the spot after his disgusting behavior. And she would have Link off her ranch as soon as she laid eyes on him again.

She slowed her pace and did some thinking. "So, what John said must be right. That horrible man *is* trying to run this ranch and my life, too. Was that what Dad warned me about before he died? He did say Link's name." And after this frightening encounter, she fully believed Link could have done a hideous thing like killing her father.

She had been careless this time, but would never leave the ranch again without her pistol. She now believed Link fully capable of trying to control her, the ranch—all of it! He was a treacherous viper in the very heart of her ranch. Remembering his reddened, angry face, she knew he could be part of the vandalism and theft going on, and even the murderer of her father. Yet recalling how helpful he'd been, she puzzled over these questions until her head ached.

Cherry felt sick and wouldn't feel safe again until she had things figured out. She put the spurs to Checky's spotted hide again and rode furiously for home as her mind whirled with questions. She needed help. Dare she turn to Carmona? Or was he a part of it, too?

CHAPTER 8

The vile thoughts churning Cherry's insides turned her stomach until she needed to vomit and pulled Checky to a halt. Hastily checking back along the trail, she saw no dust. She safely dismounted and hurled her scant stomach contents into the brush along the trail. Chin up, shoulders squared, she remounted and headed home

Until Link was gone, she'd best have someone with her if she left the ranch again. It infuriated her to have to consider this, but she would never leave the house without her pistol again, either. It was another reminder that a woman running a ranch on her own invited problems.

Margarita took one look when Cherry rushed into the ranch house, distraught, and cried out, *"Que pasa?"* She folded Cherry in her arms and crooned in Spanish, *"Mi hija, pobrecita."*

Taking refuge in those ample arms, Cherry was comforted and soothed as Margarita waited to hear what had happened.

"I met Link out on the trail," Cherry told her. "He threatened me—he put his hands on me! I'll fire him. He can't stay on here—not after that!"

Margarita raised her eyebrows. "Ooh, you can do that, Cherry?"

"Of course I can, but I'll wait until Mr. Carmona returns." Her voice softened when she said his name. She would feel safer with John, a man she barely knew, than with Link. She had stepped into her role as ranch boss, but she'd feel a whole lot better with some backup.

જ્જજ

John and Waddie worked all day. They *choused* strays from the many surrounding brush-filled gullies and wrangled mother cows and their bawling young calves out of nearby canyons. After several hot hours, they shoved the reluctant beasts into some semblance of a herd and pushed them out into a larger open valley. They left them to graze until the next day's drive to the roundup area.

When it grew too dark for more work, Waddie headed up into a small grove of trees and brought them to another rudely built, line shack. This one proved to be far more weathered and barely good enough to keep out a decent rainstorm.

"We'll camp here for tonight," Waddie said. "Tomorrow, if we're lucky enough, and the herd ain't scattered too damned much, we might get this bunch to the roundup valley by nightfall."

John smiled at the resourcefulness of the plucky young rider

They unsaddled the horses, put them into a rudely built grassy corral, and fed them a bit of oats. Waddie shoved the poorly hung door into the line shack wide open, "Ain't much, is it?"

He laughed as he went in and John appreciated the kid's cheerful spirit, tired as he was.

"It'll do," John replied. "What's for chuck?" He couldn't help thinking of the fine meals served at Cherry's table.

Waddie dug into a box attached to an outer wall. "Wal, there's canned tomaters, beans, and dried jerky around here somewheres."

Protected on the outside by heavy wire mesh to keep the critters away, the box acted as a cooler, being shaded all day by the tall pines growing close around.

"Here's the jerky." He pulled out a canvas bag of the stiff, hard, dried meat that had been cured by drying in the sun. "Let's see what else we've got." He rooted around in a cupboard, pulled out a few cans, and a bag of flour kept in a solid wooden box. "Hope the critters haven't eaten the flour." He pulled it out and aside from a few mealy bugs found a decent supply.

John had the cast iron stove started and Waddie pulled out a rusty frying pan and placed it on the stove to heat. He then set to making biscuits by pouring water and bacon grease into the bag of flour. He sliced the dried jerky with his knife, opened a can of beans, and put them in the pan with the meat. When he decided the oven was hot enough, he placed the ill formed biscuits onto a bit of tin and shoved them in to bake. With that done, he dug out the coffee and made a pot from water out of their canteens.

Again, John found himself charmed and impressed by the efficiency of this young cowboy. "You'll do, son," he said, "and just about anywhere."

A man of few words, unless cussing out the cows, Waddie merely shrugged in reply.

After a bit, they enjoyed a good supper. John picked out a bug or two, but only if he happened to see one, and he didn't spend much time looking. His ravenous hunger made such things unimportant.

The lantern made a decent light that highlighted the interior of the shack, and rough though it was, he found it comfortable. They shook out their bedrolls. He was given the bunk and Waddie settled across from him on the floor. Sleep found them in short order.

ɛɔɛɔ

John went out in the dimness of early morning and immediately saw the poles had been removed from the rustic corral holding their horses. Both mounts were missing. Instinctively, he took it as a warning to himself, but most likely, not to Waddie. Chuckling, he put his fingers to his lips and blew. At the piercing sound, he heard an answering whinny and the pounding of hooves. His big buckskin thundered through the trees and came up to him. "Hey, you yellow-hided son-of-a-bitch, who in hell let you out last night, eh?"

Waddie's horse followed Muley at a distance. John got the feedbags and put a measure of oats in each. He had no trouble putting a rope on Waddie's mount after that.

"What the hell happened out here last night? That corral was in decent enough shape to hold those two," Waddie observed, standing there with a puzzled look across his homely face.

"Looks like we had us some company in the night. Some bastard's gone and let our horses out. Normally, they'd have gone back to the ranch, but my horse won't leave me that way. He's trained to stay close."

"Well, come get a bite of breakfast. Ain't much, but with a bit of jerky we'll make out."

John followed Waddie into the shack while the horses stood at their tethers munching their oats.

Shortly, they were back gathering the cattle for the long trek toward the roundup valley. As always, some didn't want to follow the herd, but they easily handled that situation, except for one crooked-horned steer who kept them on a constant vigil with his antics. He was a natural leader and had a good many followers trailing away with him. Waddie directed as many and varied cuss words as his vocabulary allowed in that steer's direction. John totally enjoyed the raw, shocking comments from the mild young cowboy's lips.

"Waddie, that's quite a line you're spieling off toward that poor animal. If he could blush, he sure as hell would."

Waddie merely laughed. They rode hard and kept the strays fairly intact. It was after the moon had risen before they had most of the stock gathered. They shoved the last bunch in with the expanding herd held in the wide valley.

Waddie said, "Might's well stay in that line shack again. Ain't much chuck left, but it'll have to do."

He headed his horse toward it. John went along, reluctant at missing another dinner with Cherry. She was heavy on his mind. He sighed. He'd have to abide for another day without the sight of that glorious creature.

Someone had ridden a long way to make trouble for him and Waddie. John had his ideas about that, too. This night, he'd keep a sharp eye on the horse corral and have a lot less sleep.

After the meal was over and the lantern put out, John slipped outside with an old scattergun kept at the line shack. Being cold at nights in this high altitude, he took a blanket off the bunk to wrap around his shoulders. The moon had brightened some, but the light was poor, although his eyes quickly became accustomed to the dimness.

Waddie agreed to take the second shift if their stake-out lasted past midnight. John huddled down behind a clump of brush to wait.

After long hours of cramped attention, listening to crickets and the soft rustling of other night creatures, John decided nothing more would happen to their mounts during the dark of night. He had decided to call the vigil off, but on hearing the crack of a snapping twig and the muffled neigh of a horse that came from neither of theirs, he realized that their visitor from the night before was still with them.

John tensed, bringing the scatter gun up and into position. The flitting shadow of a figure approaching the horse corral appeared in the dim moonlight. John then saw the faint outline of a bow and arrow shadowed against the deep shades of the surrounding trees. It was poised and ready to launch sharp arrows into their horses. Whoever lurked out there planned to kill or maim good horseflesh and this angered him in the extreme.

"You damned dirty bastard!" John muttered between gritted teeth. He aimed the scatter gun and pulled the trigger. Smoke belched and flames flashed from the end of the muzzle. The figure with the bow and arrows threw his arms out and began howling in pain. The man tried to run for it, but his legs must have gotten the full brunt of the blast because he limped severely and then cried for help.

John quickly caught up with him and shoved him facedown onto the ground. "Who in hell are you, and why cripple our stock, you goddamned bastard?" He pulled the man's head up. He couldn't see the culprit well in the dimness and didn't recognize him.

Waddie came running. "What the hell's goin' on out here?"

"This son-of-a-bitch was fixing to cripple our horses— and with arrows!" He pulled the whimpering man up by the scruff of his neck and asked Waddie, "You know this hombre?"

"Hell yes, he's one of our hands, John." He looked at the man cringing on the ground. "What's got into you, Larry? Whose idea was this and why use your bow and arrows?"

"I just done what Link ordered me to do. You know how damned bad I need this job. But right now I'm thinkin' I don't need it this much," he sniveled.

John snorted in disgust. "Well Larry, you won't be working on this ranch after today, and if I don't kill you right now for trying to shoot my horse full of arrows, I sure plan to beat the livin' hell out of you if I ever see your face around here again."

"You shot the hell out of me already," the wounded cowboy retorted. "I'm bleedin' like a stuck hog, an' who'n the hell are you, anyway?"

John ignored the question. "Come on Waddie, let's get this fool inside and light a lamp."

Together they hauled the man to his feet, half dragged him into the line shack, and sat him on the wood box. "Don't need you bleeding all over the bedding."

Waddie agreed about the bedding as he filled John in. "This here's Larry Price. He works on the ranch, mostly the other ranges." Waddie rounded on the culprit. "Larry, what in the damned hell got into you to pull somethin' like this?"

"Wal, you know, my mother's sick, and sure as hell, I *can't* get fired. She needs a lot of doctorin'! Link said he'd fire my ass if I didn't put a kink in this here feller's plans. He sure as hell wants you off'n the place, mister—real bad."

Larry didn't try to hide the begging tone in his voice, and John believed the kid would be groveling soon.

"No news to me, son, but I'm not going," he scoffed. "Link, eh? He'd better get his own bags packed because he won't be working here after I get back to the ranch." Muley was important to him in many ways, and he was ready to string up anyone who would harm the big horse. But by now he had formed a good bit of sympathy for Larry, the poor miscreant, and eased up on his temper. Together he and Waddie worked to pull buckshot out of Larry's hide, and bind up his wounds.

"You'd better be damned careful, mister." Larry coughed. "Link's got a lot of irons in the fire. Got friends in town, too." His face was pale. His dirty brown hair stood awry in the lantern light and, all in all, the young man didn't look overly smart to John as he added, "He's had some men lookin' around here for somethin', too. I seen 'em more than once, but I keep my mouth shut, needin' work the way I do."

The young man had actually become overly informative since he'd been caught. John wondered if imparting what he knew was his way of making up for the damage he'd tried to do. "Thanks for the warning, son." Going back to what the men had been scouting for, John casually asked, "Any idea what they were looking for?"

"Not sure what they was after, pickin' around in the rocks that way. Sure as hell didn't look like cattle men, I know that much," Larry replied, groaning from the burning pain of his buckshot wounds. "God, that buckshot hurts like hell's fire."

Ignoring the injured man's complaints, John slipped easily into the local jargon and said, "Well, that's something worth knowin'. Might have to do with some of the goin's on around this ranch."

"Got any whiskey? I'm a hurtin' like hell since you picked out them pellets. Damn! What was you usin, anyway?" Larry's face shone white in the lantern light. His leg still bled a little and his trousers lay on the floor, torn and bloody.

Waddie found a bottle and, giving him a good slug in an old glass jar he found, snorted. "I knew damned well messing with that Injun stuff would' get you in trouble someday." He chuckled. "Bow and arrows, huh? Dumb ass."

Larry choked and gagged on the stuff but didn't refuse a second round.

After John's temper cooled, he decided Larry was just a desperate kid trying to help his mother and advised, "You know, you'll get yourself killed one day following orders like that. Killin' a man's horse, you sure as hell will."

"You're right, Mr. Carmona, I see that now." Larry looked down and shook his head. "Got caught up in worryin' over my mother. Sure sorry, fellas."

"That's all right, kid. We'd better catch a few winks, boys. We got a lot ahead of us in the morning," John said. He figured when he got back to the main ranch, he would have it out with Link.

Madder than hell over what the man had tried to do, he determined, *That ornery bastard'll rue the day he tried to harm my horse*. He and old Muley had been together over too many trails and seen too much to have it end with him shot full of arrows.

CHAPTER 9

In the morning, John shared a hastily-made breakfast, thinking Waddie had done a good job with the scanty supplies left.

Larry frequently moaned in pain, but declared, "My legs are shot to hell in front, but I can sit a horse long enough to make it back to the ranch."

He didn't eat much, just chugged a couple cups of the thick, strong coffee with another slug of the rot-gut whiskey that Waddie cheerfully poured for him. The shack could stand restocking when they got the chance. Thinking of it made John realize he felt a part of this ranch.

It hit him dead center. *That black-haired lass has got me over a damned barrel and she has no idea in hell about any of it.* He couldn't hold back the smile that spread across his face.

"What the hell's got you grinnin' like a damned monkey this morning?" Waddie shot at him while he cleaned up after the hasty meal.

"Nothing at all. Just feelin' damned good today, so let's get that ornery bunch of beef down where they belong."

John felt a deep happiness flooding through him as he went out the door.

Larry limped out with them and leaned against a tree while Waddie saddled up for him. "Might get limbered up enough to *chouse* a few head when the sun gets up a bit more," he said, groaning loudly as he hauled himself into his saddle.

Hearing Larry's complaints, Waddie replied, "Aw, shut the hell up. You're lucky to be alive this mornin', you damned jackass."

John smiled, thinking both men were well worth their pay.

With that, they rode out to gather the sprawling herd and, along about ten in the morning, had them bunched enough to push them toward the roundup location nearer the ranch. John thought the beef looked in good shape.

"Looks like decent grazing most anywhere on this ranch," he said to no one in particular.

He rode among the greatly increased herd of bawling, milling stock, feeling again like he'd become a part of this wild mountain scenery and as though some part of everything on this ranch had to do with him in some crazy way. *Either I'm loco, or the beautiful Miss Cherry has staked a hell of a lot bigger claim on my heart than I realized.*

It neared dusk when the three of them finished adding this large bunch to the ever expanding herd in the roundup valley. Cattle dotted the plains of that vast open area as far as the eye could see. John saw that poor, wounded Larry was nearly washed up, but he'd added his efforts to theirs and done a decent day's work despite his injuries.

"Young man, when we reach the home ranch, I'll sort this out with Link," John said. "It's me he's trying to run off. You'll have your job when I'm done with him."

"Thanks, Mr.," Larry mumbled. Grateful and embarrassed, he pulled his bridle and headed to the ranch.

The three rode in silence, tired, yet satisfied with the haul of cattle they had added to the main herd.

Entering the ranch yard, John went straight to the bunk house, but found only Booker working over the cast iron cook stove, making chuck for supper, "Link around?"

"Ain't seen 'im all afternoon." The grizzled old man turned away to fuss over his stew, his attitude less than friendly. He rattled the pots and pans loud enough to let his feelings be known.

John looked out the door, hoping to catch sight of Cherry, thinking another dinner invite would be nice and a walk in that orchard would be even nicer. She was nowhere around.

His senses came alert on hearing Booker step close behind him. "Say, Miss Cherry says you're to come for dinner if you've a mind to."

He turned to see an icy frown cross Booker's face, affirming him as solidly in Link's corner and not to be trusted behind John's back.

"Thanks, Booker." Despite his failure to confront Link, he felt elated to have dinner with Cherry again. There would be time enough for Link later if the horse-killing bastard showed. He went to the horse trough and washed up before donning a better shirt. With his black hair slicked down and his heart beating double time, he walked to the front door, knocked, and waited.

Cherry opened the door and, reaching out her hand, took his and led him to the table. "How'd your drive go?" Her violet hued eyes were full of curiosity. That, and the touch of her hand, kept his heart beating like a trip hammer as he tossed his hat in a handy corner and sat down.

"We brought in every animal we could find up in the area. My guess would be you've got a sizable herd right now despite your losses. " He didn't expect to mention any difficulties to her. He'd wait until Link showed up. They would discuss things in private, and John looked forward to it.

"I expected to find Link around," he said. "But he's nowhere to be seen. I had something to say to him. Isn't he usually around by this time?"

Cherry shrugged, didn't answer his query, and indicated for Margarita to begin serving. She settled across from him and placed a napkin in her lap, a small, insignificant action he hadn't seen in a while.

She was bright, chirpy, conversational, and downright pleasant, but something hung in the air. John had the feeling nothing was right tonight. Unspoken words, fears, or accusations, he wasn't sure as he waited for the ax to fall. It didn't take long.

"Mr. Carmona, you played cards with my Uncle Omar that night? How did that happen?"

He didn't miss the hint of distrust in her eyes. "Theirs was the only card game in the place. Of course, I didn't check on the other saloon that night." He turned his eyes on her. *It's Mr. again, is it? What in hell's on this lassie's mind, now?*

"It seems very strange to me and hardly a coincidence. Tell me again, why you're in this part of the country? I can't get over the feeling you might be spying on us for some reason." She shrugged. "Sorry if that insults you, but I'm on my own these days, and trying to find out who killed my father, if not my uncle, and why." She blinked back a few tears and went on. "So many strange things have gone on around here that I find myself suspicious of everyone."

"You've certainly got the right for that, Miss Cherry. As I've said before, I was passing through this country to see about certain rare minerals needed by the government. I have papers to prove my claim if you'd need to see them." He wanted to add more but waited for her reply.

"So you've said." Her shoulders slumped a bit. "I guess I'll have to believe you." He saw reluctance in her lovely eyes. "I'm upset and angry just now and need to get my head straight." She cast her eyes down and took a deep breath. "I guess I'd better tell you what happened."

She hesitated a bit before going on. "I went for a ride to a special place of mine, two days ago and—Link—he actually accosted me out on the trail. He put his *hands* on me!" Pale with anger, she raised her head, along with her voice. Her eyes flashed fire. "I plan to fire him, but I also wanted to see how you'd answer my questions. I want very much to trust you, even knowing so little about you."

"Oh God, that bas—" He flushed. "Excuse the language, miss, but I have a few things to take up with that gent myself when I see him."

"I'll never allow that man inside this house again after what he did," she said. He saw the tears begin and how she fought them. "I haven't seen him around here since. I don't know where he is."

John sighed. "Try not to worry so much. I can sort things out, given a bit of time. If you'll trust me to have a free hand around here, maybe I can find some of the other answers for you while I'm at it." After a long silence, he asked, "Who owns the land on the other side of the mountains to the north of here?"

"It belongs to a friend of mine, Hettie Jamison. Why do you ask?"

"Just curious, I suppose," he replied. "Wondered who the land belonged to and who lives nearby."

"Of course, I know. I've lived here all my life and know my neighbors." She thought his answer meant nothing and didn't answer her question, but she didn't go into it further. His curiosity about her neighbor's land only added to her confusion about him. It made her feel uncertain about him all over again. *Why would he be curious about Hettie's place?*

They ate in silence until desert came, served by a smiling Margarita. The woman doted on the sight of the big man across the table from her and spoke fondly of Señor John at every opportunity. She practically fawned over him and Cherry found it unsettling. She planned to speak to Margarita about it later, but she knew that gentle soul would hear no words against the man.

She got up from the table and asked, "Would you like to sit in the big room there?" she asked, indicating the large room where they had first spoken, "or walk outside for a while?"

Maybe she didn't trust him, but she didn't want him to leave so soon either, John decided. Feeling a bit of deep satisfaction, he replied, "How about walking outside? I'd like to see more of that fine orchard out there."

It had grown nearly dark as they walked out across the wide, paved patio. The moon had risen big and full, shedding a soft, mellow glow over everything, creating an almost magical scene.

Cherry led the way off the patio and into the grove of fruit trees. The trees emitted that familiar sweet aroma of rapidly ripening fruit, mostly apples at this time of year, he believed.

She indicated a shadowy growth of smaller trees surrounding them. "My father planted this orchard many years ago and we get quite a bit from it. We'll be picking apples and pears soon. The peaches came earlier and are canned or dried. I love it out here. Smells nice, doesn't it?"

"Sure does," he replied softly. They walked a bit farther before he broached what lay on his mind, hoping for a few answers for himself. "I've wondered how things are going for you. How you're handling everything. This is a big ranch, and it'll be a lot of work for you without your father."

Would she admit that things weren't on the up and up? He knew they weren't, but wanted to hear her say it and confess her need for his continuing help.

"I was born here," she began. "Dad said he loved this location from the moment he set eyes on it. This part of

Arizona is far away from the bigger towns like Flagstaff or Prescott, but we go there, too, when we need to." She hesitated, "John, I know you're still very much a stranger, but I find you easy to talk to. And since you ask, no, things haven't been right on this ranch for a long time. Riders don't stay very long, cattle are continually missing, lost, rustled, or go missing, and fences are torn down." She paused, took another deep breath. "It's been happening for the past two years or more. Link has always been the one who stayed faithful, but I certainly can't have him on the place any longer."

She looked him in the eye and uttered a soft laugh. "And now, with all those losses, I have no foreman, either."

He nodded. He didn't want to mention what the man had tried to do to his horse until he'd had the chance to settle the score on his own, but his feelings crept into his voice, "Link, eh?"

"Yes, the one we always counted on." She uttered a derisive laugh, but John heard the tones of despair she tried to hide. "Seems I'll be doing more hiring with roundup coming on." She frowned, "With Link gone, maybe now they'll stay and work a while, instead of disappearing."

"Well, I've a score to settle with that hombre, myself, before he goes. I hope you feel you can count on me." John smiled down into her upturned face. The moon had cast lovely shadows across it, deepening the set of her eyes. "I'll do my best for you, Cherry."

"What score do you have to settle with Link?"

"When we were out at that far line shack, he tried to kill my horse. He'll answer for that, and plenty, if I get my hands on him."

"He tried to kill that wonderful horse? I can't believe he'd be that low down mean after all the years we trusted him." She shuddered, visibly upset. "How'd he do that?"

John reached out and laid a hand on her shoulder. "I'll go into it later, but don't you worry, I'll sure as hell take care of Link." He was being familiar, touching her, but she didn't shrug his hand away. Instead, she placed her hand over his and moved closer to him.

In these few magical moments, John burned with a mad desire to sweep her into his arms, crush her slim body to his, and cover that lovely face with kisses. The perfume of her body, lavender-scented clothing—everything about her—had about driven him near the edge of insanity. He held onto his self-control the best he could, fighting his maddening thoughts and desires.

She moved away. "I guess I'd better go in now, Mr. Carmona. It's getting late." He heard the regret in her voice as she turned away to return to the house. He knew she was drawn to him whether she trusted him or not.

"Why not just call me John." His voice was barely above a whisper, but she heard him. "You have a few times already."

"If you'll call me Cherry." She smiled at him. Her eyes shone black in the darkness as she turned to lead the way back across the patio.

He followed her toward the sprawling house and, before turning to leave, took hold of her hand. "Good night, Cherry." He held it too long, but she didn't seem to notice. Or did she? Not wanting to press his interest in her too soon, he released her hand and left her there at the edge of the patio.

Cherry walked back into the house. A soft glow had taken hold, deep inside of her, and she still felt the firm pressure of his hand. Unable to quiet the feelings he aroused, she washed and went to bed, still excited and flushed. Seeing deep gray eyes and that long, tall form in her mind made her heart race and kept her awake with thoughts of things...most disturbing. Finally, after many long hours, sleep claimed her.

CHAPTER 10

John entered the bunk house, receiving a terse greeting from the cook in the form of a grunt. Booker sat alone at a small table shuffling cards and neglected to invite him to join in a hand.

"Link not back yet?" John asked.

"Dunno, ain't seen 'im fer two-three days."

The man's absence from the ranch told John that he was afraid to show his face after accosting Cherry.

"He'd damned better be afraid to show up around here after trying to kill my horse," he muttered under his breath, figuring Booker didn't hear, but added in a louder voice, "If you see Link, you can tell him I'm looking for him."

"When he comes back, you'll see 'im all right." And with that, the disgruntled cook blew out the lantern and took to his blankets.

John settled into his own bunk. He lay across from the ornery cook wondering just why the man so disliked him. *Hope the bastard doesn't poison my chow in the morning.*

The fatigue of three days hard work overtook him and he'd nearly drifted off when Waddie and Larry came in.

The wounded cowboy worked his shot-peppered body carefully into his own bunk, and John grimaced on hearing his painful moaning. Still, the miscreant had the will to work in spite of his injuries. John figured the other boys were out at a line shack for the night.

He wanted to consult with Cherry on hiring a new foreman. She had a lot of decisions to make, and he looked forward to seeing that beautiful face again under any circumstances.

Still filled with anger at the attempt on Muley, he awaited the chance to brace Link for his attempt to main or kill his horse, but more so for what he'd done to Cherry. She couldn't blame him for her loss of a foreman, and she might even thank him for giving the bastard what for.

Those violet eyes and thick curling black hair created a bewitching vision in his mind that kept his whole body in a constant glow. *That girl's got to me in a thousand ways. Oh Lordy, Lordy, there'll come a day...*

⌛

In Parson's Grove, Link sat across from Harry Bourdain and Wilmer Mains. "Looks like I've run into some trouble out to the ranch," he admitted. "Some damned slicker has turned up and sure as hell, he's caught that fool girl's eye. The goddammed bastard follows her around like a hound dog and she don't brush him off like she done me." He shuffled his feet and sat, head down, his hat in his thick hands, thumping the dust off it. "Anyways, her and I had a little dust-up out on the trail a couple days ago, and she's set to fire me soon's she sees me."

Mains sat listening, his cheeks filled with a healthy chunk of chewing tobacco. Bourdain had a nasty scowl across his face that made Link nervous.

"Anyways, dammit, I was figgerin' on a marryin' that girl," Link fumed. "That big bastard's moved in on the place and she's taken up with him. I saw that right enough. And didn't she go an' hire him to work around the place for a while against my advice? Man ain't even a stockman."

Bourdain's pale features were set stone-like with anger. "You dumb bastard! Had to get yourself in a hurry, didn't you?" His frustration appeared to mount rapidly. "You know we need access to the place, dammit! If those ore samples are what we think, we'll be making out real fine. Now you've gone and made that woman shuck you off like a damned rattler!" His look of disdain made Link's nerves tighten up. "We'll have to take care of that gent right off."

Bourdain hesitated and his eyes narrowed. "You saying he's that same stranger that was in the card game where Jeems got himself shot?"

Anxious to please, Link hurried to answer. "Right enough, that's what he told the girl. I overheard the two of 'em talkin'. Nice as pie they was together with him handin' her a bag of money he said old Omar won." Link, clenching and unclenching his hands, snorted a half-laugh and stuck out his chest. "She threw it back at him. Didn't believe his story a'tall."

Link needed these men. Now Bourdain acted mad as hell. Old Wilmer hadn't said a word, just worked his damned chaw of tobacco around to his left cheek, fixin' to spit.

Bourdain snorted in disgust. "Hell, you say! That stranger was the one with the big hand and the bastard used his bag of money to get next to her." He shot a glance at Link that made his insides shrivel up. "We need to know who the hell that stranger is and why he's come here. What's he snooping around for?" He scowled and scuffed his boot across the floor. "I'm not liking this business one damned bit!"

Link started to rise, but Bourdain wasn't through yet. "You damned fool, we needed you on that place. Especially now, if it looks like we're dealing with something more than a traveling cowhand." He frowned. "Wonder why Miss Cherry threw it in his face?"

"I've heard Miss Cherry say plenty of times how old Omar never won anything—always lost," Link was quick to say. "Guess she didn't believe his story."

Events had taken place beyond Link's ability to grasp them. It frightened him. The way things were shaping up he was set to lose everything he'd worked for.

"Miss Cherry! Miss Cherry! Good God, Link, you poor bastard, can't you get your mind on anything else?" Wilmer exclaimed as he spit a large, brown wad into a spittoon.

"Well, she's played a big part in all of it for me. I had my plans all worked out when that big son-of-a bitch showed up."

"Well, he won't be around a hell of a lot longer, I'll see to that." Wilber smiled. "You just get back there and don't let her run you off, you hear? Didn't you say her father told you to take care of the place?" His smile turned sardonic. "And her, too, if you get my meaning."

"He did tell me that a while back, but lately he was gettin' mighty damned cool towards me. I did what I had to do." Link suddenly stopped talking. He'd spilled way too much. Seeing Bourdain's eyebrows raise at what he'd just admitted, he gulped in fear.

"You slick bastard, it was you did Bender in, wasn't it?" Bourdain growled. "I can see you did." He scoffed. "And now you want to marry the girl. Well, never mind about that, long as she's got no idea about you doing her daddy in, and she don't, does she?"

"Hell no, she don't know a damned thing about that or anything else," Link barked defensively. "He was so beat up and dyin', anything he'd have said to her, if he said anything, wouldn't a made a lick of sense. She never acted toward me like he'd said anything. Anyways, I had my face covered at the time."

Remembering how he'd come to the rescue, he added, "Hell, I was the one who helped out, carried the old dude up to the house and all." He puffed up with pride. "I was the strong one. I took care of things for her when she needed me. She outta be thinkin' real high of me for that." He thought for a minute then added, "Well, she did until that interferin' son of bitch showed up."

"I see you're sort of bitter, Link," Bourdain said. "If you'd take care of that so-called interfering son of a bitch, we'd all be better off." He smiled, his eyebrows arching. "Any ideas?"

Frustrated, Link shook his head. "No, but I'd sure as hell like to see the last of that goddamned Carmona."

Bourdain shot him a wolfish smile, as if he'd just figured a way to get rid of the interloper. "Go to it, Link, and let us know how it goes. We'll be needing to make a trip out there in another day or two." He leaned closer, his voice low and confidential. "Find anything over at the Jamison place?"

"Naw, nothin' of interest, looks to be a dead end out there." Link uttered a soft laugh. "Well, except for that widow woman."

❦❦❦

Morning came and Link hadn't returned. John slicked up the best he could and went up to the house. At his knock, Margarita opened the door. *"Si, senor?"*

"Miss Cherry around?"

"Si, senor, una momento." The amply formed woman stifled a big grin and opened the door to him. She ushered him into the large front room where he had spoken with Cherry before. While waiting, he surveyed the room, seeing again the rustic furnishings softened with feminine touches here and there.

Cherry's fine hand was in evidence everywhere. A soft, embroidered pillow to rest against and flowers in a vase displayed on a small table set against a colorfully woven Indian rug fastened to the wall with wooden pegs. He stood there looking about in a home that, once so warm and inviting, had been darkened by death and multiple troubles.

After a short while Cherry entered the room. "You wanted to see me?"

"Yes, ma'am, Link's been gone a couple days now. Think he'll show his face around here again?"

Her cheeks flamed red, but she held her head up and looked him square in the eyes. "I was hoping you'd back me up if he does and tries anything."

John saw the distress written on her face and offered his help. "You know I'll back anything you want, ma'am. He ran off your cowhands. Waddie said it, too." John, elated that she asked him to take her part, was more than ready to settle with Link on her account. It pleased him to stand up for her, however, his own score remained to be to settled with Link as well.

"The day he accosted me, he claimed my father put him in charge of the ranch, and of me, too." He saw the anger flashing in her eyes. "No man owns me, John. I don't care how long he's worked here. My father would never turn me over to anyone that way, especially a man like that!"

"He'll never bother you again. I'll see to that." His anger boiled, thinking of the heavy-set cowboy manhandling this lovely girl. "I've got my own score to settle with him. He won't be trying to shoot my horse full of arrows again, you can count on that."

"I can't believe any man would do that to a horse."

"I already told you some of it. We were way out in that far canyon where we'd been gathering cattle for the roundup next week. Link sent Larry Price up there to shoot our horses full of arrows. Larry told us he was planning to use arrows so it wouldn't make a lot of noise and wake us. Someone had let our horses out the night before, so we knew something was up. I sat outside waiting and, when I saw a man aiming at the horses, I let him have it with a scatter gun they keep at the shack up there."

He shrugged and ventured a smile. "Larry told us everything. At first, I wanted to kill him, but he said he was doing what Link had told him to do to keep his job. His mother's sick and needed a whole lot of doctoring, more than he could afford."

She furrowed her brows in the way he absolutely loved. "I'd hate to fire the man when we're so short of help, but can he be trusted?"

"The kid's okay. He learned a tough lesson though. I told him he wouldn't lose his job over it if that sets all right with you." He chuckled. "Larry's kinda stove up with what we did to him, but with all the whiskey we poured into his wounds, and him, too, he'll mend well enough. Rode all the way back and worked the best he could. Old Muley's been with me on many a trail. Shooting arrows into his yellow hide would make me mad enough to do damned near about anything, beg pardon ma'am, for cussin'."

"I'd want to cuss, too if someone shot at my Checky, but I'll just say thanks to you, Mr. Carmona—John. I do value your opinion."

She went silent, thinking, then said, "You seem to be the sort to take care of things right when we need someone, don't you?"

He saw a glimmer of trust building in her. It'd be a solid beginning for him if he could earn her confidence.

He already knew he had her interest. She had always looked at him with more than a little of that. If she believed him and trusted him, it'd make his life a lot easier because by now he knew he wanted this girl in his arms, his bed, and, for damned sure, in his future.

"Well, I came through this country for more of a purpose than bringing your uncle's winnings. I believe I mentioned something about that earlier."

"Yes, you did." Curiosity deepened the violet of her eyes and he enjoyed the sight of them all the more.

"There're other minerals the government's concerned with, not just gold or silver that most folks look for. Some of those discoveries might be in the works. Don't know if any of the men around here would know about that, but the mineral in question is often found with gold. Maybe the hope of finding gold is the reason behind some of the things going on around here."

"Do you suppose that mysterious mineral is here on this ranch and because of it, someone's trying to take our property from us?" Cherry asked, choking back a sob. "That would surely explain a lot of our problems of late, but certainly it wouldn't have led to my father's death."

John felt her grief and wanted to console her. Taking Cherry in his arms to comfort her burned on his mind, but dare he try for that much closeness? Not yet, he decided. "It couldn't have been anything else to my way of thinking."

Her laugh was derisive. "We've called the sheriff endless times without his actually doing anything," she told him. "He's never found our rustled cattle or discovered who torn down our fences. I wouldn't be surprised if he might be in partnership with those working against us!"

"Why don't we see what happens when Link shows his face. We've plenty to sort out with him, and if I have your leave to fire the man, I'll do that, too."

"Why yes, you certainly have my permission. I'll not be sorry to see him gone. I'd never trust that man around here, not anymore." She hesitated. "John, will you consider acting as boss in his place?" With those words, Cherry realized she had just granted John Carmona the status of ranch foreman, trusting him to be who he said he was.

"Certainly, I will, Miss Cherry. I'll do my best for you, ma'am, considering, I'm no cowhand. But I thank you for your confidence in me." He tipped his hat. "Well, I'd best be going then." With reluctance, he left the beautiful girl and headed for the bunk house when going into the garden in the moonlight was what he really wanted.

CHAPTER 11

By the next day, Link still hadn't shown his face at the home ranch. If he was elsewhere on the property, John had no idea where. He sat with Larry, Waddie, and another man who had come in during the night.

"Name's Monte Blue. I've been ridin' the west ranges mostly. Come in to see what Link wants done, and like you say, I haven't seen 'im for a while, myself."

He held out a hand.

John shook it. "Pleased to meet you, Monte. I should tell you that the boss lady has asked me to be foreman in Link's absence." He saw a dark scowl cross the cook's face. That this news didn't set well with Booker was no surprise to him. He saw the man quickly wipe his hands and leave the bunkhouse.

Monte scoffed. "Guess ol' Booker ain't takin' to that news real good, bein' they was buddies of a sort."

He was a quiet man and said no more on the subject, but John noted his obvious distaste for Link's toadie of a cook.

"Boys, I'm new here and never wanted this job, but for now I want to help Miss Cherry, and I'd appreciate any help you fellows might care to offer. We've got a good sized herd over in that big valley set up for the roundup and might need another hand or two for that."

"I can think of a few boys that Link ran off. Might get them back if you'd let me go after 'em," Waddie offered. John nodded his go ahead.

With things settled, he decided to have another chat with Cherry. He sent the boys out for a day's work and headed for the house. She met him at the door, dressed for riding.

"Oh good, I was coming to find you. I want to go riding today, but I'd rather go with someone, if you wouldn't mind riding out with me."

"Not at all, I came to see you about taking a good once over look, at your ranch. I find it difficult to give orders when I am not sure where things are located and what they're named. If you'll ride along and point things out to me, it'll help me do my job some better."

"I'll go get Checky, then," she said with a smile and headed for the corral.

He watched her fetching figure, walking along in her split, leather riding skirt. She had a good, healthy stride and when she reached the corral her horse nickered and came straight to her. *She's sure got a good way with animals and if she only knew it, with me, too.* He envied the horse for the way she touched and caressed him. It made him quiver in anticipation, watching her hands move across Checky's silky hide. *Makes me wish I was a horse.*

He caught up Muley. They saddled quickly and were soon on the trail. "I love it when the weather is this nice." She chatted happily as they jog-trotted towards the west side of the ranch where she pointed out areas where certain herds were run at different times of the year to facilitate good grazing. With all the knowledge she displayed, he realized the young woman knew the workings of her ranch far better than he ever would.

He had difficulty remembering much of what she told him as he watched that graceful figure sitting her saddle with ease of long practice. Her horse was sure footed and eager to run if she gave him his head which she did a few times. Then she would laugh and look back at him, waiting while he came up to her.

Along about noon, she stopped and asked, "Are you hungry?"

"I could eat," he said, hoping to find out if her skills in a line shack equaled those of Waddie.

"We'll find one of those line shacks around here. It's over at the edge of those trees." She pointed the way, turned Checky, and led the way. John saw nothing ahead, but she seemed to know where she was going.

As they neared the trees, she pulled up. "Someone's there, I see the smoke rising above the trees." She looked at him, her eyes growing large with a touch of alarm. "No one's working this area as far as I know."

They pushed ahead and coming into a slight clearing. He saw a small, grubby shack, not unlike the other two he'd seen. A thin trail of smoke trailed upward, barely clearing the chimney before the breeze took it. A large bay horse grazed at grass and weeds in the small pole corral.

"That's Link's horse!" she exclaimed,

"Hold on, Cherry. If it's him, we'll likely see trouble. He won't want to see me, or you either, after what he's done."

He bade her wait, rode closer, and hailed the cabin. "Hallo in there. Link, if you're in there, step on out here!"

The flimsy door shoved open and the burly cowboy slid out crouching sideways, a gun in his hand. "What the hell *you* wantin' around here?" His snarl showed surprise as much as animosity. John knew he was the last man Link wanted or expected to see.

"I came looking for you to fire your sorry ass out of here and off this ranch. I know you insulted and put your dirty hands on Miss Cherry, and I sure as hell know what you intended for my horse." Speaking of those foul deeds, John grew angrier. "You can get your bloated carcass on out of here. I've got orders to fire you off the place, and I aim to see it done, and pronto! Those are the orders from me, and my boss," he said, emphasizing the last word.

"You can jest go straight to hell, you interferin' no account bastard. Her father left me in charge and I aim to see things carried out like he wanted!"

He held the gun as steady as he could in his trembling hands, but fear of John held him back and he didn't raise it to shoot.

"There's two ways you can leave the place, flat out dead or ridin' your horse. Your choice!" John waited, his hand held out, ready to pull the six-gun he kept oiled and ready in its holster, low on his right leg. "Any way you want it, Link."

Link stared angrily at his nemesis and saw his great disadvantage. He was ready to raise his gun, but looking things over, decided he'd be dead in a flash. "I'll be leavin' soon's I get my horse and gear." He flashed a look of utter hatred, the kind John hadn't seen in a long while, and went into the shack for his gear. Cherry rode up, pulling Checky next to him. They sat side by side on their horses, waiting while Link made ready to leave.

The man came out of the cabin, his pack slung over his shoulders. Seeing Cherry, he flashed an ugly scowl. "Sidin' with this sneakin' bastard, are you?" He spat a brown wad of tobacco into a nearby bush. "Better be watchin' your back with this stranger, girl. You jest might be sorry. Keep in mind what I say. The man ain't what he says he is."

Cherry flushed in anger as he called her "girl" again, but she said nothing.

Link's face was white with bitter hatred as he saddled his horse, mounted, and rode off. Cherry hoped that scowling face was the last she would ever see of the disgruntled foreman.

She faced John. "Thank God, I'm so glad that nasty business is over with. Thank you, John, for taking care of it for me." She heaved a long, shuddering sigh of relief

He gestured toward the line shack. "Still hungry? Want to go in there now—after that?" Seeing the distaste on her face, he knew she didn't.

"No, please, let's get away from here. I feel sick to think that man's been in there." She shuddered in disgust and turned her horse for the ranch. John followed her and seeing her shoulders shake, caught up with her.

"You all right?" he queried.

"Yes. That was unpleasant enough, but now I'm thinking he might try to kill you, John, and I'm worried." A look of concern for him crossed her lovely face. "As much as I'd like to think so, we haven't seen the last of that man. I saw the way he looked at you and he'll be trouble. He's not one to give in that easily. Never has been. I know that much about him."

"I'm ready for him if he has the gall to show his face on this ranch again. Don't fret yourself about that." He wanted to soothe Cherry, but figured he had best keep an eye out for an ambush. It could come from any direction and he wouldn't be surprised if Cherry hadn't made a dangerous enemy for herself in the bargain. He knew *he* certainly had. "The boys said he had friends in town. What do you make of that?"

"I don't know, but nothing surprises me. Might have something to do with the strange happenings around this place."

They rode silently side by side through the rangeland. All he wanted was to stop, pull her off that horse, and comfort her. The idea held his mind, filling it with pleasant images, but he'd wait his chance for something like that.

It wouldn't be long before they would walk out into the orchard again. *I wonder how she would take to my idea of comforting?* His mind raced with thoughts of how he'd go about it, taking her in his arms and holding her close, kissing her soft lips.

Cherry rode along beside him, deep in her own thoughts. They roiled about in her head. She wanted to trust John completely, but Link's threatening words clung to her mind. *What did he mean, he's not who he says he is?* She frowned, her thoughts totally conflicted. The man beside her and the passing scenery went unnoticed in her turmoil.

Near nightfall, they sighted the ranch house in the distance. "There we are!" Cherry cried out, forgetting her dismal thoughts. Her home had always been a place of refuge and rest for her troubled mind, and in her eagerness to reach it, she let her horse out. He took off at a gallop, though she found him less eager to run, even with his barn and corrals in sight.

As they unsaddled their sweating mounts, she asked, "Will you come for supper tonight?"

More than happy to oblige, he nodded. "Certainly, if we can go into the orchard and talk awhile."

He saw her stiffen a bit at his request. "Well yes—I guess I'd like that too." Saying no more, she walked to the house.

He took his time, washed himself carefully in the bunkhouse, and slicked his hair down to a black, shining mat beneath his hat. He'd needed a haircut for some time, but he did the best he could with an old pair of rusty scissors. The result was uncertain at best and his hair appeared uneven. He went to her door and knocked.

She opened it for him. "Come in, John."

Her voice, so quiet and controlled and her manner, so very reserved, made him wonder if she really trusted him. Despite any other consideration, she had dressed carefully again tonight, and that was not lost on him.

He tried to figure out what had brought about her increasingly reserved mood. He'd but never been sure of a woman's thoughts and was happy to be asked to dinner at all. Confused, he shrugged and followed her to the table.

For Cherry, the sight of this big male sent her heart into wild spasms she didn't understand, and while that puzzled her, it both angered and excited her. This man could set her on edge without saying a word. Yet, although she had tried to remain distant and wary, she had dressed, brushed her raven-hued tresses into shining lakes of fire, and waited his coming to supper with unbelievable eagerness. *What is wrong with me? This man turned me to jelly the first day he came here and the madness hasn't stopped!*

Margarita watched her young charge with great interest and enjoyment. She'd come to love Cherry years ago as a cherished daughter and understood the tension between Cherry and John Carmona. He was such a man—and Cherry couldn't take her eyes off him. With loving joy in her heart, Margarita quietly watched their growing love for each other unfold before her eyes. She bustled about putting a thin soup before them, followed by roasted chicken, and fluffy biscuits. The garden had generously filled out the rest of the menu with vegetables. She served flan for their desert, and after that, with a secretive smile, she made herself scarce.

After they'd had coffee, Cherry rose from the table and John followed. Silently, she led the way across the nicely-laid flagstones of the patio, out to the bench beneath the apple trees. The aroma of ripening fruit scented the air, thicker and richer than before. It filled their nostrils with the subtle promise of nature in the fullness of time.

The tension between them had become a heavy, choking thing. He knew part of it had been Link's parting words, and he didn't know how to lighten the new suspicions those words may have caused. The easy camaraderie they'd enjoyed on the ride earlier had disappeared all over again beneath a thin veil of suspicion.

He ignored that worry for the moment. "I enjoy coming out here after a good meal." Following her to the bench, he joined her there. "Why so quiet, tonight?" he asked, his voice as soft as feathers.

"I don't know, John. I feel strange sometimes and so much has happened." But it was so much more than that, she thought as she sat in a heated glow next to his big body. His nearness affected her so much she could barely speak. Unconsciously, she wrapped her arms tightly around her body, keeping herself locked away from him. Unable to look him in the eye, she waited, without knowing what she waited for.

"Cherry, have I done anything to upset you?"

She turned to him with alarm in her eyes. "Oh no, not at all, John." She began to shake and tremble, unable to stop.

"Here, here, come now, what's wrong?"

He pulled her into his arms and she allowed it. He pressed her against his chest and held her snugly against his body, taking in the blessed feel of her pressing against him. They stayed close for a long time while he crooned soft words of comfort. He nosed into her fragrant hair, caught the aroma of it, along with her female scent.

The heat of wanting her possessed his mind until it set him on fire. She hadn't objected to his touch thus far, and that added fuel to the turmoil building within him. Unable to help himself, he held her even closer.

Cherry tried a few feeble attempts to move away from him, but the man's comforting body, the warmth of his encircling arms, though gentle, felt like bands of steel. He held her against him and that closeness affected her even more. With her head on his chest, she heard the deep hammering of his heart, beating the same frantic drum as hers. It made her realize she had an effect on him, too, the same one he had upon her. Oh God! It felt like heaven. Yet, after a time, feeling it must be wrong, she tried to pull away.

"Stay right here just a little while longer," he crooned softly into her hair. "Cherry, you feel good in my arms—in fact, you feel just right." He uttered a joyous laugh and hugged her tightly. "You're some kind of woman, Miss Cherry Bender. I want to help you, and I will, but I'd like a whole lot more of this, too. My God, you have no idea how much I want this—how much I need you."

She finally found the strength to pull herself away. "You need me?" Unable to believe a man like him had a need for anything or anyone, she was surprised at his words. He seemed so strong and able to handle anything, how could that be? Puzzled, she drew away. "I'd better go in, John—I think I must." She had turned away from him to lead the way back to the patio when John caught her, took her in his arms, and kissed her upturned lips.

She gasped. "What are you doing?"

"Just a little kiss is all, Cherry, just like this."

He crushed her to his chest, laid his lips on hers again, and gently kissed her. He increased the pressure until she felt the tip of his tongue seeking an opening. She struggled against him at first, but finally opened for him. He gently explored her mouth with his tongue until she frantically pressed her body against him, unable to understand why she felt a need down deep in her body—but for what, she didn't know.

She answered his passion, moaning with pleasure, until she realized she'd let this man go too far—*way* too far. Getting herself under a semblance of control, she struggled against him.

"Stop it! Please stop this!" She jerked away from him. He moved to catch her again, but she put up her arms to ward him off. "You're some kind of a devil, aren't you?" She hissed the words at him as she backed away. What are you trying to do to me?"

"Darling girl, any man worth his salt would do the same. A woman like you is a rare and wonderful thing. You're beautiful. I can't seem to keep my hands off you. I'm sorry, Cherry, or I'm trying to be." He watched her stricken face, trying to keep a wide smile off his own.

"I'm going in, John. Good night!" She turned in a huff and left him standing there. He heard the muttered word, "beast," as she hurried away.

"Good night, my lovely girl," he called softly after her, watching with regret as her trim figure retreated into the dark. His entire body burned and glowed from holding and kissing this bewitching young woman. "Whew!"

He grinned from ear to ear. "God help me, I'm sure as hell in love with that lovely girl!"

CHAPTER 12

John crossed the open space of the ranch yard, intent on heading towards the bunk house and his blankets. A shot rang out and the rush of air from a bullet whizzed past his ear. By pure luck and the encroaching dark of night, he wasn't hit. But he sure as hell knew it had to be Link. "You son of a bitch!" he yelled as he crashed through the bunkhouse door.

Waddie sprang up from his Poker game and ran to him, his worried face a dim glow in the lamp light. "I heard the shot. What the hell's goin' on, John, you got somebody shootin' at you out there?'"

"I fired Link today and I'm thinkin' maybe this is his idea of leavin' a calling card. He's not much of a shot, I'll have to say that." John felt around both his ears but found no blood. "Rotten bastard missed me by a mile."

He smiled, forming a plan. This evening wasn't over by a long shot.

Over in the corner, Booker wore a half grin on his face. "Maybe he won't be missin' the next time."

Waddie slipped out and after a short while, returned. "I heard a horse runnin' like blazes, John. You won't be able to catch him in the dark like this," he said, his shoulders slumped in disappointment.

John stayed cool. "Runnin' off, like the damned rat he is, Waddie." He'd seen the sly look on Booker, but had no time to waste on scum and paid him no mind. He turned in, or gave the pretense of it, saying, "Get some sleep, boys. We've got a big day tomorrow."

ᘓᘓᘓ

In the house, Cherry and Margarita both heard the shot. Alarmed, her heart racing a mile a minute, Cherry ran to the window. "John fired Link today. Could he be out there trying to take revenge?" Trembling, she paced the floor.

Margarita placed a comforting hand on her arm. "Oh, *mi hija,* is Senor John hurt?"

"I don't hear any shouting or calling for help, so maybe not."

Cherry lingered under a languid spell from the way he'd held her against his body and made her burn inside. She didn't want to admit it, but his touch had struck her deeply. It was a new and strange sensation. She couldn't shake the memory of it and longed for more.

Margarita nodded. "This big man, he take care for those shots."

Cherry recognized the look of admiration on Margarita's face. The woman held John in the highest regard and had from the beginning.

"*Mi hija*, you care for this man, no?"

"Oh, Margarita, I don't know. He's strong and he's smart. He knows things—maybe too much. What do I do?" she cried out, still on edge after her encounter with him in the orchard.

She'd just learned how quickly her body would betray her, if things were right for it. *He said he needs me.* The feel of his hands on her body still burned, and the feel of his lips on hers had seared her soul. *I wonder what he meant by he needs me.*

"I say before, he will show you what to do. He much man. I think he love you. His eyes, they follow you everywhere." Margarita's conspiratorial grin didn't help at all, especially as when nodding, she repeated softly, "Your eyes—they follow him, too."

"I'm going to bed!" The truth of it was too frightening to face, and Cherry rushed from the room.

What did she really know of the man? Nothing except what he'd already told her. In her confusion, she agonized over everything and remembered again Link's veiled warning: '*The man ain't what he says he is.*' It lingered in her mind and threw doubts about John into her path. Had she just become the world's biggest fool?

Cherry threw herself on her bed and lay there going over the passionate way John had held her and kissed her. The way he'd touched her and the way the heat from his kisses had raged through her body, making her legs so weak she feared she'd fall if she tried to run away. She clenched her fists, anger at herself climbing rapidly. She was to blame. She'd allowed that heated interlude in the garden to happen.

"I don't even know the man!" she fumed as she punched her pillow in utter frustration.

∽∾

John slipped out of the bunkhouse carrying his boots in hand. He'd waited until the boys were asleep. Listening to their heavy snores, he knew it was time. If no immediate action was taken, the shooter would hang around, waiting for another chance. Link had missed his mark. He'd be back. John pulled his boots on, slipped quietly into the trees at the edge of the ranch yard, and waited.

After another hour had passed, he heard a soft thunk, audible but not loud enough to arouse a sound sleeper. Shortly after hearing the noise, John saw a figure emerge from the shadows of another outbuilding and edge carefully towards the bunk house. The dull gleam from the rising moon identified the kerosene can he carried.

John recognized the robust outline of the man. It was Link. *That bastard is planning to fire the place with his own buddy in there, for God's sake!*

John gripped his rifle, and as the figure closed in on the bunkhouse he stepped out and raised his rifle. "Hold on there. Who are you, and what's in that can you've got there?" He received no answer. The figure tossed the can onto the sand and swiveled his body around, pulling leather. John pulled the trigger.

Two shots rang out. The man crumpled to the ground and John stepped closer, his rifle at the ready. "Let's see who we've got here." With his boot, he rolled the man over to see Link's face, barely visible in the faint moonlight. Even in that dim light, he saw the man turning pale and gasping for breath in his death throes. John cursed. "You damned, stupid fool!"

The bunkhouse door opened and the boys piled out in various states of undress. "What the hell's goin' on?" Waddie yelled. He rubbed the sleep from his eyes and stared down at Link's body. "By damn, he did come back!"

John went to the can and smelled the fumes as kerosene leaked into the sandy soil of the ranch yard. "Looks like he planned on burnin' me out, and you boys right along with me." He righted the leaking can. "Look at this."

Out of the corner of his eye, John saw a sick expression cross Booker's face. He apparently realized his good friend Link didn't seem to mind if his faithful buddy burned up right along with the rest of the boys.

The door of the ranch house sprang open, and Cherry rushed out clad in a heavy robe. "What happened out here? We heard shots."

Margarita stayed back, hovering on the wide front porch as Cherry approached the men. Her feet bare, she'd rushed out quickly with her robe wrapped snugly about her slim figure. The men, gazing at her slim little feet in the dim glow of the moon, made John smile. He knew the sight of their boss, dressed like that, made the men momentarily forget what Link had done.

John approached her. "Sorry ma'am, but Link was set to burn us out tonight while we slept." He didn't want to touch her in front of the men, but he did take her elbow, ready to escort her back to the house. "I had to shoot him, Cherry. He pulled his gun on me."

He saw the blood drain from her face. "Was it Link who fired the first shot we heard?"

"I believe it was."

"My God, John, terrible things just keep happening when you're around, don't they?" She sighed. "We'd better notify the sheriff about this. He won't do anything, he never does, but he's the law here." Following her gaze in the direction of the dead man, John noticed the cowboys had already thrown a blanket over Link.

Cherry turned to go back inside. "What next?" he heard her mutter as she walked away, shrugging off his offer to go in with her.

He stood alone in the ranch yard, wondering what had Cherry's tail in a twist now. He shook his head in frustration. Women often had had him buffaloed. "I'll send someone to town in the morning." He flung the words at her fleeing back.

Cherry froze, thinking of Link, a long time faithful employee, now lying dead on the ground. Remembering again his last words to her: '*The man ain't what he says he is.*' She felt angry with herself. She'd gotten tied up with John—maybe closer than was healthy. She wondered why he was so fast with a gun—and so quick to kill.

And now, another dead man lay outside her door. Did that prove Link's claim? True, he had laid a hand on her and tried to burn his own men to death, but he was another man who lay dead. That made her feel a deep sense of guilt. She struggled with those facts, wishing her father was here with his steady hand and calm head. She needed him now more than ever.

✿✿✿

The next morning, John made ready for his trip to Parson's Grove. He would alert the sheriff himself and do a little business while he was in the village.

After he'd lined out the cowboys' work for the day, John went up to the house and knocked. Cherry came to the door, her expression blank and dark circles beneath her eyes.

"I'll be headin' in town to see the sheriff. If you need supplies, I'd be glad to take care of that, too."

Wordless, she turned away, but did not ask him inside. He waited. After several moments, she reappeared. "Here's the list." Her lips were firm and she kept her eyes on anything but him.

"Wondered if you'd want a trip to town, yourself, ma'am."

"No thank you, I wouldn't." She turned away and shut the door, but not before he saw her lips quivering and moisture beginning in her eyes.

"Damn! Women are hard to figure sometimes." He shrugged, even grinned, as he hitched the team to the smaller ranch wagon and headed out. He planned to visit the telegraph office while he was in town, hoping the vital information he awaited had come in.

cɔeɔ

It was near noon, and John's rump sorely felt the wear from riding the wagon seat, when he hit the dusty street of Perkins Grove. He left his team at the stable for a good feed and went into the Rose Hotel for a bite to eat. The place was half full of diners. He pulled out a chair and sat down at an empty table. After giving his order, he looked around to see who might be in the room, an action he always practiced.

He noticed a pair of gents giving him the eye. One of them rose from his chair and sauntered over.

"How'd ya do?" he offered. "I'm Harry Bourdain, in business here in Parson's Grove." John shook his proffered hand and eyed him carefully. He'd wanted to meet this man and that shady friend of his, too. He'd heard their names before.

John introduced himself, and their immediate reactions set him on alert. He had the idea these men were Link's associates. "Know where the sheriff might be, today?" he asked Bourdain.

"Got business with him?"

"'Fraid I do, yes." It was none of the man's business, although he sensed his curiosity. "Had a bit of trouble out at the Bender place," he added.

"Don't say." His barely concealed curiosity peaked, but he didn't ask for further details. "Sheriff's in his office, or was, might show up right here to have a bite, too. Usually does, most days."

The man went back to his table and shortly after Monte Delavan walked in and joined Bourdain and his companion. John didn't miss the easy familiarity between the three men. It fit with his idea they were working together in secret dealings of some sort. Bourdain gestured in his direction and the man with the star walked over.

"You wanted to see me?" He took a closer look. "I remember you now, from the night Omar Bender got himself shot, wasn't it? How do you do?" He held out a hand and they shook as he took a seat across the table. "Trouble at the Bender ranch, they said?"

John explained what had happened during the night and, seeing the man blanch pale, wondered about it.

"I'll head out right after I have a bite. Always somethin' or other out to that damned place," the sheriff grumbled and took a table of his own to order his meal. Soon after, Bourdain and the other man went to the sheriff's table and joined him.

Muffled conversation from that area confirmed further the secrecy and closeness between the three men. Their association cemented things with John. He had known the name of one of them because of ore samples sent to Phoenix. They'd taken specimens from land where they had no rights. Now John had a face to match the name.

Finished with his meal, he left the Rose Hotel and headed for the telegraph office, several doors down. Once inside, he asked the slightly built young man behind the counter, "Anything for John Carmona?"

"Just a minute, sir." He dug through a small pile of yellowed messages and handed a sheet to John. "Right here."

John read the message: *Materials sent appear likely stop keep on with your work stop.* He wrote out a reply, stepped up to the window, and handed it to the young man. "I'd like to send this off."

"Certainly, sir, right away," the operator said and took the message. John heard the ticking of the metal keys as he left the office. He spent an hour or two buying the needed supplies at the general store and listened carefully to any conversation he could overhear while inspecting the layout of the store and the supplies it offered. He heard nothing he cared about.

After loading the supplies Cherry had ordered, he headed his outfit back on the road out of town. It had grown late in the day, and he found himself thinking of the black hair and violet eyes waiting at the ranch for his return. In a few days he would return to retrieve a reply to his last message at the telegraph office.

The day had faded into the magical deepening of purple shadows that rapidly approaching dusk always settled over these vast ranges. The air had taken on a chill by the time John pulled his sweating team into the ranch yard.

The cook stood in the bunkhouse door, and with surprise, John thought he saw a welcoming expression on the man's face.

"I'd like a hand here, Booker." The man seemed more than eager to take care of the supplies and rushed out to lend a hand.

"You go on in and eat, John. I kept supper for you. The other boys haven't come in yet. Gonna be a late one tonight, looks like."

Wondering at the change in Booker's attitude, John decided being cooked alive by your ex-foreman didn't create a lot of loyalty. He felt relieved that the man was capable of a little common sense after all.

"Sheriff been out here?" he asked.

"Yeah, he saw everything and was in to see Miss Cherry. Spoke to a couple of the boys and saw the kerosene can laying right there where we left it, too." He shuffled his feet and continued. "Hurried himself right back to town like he didn't give a good goddamn what happened to Link." Booker frowned as he added, "We stuck him in the tool shed for now, but we'd best get him planted by tomorrow, seems like."

The man was asking for instructions, and by this John knew he had been fully accepted as the new boss by Booker.

"Link have any family you know of?" John asked.

"Never heard of any. Guess we could look in his personal gear. Good job for you, I'd say."

"I'll ask Miss Cherry where she wants us to put him, then," John replied. "Thanks, Booker." With a good reason to go up and see her, John felt a wide smile cross his face, and his heart rate soared.

Margarita answered his knock on the door. "*Hola, Senor* John. I help you?"

"I'd like a word with Miss Cherry." He waited, his heart racing rapidly in his chest.

Cherry avoided meeting his eyes, but she opened it for his entry. "You wanted to see me?"

She frowned and he knew she still carried a grudge against him for some reason he couldn't imagine. *Could be she remembered what Link said the day we fired him.* Or was it from the unexpected excitement of their encounter in the orchard? *And she blames me for the way she feels.*

He smiled at her. "We were wondering where we should bury Link in the morning."

"Oh yes. I guess that has to be done. I'm not crazy about having him in the family cemetery, but anyone who's ever died here has been buried there. It has to be done, of course. Maybe along the outside somewhere. We can look in the morning." She led him to the door. "I'll choose a spot."

He left without a word. *I'm guessing I got too close in the orchard and now she's feeling huffy after she realized how much she liked it—and she damned well did.* He chuckled softly as he walked back to the bunkhouse. *There'll be another time, my darling Cherry.* He wore a big grin across his face. He'd wait for the next chance and it wouldn't be long. *She'll fight me all the way, but she won't win.*

CHAPTER 13

In Parson's Grove, Bourdain sat with the sheriff and Wilmer Mains. "So, Monte, did you find out what happened to old Link? I give the man a job and he turns up dead. First Jeems, now Link." He shook his head in disgust. "Can't figure on anybody anymore."

"Looks like he figured on burnin' out his own crew and got himself shot for his trouble." Delavan frowned. "But, dammit all to hell, a man who'd treat men he worked with that way ought to be shot. Serves the damned fool right. I couldn't arrest anybody out there." He shrugged. "Sure would've been my pleasure to put that big honcho out of the way, but the cowboys out there stood behind what he done."

Bourdain snorted. "Looks to me like you were glad you didn't have to brace that big honcho. 'Fraid of him, are you?"

"You weren't there the night of that card game," Delavan growled. "I saw that lightning-quick draw

Carmona pulled. I'll never forget it. I got a damned good memory."

"What happened out at that ranch that got Link so riled?" Mains asked.

"The new guy fired Link. Men didn't say what over, but it's my guess it's the girl. I 'spect ol' Link was keepin' her for himself, or tryin' to. Never heard for sure, though."

"Looks like we'll need some new blood. We might have to bring in *El Tigre*. He's a bloodthirsty devil, and I've never wanted to do business with the sadistic bastard," Bourdain said with a frown. "If that Carmona's a crack shot like you say, I sure as hell don't plan to make a target of *myself* out there."

"Any news from that assayer's office in Phoenix?" Delavan asked.

"Nothin' yet. Can't figger that either—something ain't right," Mains replied, leaning back in his chair. "I'll look into it, but maybe it could wait a bit longer."

Bourdain sent a snarl his way. "You always were one to put things off, you damned jackass. We'd best do some checking on it, so get down to the telegraph office in the morning and fire off an urgent request for an answer."

A knock on their door caused instant silence. Each man tensed as they waited. Bourdain opened it to find Casey Milstead, telegraph operator, mail clerk, local bookkeeper, and part time lawyer, standing there.

Bourdain welcomed the slightly built young man to a chair. "Well, how do, Casey. What you got there?"

Fidgeting, Milstead barely took the edge of the proffered seat. "Just might have something for you," he said, his voice tight. "This afternoon, early, a man came in and sent off a telegram to an assayer's office in Phoenix. The message asks if any further ore samples have been taken in this area, and if so, what kind." He flushed with embarrassment and a downcast look of shame as well. "Uh, well, I can show it to you."

"Describe the man," Bourdain demanded, ideas forming in his head.

"Big fellow with sharp gray eyes, the kind that bore clean through you, is all I can tell you. He didn't say a thing besides asking me to send this off." He produced Carmona's carefully written message. "If the company knew I'd breached the man's confidentiality, they'd have my hide, you fellows know that."

"Yes, well thanks, Casey, we really do appreciate your help. We have to stick together around here, if you know what I mean." Bourdain let his voice exude confidence, but he couldn't see that it soothed the man's agitation.

Casey hesitated, guilt plain on his face. "Yeah, sure—I know, just trying to be helpful whenever I can."

The other men in the room had no problem with what he'd done. They often slipped the younger man extra business and a few other perks along the way. Things like that kept Milstead believing he owed them for helping him set up his business and for keeping it going, as well.

Casey left them holding the message in their hands. "I'll be back to get that in the morning." His voice nearly begged them to return it. To Bourdain, the young man sounded like a mouse, dealing with several mangy alley cats, and he could see that it didn't set well with Milstead. He began to worry that the telegraph operator had a conscience. If so, it could mean trouble later on.

The three men checked the message with careful scrutiny, noting the firm, precise hand that had composed it. "Sure as hell, this Carmona is no passing-through cowpoke. Wonder what that man's up to and who'n hell sent him." Bourdain' had begun to worry. "I'll send off a telegraph of my own in the morning. By damn, we'd better send for that damned *El Tigre,* and soon. This is getting out of hand. Our plans'll all be shot to hell if we don't put an end to that interfering hombre."

"You're scaring the shit out of me, Harry. I don't like the way this is shaping up. I don't like it one damned bit!" Mains shot a wad of chew over six feet into a brass spittoon right near Bourdain's feet.

"Watch it, you bastard! I just got these boots from Denver."

"Aw, forget about it. They ain't so damned fancy as all that! So when's that killin' son-of-a-bitch gettin' here anyway?"

"How'n the hell do I know. I haven't sent the damned telegram yet."

❧❧❧

The ranch hands and a few neighbors laid Link to rest along the fence near the back of the graveyard. Cherry reluctantly came to see Link buried. She had asked a neighboring rancher, who at times acted as a preacher, to do the honors.

John waited until the words had been said and the shoveling done and then went to the bunkhouse to see the men. "Boys, we've three new riders coming, thanks to Waddie here. I'm askin' you fellows to manage the roundup for the next three days. There're several things I need to take care of, and then I'll be back."

They nodded their compliance until he added, "As you know, cowboyin' isn't really my line of work. I'm helping Miss Cherry for now and thankin' you for your help. She'll expect a full accounting of her stock and I'm asking Waddie here to take things in hand until I get back."

The look on some of the cowboys let him know they thought Waddie wasn't man enough for the job, but John, having worked with the young man, was fully confident that he was. Waddie could handle the job better than John could, any day of the week, and he was glad to make use of him.

ひのひ

Despite her niggling mistrust of John, Cherry was more than eager to catch sight of that gray-eyed devil. He occupied her thoughts day and night, but he hadn't been up to the house since she'd been so cold toward him.

Thinking constantly of how deeply he had affected her during their encounter in the orchard, she had come to realize the power he had over her. His touch and kisses made her body feel strange and weak. They set off a burning inside her in some crazy way she didn't understand.

She wondered about the weakness she had felt in his arms and in his presence.

Because of her worry over that mysterious power, she had treated him with a coldness she'd never felt. Since then, he hadn't sought her company or even tried to see her. She couldn't discuss it with Margarita. The woman seemed to believe the man could do no wrong. She would only smile mysteriously and say, "He will show you many things, *mi hija.*"

I can just imagine what things he'd show me, she thought as she huffed about her room. Restless and haunted by visions of that hawk-like nose and piercing gray eyes, she didn't understand it, but another woman might. She thought of her friend Hettie. *She'll know about things like that. Of course she will."*

Wanting to feel the wind in her face as she rode Checky, she decided that while the boys were working the roundup, she should be able to ride where she wanted on her own ranch. She quickly threw on her riding skirt and boots. After her encounter with Link, Cherry made sure to buckle her gun belt around her waist and keep her pistol checked and loaded. She said goodbye to Margarita and left for the corral.

Checky came readily at her call. She saddled her horse, rode out of the ranch yard, and let him have his head. He lengthened his gait into a dead run for a mile, then settled into a soft jog-trot that covered ground and felt comfortable to ride.

She headed for the pass in the mountains that led to Hettie's ranch. The Lazy J was a small outfit, and her friend ran it alone after her husband had been thrown from a horse and died. Damned prairie dog holes, they were ever a menace to a running horse, and in Hettie's case, it had certainly put an end to a very happy marriage.

After a couple of hours, she rode into the Jamison ranch yard. The place was well run and cared for by the way it looked. She saw the usual accoutrements hanging from pegs along the porch walls and heard footsteps. Delight filled her when Hettie ran out the door to greet her.

"*Hola* friend, I'm so glad to see you!" Hettie said then demanded, "All right, what's going on?" She waited, hands on her hips, while Cherry dismounted and flung the reins over the hitching rail.

Cherry tried to hide her agitation behind a wide smile. She laughed gaily and ran up the steps to hug her friend warmly. "It's good to see you, too, Hettie. Let's sit a while if you've got time. I need to talk a bit."

"Troubles?" Her friend's face crinkled with concern. They'd been close for years. Cherry had seen her through the deep romance of when Hettie and her husband had met and married and stood by her when she'd suffered his loss. Hettie had been there for her in the loss of father and uncle as well.

"We always have trouble at our place. But this time, it's worse, and different." Cherry told Hettie about Link and hiring the stranger in his stead.

Then, she went on about John Carmona. "I don't know how to handle this man." She knew she was blushing like a teenage girl as the heat rose up her neck into her cheeks. "He scares me in some ways, yet I can't stop thinking about him or longing to see him. Something about him draws me to him. I don't know what to do." She flung out her hands in her helpless frustration. Then she mentioned Margarita's attitude and laughed as she mimicked her, "He will show you, missy or *hija*. That's all she ever says!"

"Sounds to me like someone's in love." Hettie laughed. "It's about time, my dear." Then she frowned. "So it *was* that ever faithful foreman, Link, who managed to chase off any possible suitors for all those years. Met his match with this John fellow, huh?"

Cherry's cheeks warmed, and the heat burned her skin at the knowing look on her friend's tanned face. "You're no help!"

"I'm telling you—I know what's wrong with you, girl. Look at you, blushing like a silly, love-struck ninny."

Hettie happily continued relaying her thoughts on the subject until she had Cherry nearly convinced of its truth.

Hettie was a trusted friend and Cherry knew her feelings were safe with her. It felt wonderful to let her fears and frustrations flow freely. Both women broke into joyous laughter. They were in tune with each other, and it felt good.

"What about you, Hettie? Any nice cowboys come around. You've certainly kept your good looks."

"I can't seem to find any of them worth bothering about, not yet anyway." She bore the sorrow of losing her husband in her eyes. Then Hettie smiled and said, "I do most of my buying in Flagstaff these days. I hear that sheriff up there is a mighty fine lookin' man. At least he's said to be. I also hear the old sour-puss never looks at the ladies, though. Not ever."

"Hettie, it must be hard to love a man and lose him the way you lost your Del. But if you find a good man again, go after him." They hugged and chatted on for a while until Cherry had to ride back.

As she left the Lazy J and headed back over the high pass between their ranches, heading towards home, she thought about her friend and smiled at the idea of another woman falling in love. "I'd sure like to get a look at this handsome sheriff she mentions."

The sky was clear, the sun was high enough, and she thought of her special place, her Eden. The big trees and running brook were always relaxing and the place mesmerized her. She had enough time to sit there for a spell and still get home before nightfall.

After her encounter with Link, it had seemed a dangerous place to her, but she no longer had that worry. She shook off the ridiculous feeling and headed east towards her goal.

After another hour or so, she dismounted and led the horse into that softly shaded grove of trees. The sound of the small stream trickling over rocks was a sound she had always found very healing. With the moan of the soft wind through the lofty trees, she sat leaning against the bole of a Ponderosa and drifted off into a gentle doze. Checky drank from the stream and grazed nearby on a patch of grass that grew where the sun managed to shine through.

Awakening with a sudden start, Cherry heard the clink of metal on rock. The echoing sound of someone hammering on a rock came from some distance away and didn't belong to anything she was familiar with. Puzzled, she rose to her feet, slipped quietly through the trees, and looked up to see where the sounds came from.

Part way up on the mountainside, she saw a good sized man digging in the rocks and frequently pounding at something with a small hammer. Cherry held her hand over her mouth to stifle her sharp intake of breath. She knew him. "It's John Carmona! What on earth is that man digging for?" A flood of disquiet flowed through her, renewing all her old suspicions.

John was digging for something, prospecting? What on earth was he looking for?

Could this stalwart, upright seeming man be the one behind all the problems they'd been having on the ranch? Her hands shook in agitation as anger and suspicion reared their ugly heads again in her mind. *What have I done? Have I made a dreadful mistake trusting that man?*

Cherry couldn't believe what she saw, yet the proof lay before her. *I trusted him enough to make him foreman and now he's out here looking for something, and its sure not lost cattle!* She stomped her booted foot. *And not only that, he's prospecting on my ranch, looking for gold or whatever, while the roundup goes on without a boss.* "I'll give him a piece of my mind when I see him!"

She turned back to find her horse. It'd grown much darker. The sun had disappeared beneath a heavy layer of clouds. A chilly, gusting wind had kicked up to create dust devils swirling and filled with debris from the dry brushy ground. *Better get on home. It's going to be a bad one by the looks of that heavy cloud bank. If we're in for a very big storm, I don't want to be caught out in it.*

Realizing the tremendous size of the sudden storm she faced, she forgot her other worries, put the spurs to Checky, and rode headlong for the ranch. She had to beat the wicked storm that threatened to entrap her and her mount. Lightning flashed, and thunder boomed. It was rapidly headed her way.

As she rode, the mystery of John and his digging grew. It confused and worried her until she pictured him as the worst of men. On the other hand, when she was with him, his winning ways allayed all her suspicions. Her frustrations mounted as high as the threatening cloud bank as she raced for her life.

CHAPTER 14

Dark, storm-laden clouds swept over the landscape to darken the sky and sudden gusts of wind whipped wildly about. John raised his head to see them lying close to the ground and spread a mile wide. His hat blew off and into a thicket. He caught it and decided to pack his equipment and head for cover. Dust devils spun in wide circles across the flats, flinging debris high into the air. "Damned, rotten luck, I'll have to wait for a better day."

Carrying his pack, he moved to find Muley, tethered a good distance away. Covering the ground in short order, and with his equipment tied back of his saddle, he mounted up and headed for the ranch.

The wind threw dust particles in his eyes. His vision, distorted for a time, cleared enough to see another rider travelling at a mad gallop some distance ahead. He put his hand over his brow and squinted into the distance. *Cherry?* He looked again, recognizing Checky and the slim figure astride him.

What the hell is she doing out in a storm like this? He put the spurs to Muley and sent the big gelding flying towards her, hoping to catch her. Seeing her again after several days absence sent a thrill through his body.

Cherry looked back, spotted him approaching, and by the way she spurred her horse into a faster gait, he knew she didn't want to meet him or speak to him. *Damn, still got her tail in a twist.* He spurred his buckskin into a hard, headlong run, and gained steadily on her until he reached her side.

He yelled over the increasing winds, "Hold on, there, wait up a minute!" He stayed close beside her madly racing horse.

Finally, realizing she couldn't outrun him, Cherry pulled her horse to a halt and turned an accusing face to him. "I saw you digging around out there. What *were* you looking for?" Angry and filled with suspicion, she cried, "Who *are* you anyway and what on earth are you *doing* on this ranch?" Her infuriated words were nearly whipped away by the rapidly rising winds.

He yelled his reply, "I'll tell you all about it, but we've got to get in out of this rain." The first huge drops began splattering down on them and it soon poured down in heavy gouts of cold, wet, wind-driven rain. Their clothes were quickly soaked. He noticed she hadn't thought to tie her slicker to the back of her saddle. He didn't have one himself.

"Cherry, we've got to find shelter. It looks like a bad one." His words were torn away by the howling wind, but she seemed to hear them.

"I don't need your help in any possible way, you low-down, sneaking coyote! You're the one behind all our troubles here, I know you are!" The anger in her voice told him how she felt about what she had just seen him doing. He had no way to explain it in the midst of a damned thunderstorm. He grimaced. Apparently he should have discussed those things with her long before this.

Lightning crashed nearby and John caught a glimpse of her whitened face as she screamed in fright. They urged the horses into a faster gallop, but the ranch house lay many miles away over a rocky trail. The wind-filled rain had grown even more intense, whipping the grass and bushes about.

When John noticed they'd neared the valley where he and Waddie had worked that first day, he shouted above the swirling wind, "Cherry, there's another line shack near here. Let's try to make it there."

If she heard his shout, she ignored it, apparently having no intentions of following him anywhere. After another loud crash of lightning struck close by, she screamed and turned to him, her face pale. Her fear of lightning crashing so close obviously changed her mind. She indicated that she would let him lead the way.

He took the lead as they raced their horses toward the trees where the line shack was located about a half mile away. Cold, their clothing sopping wet, they pulled up before the rustic shelter. If a cowhand needed a place to spend the night, it often saved a long ride back to the ranch.

He dismounted and seeing her drooping figure plastered with water, reached up to help her off her saddle. He held her in his arms a moment, savoring the feel of her in spite of the stinging rain.

At her struggles, he loosened his grip and helped her through the pouring rain to the shack. The heavy downpour didn't stop him from noticing how well the feminine curves of her body were outlined by those wet clothes plastered snuggly against them. And nothing could stop his smile of appreciation.

"Come on, we can stay here a while and maybe get dried out." He shoved the door open and pushed her inside. "I'll see to the horses."

Fighting against the driving rain, he removed the saddles and covered them with a tarp. He put the animals into the corral, noticing it boasted a partial lean-to where they could shelter from the rain. Then he made his way through blinding sheets of water back to the shack and the wet, frightened young woman inside.

He found Cherry huddled on the bunk, shivering, and trembling. He reached for one of the blankets lying on the bunk and drew it around her shoulders, clasping her close for a quick moment. "I'll make us a fire." He turned to open the iron lid on top of the little stove, ignoring the angry glare she sent his way. He set bits of wood carefully inside and nursed the fire into a decent blaze.

When the small fire flickered and took hold, bringing the first bit of heat into their shelter, Cherry tried to speak. "I'm so c–cold, I c–can't stop shaking." Her teeth chattered so hard, clear speech had become difficult. Desperately shivering, she hugged herself as the little warmth from the rough blanket he had put around her didn't seem enough.

Looking at the bedraggled figure huddled beneath the worn, thin bit of blanket, John's heart went out to her. "Hold on, Cherry. I'll make it warm enough for you." He built up the fire until it was blazing then turned to her. "Better get some of those wet things off you before you catch pneumonia, cold as you are." He picked up the other blanket, a sorry sight, but she needed the additional warmth it offered. He helped her off with her jacket, then, pulled off her boots. Her socks were dry enough and he was glad to see it. Warm feet would be a big help in this situation.

"T–thanks, John," she stuttered, trying to unbutton her dripping, wide legged riding skirt. "I can't seem to get these buttons open. My hands are frozen stiff."

"Here, let me." He reached to undo her buttons and saw her eyes searching his face. Her previous anger had faded away in the face of her plight.

"Will I be all right here with you, J–John?"

"Of course, you will. I'll take care of you. Don't waste your time worrying about being here with me. Right now we've got to get you warm." He worked the wet leather riding skirt off her hips and laid it dripping over one of the broken down chairs near the fire. "Maybe this skirt-thing'll dry out a bit after a while."

He looked outside and saw thick, gray-black clouds near to touching the earth. The fierce pounding on the metal roof told them both that the rain had only gotten heavier.

"Looks like this'll last a while," he offered. She continued to shiver uncontrollably and he told her, "You can cover yourself with these blankets, but you need to get that wet shirt off. It's sopped and making you colder." He reached for the buttons, but she stopped his hand.

"I can get these." Her face flushed with embarrassment, but she couldn't stop the mad shaking from the cold.

John's blood had reached the boiling point. The few glimpses he'd had of her shapely legs and rounded hips, nearly drove him mad with hunger to touch and caress those parts he had only guessed at.

She unbuttoned her blouse with cold-numbed finger and finally pulled the sopping shirt from beneath the blanket. "What about you?" she asked, seeing his own chilled condition and soaked clothing. "Men get pneumonia, too." It worried her. "Aren't you going to catch your death from the cold, same as me?" She handed her wet things to him.

"I'm all right so far, but I am wet as hell," he confessed. "Keepin' busy helps keep me warm." He turned and chucked another stick of wood into the old flat topped stove and noticed with sudden alarm that they only had a few more good sized sticks of dry wood. If the rain didn't let up right soon they were in for a damned cold night.

He fed the fire and as the shack warmed, he took off his jacket. His shirt was dry in spots, but his trousers had taken a lot of water and the wet fabric clung to his wiry hips. She kept her eyes on him as he set about making coffee. "I'm feeling warmer now, John. Thanks." She snuggled deeper into the ratty blankets, they covered her vulnerable state of undress and she was not bothered by their unseemly condition. The warmth they provided did matter and sorry as they were, they were life-saving and she knew it.

Her cowboys used these shacks when they were out like this and on occasion, she did as well. She watched the big man work over making something to eat. He pulled the makings for a batch of biscuits out of the rough built cupboard. It bothered her that he took care of her and neglected himself. His trousers dripped with water. It prayed on her mind now that she was more comfortable.

He formed several oddly shaped biscuits and shoved them into the oven on a sheet of tin he had found and then cut some jerky into a pan. The smell of coffee filled the shack and her stomach rumbled.

She decided to ask him what he had been looking for when she spotted him. "What were you digging for on the mountainside? Yes, I saw you up there, but I didn't know what you were doing."

Her voice held unspoken accusations, but he merely shrugged. "I guess I'd better come clean about myself." He smiled at her and sat near her on the edge of the feeble chair. "I'm not the bogeyman or anything like that," he began. "I have some interest in finding rare metals. An assayer friend of mine in Phoenix let me in on some samples of ores found in this area. I'm not looking for gold or silver, but there is very likely another particularly rare mineral the government keeps track of.

"I believe I've mentioned this before," he added. "My expertise is more as a geologist than a cattle man and I came here to check into what the assayer told me. I think you can believe that." He didn't feel the need to go into his years as a Texas Ranger and a few other things he'd done.

"Why look on my ranch?"

"Some of the ore samples we became aware of appear to have been taken from your ranch and that of your neighbor's as well."

"Hmm, thanks for telling me that." She looked up at him. "Why couldn't you have said so in the first place? Why all the mystery?"

"Maybe it's just me. Never was much of a talker." John relaxed. She knew what he was about, or believed she did, and if she still hated him, it wasn't showing as much.

He got busy and put together the few soggy biscuits and some jerky gravy. Try as he might to emulate Waddie's expert performance at the stove, the result wasn't half as good. Outside in the pouring rain, it grew dark. Needing light, he found where he had left the matches and lit the lantern.

She ate with a good appetite and choked down the beastly coffee.

He smiled at her. The admiration on his face was plain for her to see. "You're a real trooper being stuck out here like this during a storm."

She laughed. "I was raised here, don't forget. We get some terrible storms around here. This one seems especially bad, though. Sometimes they last for several days. I don't mind the storms, but the lightning..." She shivered again. "It frightens me out of my wits," she muttered with a nervous laugh. "How are we fixed for wood, then?"

John hesitated. "We're about out, I'm afraid. It's going to be cold as hell in here right quick this time of year, sorry." He looked out the window at the heavy sheets of rain pouring down in the deepening dusk. "Looks like everything out there is soaked too."

Cherry looked about the shack. "Any more blankets around?"

"Don't appear to be."

She hesitated to ask the question burning on her mind, but had to bring it up. "How will *you* stay warm? That worries me, John."

"Guess I won't." He sat on one of the rugged chairs. "We'll see how it goes. If I get too bad off I'll burn these chairs."

The fire went out, having eaten up all of the wood. Cherry grew increasingly nervous as John began shivering almost uncontrollably. Fidgeting under her blankets she finally said, her voice very soft, "John–uh–if you'd promise to be good, you can get in here under these blankets next to me. I don't believe I could stand to see you freeze to death to save my modesty. I just couldn't do that," Her voice quavered, her face reddened to a bright crimson, but her chin was firm and she meant what she said.

He looked down at her in the flickering lantern light. "If it gets as cold as I believe it will, we may have to try it." He hesitated a moment. "But Cherry, I have to warn you, I'm a man, only human, and my God, you are a very beautiful woman."

As time wore on, the weathered old shack quickly leaked out what pitiful heat the stove had given off. John kept the lantern lit, he could see by it, but it gave off little or no warmth. The insidious cold crept into the shack and deep into his very bones until his teeth began to chatter.

Cherry watched him shaking in his wet clothing until she finally overcame her fear, "You'd better climb under these blankets, John. We only have the two and they're barely keeping me warm. I'm becoming awfully cold now and I have them both." She moved as far back on the bunk as she could, feeling the chill of new territory against her back and legs. It was rather narrow for one person, let alone for two, especially when one of them happened to be a big man.

Getting into the bunk with a woman like Cherry would realize any man's dream, and John's in particular. While wanting to keep the faith of decency with her, he was not sure he was equal to a task like that, but he would try.

Right now, he was so cold, getting warm was all he had on his mind. He had to crawl in beside her or freeze to death. He sat on the side of the bunk.

Cherry felt the weight of his body press the thin mattress down as he tugged off his wet trousers. Her heart thundered in her chest. She faced a very long night lying against this man's strong body. *How did I get into this frightening fix?* She shrugged in her helplessness. Shaking with cold herself, he was colder, and she saw no help for either of them.

Forced by plain human kindness, she allowed him to come under the blankets for the little warmth they had to offer, and held them open for him.

He carefully slid his legs in under the blankets and she shivered at the feel of his icy skin. "Oh, John, your legs are frozen!" she cried. "I'm sorry I made you wait so long."

"I understand how it is, Cherry, and I sure thank you for sharing these sorry excuses for blankets with me." He shuddered. "God! I'm cold! I can't stop shaking." The cold that had slowly taken over his body after the stove fire died out had seeped deeply into his bones. The coldness in the shack tonight reminded him of the coming winter with the nights getting progressively colder and longer. He'd tried to stay out of her blankets, but his body had gotten cold, and her invitation was more than welcome.

CHAPTER 15

He felt her hand glide over his shoulder. "John, you're shaking like a leaf." She moved closer, placing her warmer body against his back and legs. "Is this better?" He heard her voice go very soft, almost crooning, and his pulse quickened.

"It sure helps. Sorry for the way I'm shaking, girl."

"I should have had you get in here sooner and I'm sorry for that, but I'm glad you understand my feelings about it." If he could have seen her face, would it look the way it felt, hot and flushed with embarrassment at lying so intimately close to a man? But believing him too cold at the moment to care, she snuggled her body closer yet to warm him.

Lying against his broad back, she inhaled his masculine scent, manly, like her father was, yet strong and solidly comforting in a different way. John smelled of wind and sage, with a touch of campfire and ashes. Close to his body as she was, they both became warmer and more comfortable. Her skin, pressed against his, sent her mind singing with a sense of rightness she was sure she should not feel. Yet every sense in her body was vitally aware of his masculinity and eagerly welcomed the contact.

"You feel mighty good laying against me." He adjusted himself a bit. "Just like that," he groaned softly with increasing pleasure as the warmth from her body slowly suffused between them. After an hour or so, he wanted to turn toward her. "All right if I turn a bit?" he asked with a voice soft as an owl's wing whispering through the night.

"I guess it would be all right." Her heart fluttered madly in her chest as she felt him turn over, with each move he made being so solid and male. His long legs had grown warm against hers and she marveled at the physical difference between their bodies. His, big, hard, and strong—hers, strong and supple, yet soft.

They became even warmer as the night wore on. She loved the solid feel of his body. A man was made so differently. She puzzled over this as she snuggled ever closer against him. "Are you warmer...more comfortable?" she queried. "You've stopped shaking."

Outside the rain continued a heavy drumming on the roof and flashes of lightning sent blinding light through the soiled, smudged windows of the shack.

His hip pressed against hers and his head, higher on the bunk, lay on the ancient pillow left in the shack long ago. His body felt warm now and so good against hers. "It feels awfully nice with you close against me," he whispered

"Yes, it does. It's so awful outside, John." She snuggled closer. "It's terrible out there and I don't know why, but I feel safe in here with you, away from that terrible lightning." She shivered slightly, remembering the fearful way it had flashed.

"You'd feel wonderful anytime to me, Cherry." He felt a slight cramp in his hip and asked, "I don't want to frighten you, but if you turned a bit, I'd be able to hold you closer against me and we might sleep a little warmer that way."

He moved onto his side and drew her against his chest, with his arms entwined around her body. She felt so warm nestling even closer against him and her excitement mounted. If John could feel her heart pounding, he would know how greatly he affected her.

Cherry didn't understand why she reveled in the comfort and warmth she found lying in this man's arms. It wasn't right and she shouldn't allow it. But it was dangerous outside this flimsy shack, and in his arms she was safe from the wildness of that storm out there in the blackness.

Feeling content where she was at the moment, Cherry forgot all her suspicions of him. He was her savior in many ways and she clung to him for the safety and protection he offered. Feeling warmer the way he held her body against his own warm chest, she relaxed.

There had been no real choice, and in her heart, Cherry was glad of the situation. It had just happened. She made no move to escape him nor did she want to. Though her heart went wild with such frenzied beating, and she could scarcely catch her breath, her troubled soul reveled deeply in his strength and masculinity. She couldn't move nor could she speak.

John felt his heart soar with the tender feelings swelling in his chest as he pressed her head close against him. He wanted to comfort her for all her losses and give her the feeling of security. But as they lay together, it wasn't long until his stirring blood wanted far more. No red-blooded man could lie beside a woman like this and not feel the way he felt. He smiled into her hair, as her head nestled into his shoulder, and breathed in the scent of it.

He nuzzled down through her hair and after a little while his seeking lips found her cheek. He moved to her mouth and gently kissed her, not deeply, but soft and loving as he held her in his warm embrace.

She gasped for breath. "I don't even know you, mister and I can't allow these liberties. I must not!" She tried to sound angry and pull away, but she couldn't deny she'd eagerly returned his kiss.

"I couldn't help that, Cherry. You're the most glorious woman I've ever known. Please don't be afraid of me. I'd never hurt you, not ever. It's just that I've had this feeling lately—don't you know—or can't you feel the strong tie that's been building between us? I think you're aware of it, too."

Cherry made no answer and he loosened his hold just a little. "Are you warm enough?"

"Yes, it's much better," she murmured. "I'd never been kissed before that time you kissed me in the orchard, well…not like that. I don't know what to do about certain things. You frighten me in some crazy way and because of it, I know I should be afraid of you. Yet your arms feel so good to me right now and I don't want to be anywhere else.

I'm warm and I find it very hard to keep my thoughts straight with you holding me like this."

He laughed. "Well, don't then!" Turning her to face him, he pulled tighter into his arms, and kissed her again. "There! Maybe that'll make up for some of the things you've missed."

She didn't struggle again, and they spent a long time lying next to each other, being warm, and listening to the pounding rain outside. He didn't want to frighten her, but they had a long night ahead, and his blood had long since reached a fever pitch of intense desire.

Delaying, trying to control and settle himself, he asked, "So who did you kiss, then?"

"He was just a kid, a young cowboy who worked here. But he left after that and I never knew why."

John detected her note of puzzlement. "It was Link. Seems he didn't cotton to any man making up to you." He kept his voice calm and non-accusatory. Link was a thing of the past on this ranch and he didn't want to get her stirred up about it.

"Yes, that must be why so many of our riders seldom stayed around." Her voice went low, remembering how Link had kept men away from her. "I wouldn't have stood for that had I known! For a man who just got here, you seem to know a lot about us."

He laughed and Cherry heard it rumble softly, deep in his chest. "It didn't take long to see what he was up to." His every move or sound seemed to go to the very heart of her being until she felt he was consuming her. She knew she should fight against this mysterious sensation, yet how greatly she welcomed the warmth of his body and the way his arms made her feel.

She'd never been in a situation like this. While fighting with her inner thoughts, and fearing she would lose control, she also knew being here in this man's arms on such a wild night, seemed right somehow. If it wasn't right...she didn't know anymore—she could barely think at all.

She'd already learned how easily a certain man could turn a woman to jelly, one that attracted her. But what about him? How did he feel when he touched her? Did his heart beat as madly as hers? As her head lay on his broad chest, her question was answered. His heart pounded as fast as hers, and hearing that wildly beating heart, she knew somehow, that as a woman, she had a certain kind of power, too. And it had to be plenty strong to set his heart thumping so rapidly. She had also noticed before today how his body tensed when he came near her.

Certain that John was a man of the world, experienced in many ways, and she but a lonely young girl, she felt that she possessed a mysterious something in herself, an allure, an essence he needed and wanted.

She lay beside him wondering what he would do next. Certain he had the knowledge and experience to take the next step if she allowed it, she wondered what would happen. What did he want? Those errantly wild thoughts about the male/female thing set her afire with a wild sort of tension inside her mind and body. This was all new to her. She had little knowledge of these things, outside of seeing animals couple a time or two. But she remembered

Margarita's words. They came back to her, exciting her curiosity.

"The man, he will show you," she'd said before, and Cherry, unable to hear more, had escaped to her bedroom. There was no bedroom for her to run away to now. She felt so wonderful and so excited, it didn't seem to matter anymore.

"Dear girl, what are you thinking?"

"Oh, nothing of importance." She was silent for a while and then she said, "I don't know what to do, John." She trembled. "I feel so good being here with you. I know it's not right, yet I like it—I want to know more of this."

His heart pounding nearly out of his chest, he kissed her again. "Cherry, there's so much more to this wondrous thing between us. I'd love to show you how it can be between a man and a woman, but it wouldn't be right for us trapped out here like we are. I believe you'd hate me in the morning."

"Because it wouldn't be right, and you know it wouldn't. Is that why I'd hate you in the morning?" She felt his hands move over her breasts, and then his fingers touched her between her legs and moved slowly upward. "Don't do that, John, it makes me feel like I'm burning up inside." He touched her again. "What's happening to me?" She moved her head on his broad, warm chest and felt his nipple against her mouth. She nipped gently on it and he stiffened in her arms.

She pulled slightly away from him. "Was that a bad thing to do?"

"No, my darling, not at all," he choked out the words and fought to keep himself honorable. Although he tried, he couldn't keep his burning erection from pressing against her abdomen, couldn't keep his wandering hands off her breasts, her back, and her feminine heat.

"I'm sorry for touching you this way. I've tried to keep my honor and yours." He shuddered. "God help me, girl, I have."

"I'm not totally ignorant, John," she murmured in his ear. "I know a little of what you are going through. I'm twenty years old and know nothing much, but some things are just there." She turned to face him and wrapped her arms around his neck. "I'm not a baby anymore."

He kissed, caressed and stroked her, until the urgent, burning need rose within her, becoming unbearable. Panting for breath, she cried out, "I'll die if you don't do something to make this aching go away—I'm on fire, John!" She was writhing in his arms. "You know everything, don't you?"

In her frenzy, she bit the edge of his ear and it sent his heart pounding. Driven even more frantic with desire, he whispered, "Yes, I'll take good care of you, my darlin', sweet girl." He kissed her, a long drugging meeting of lips. As her lips parted on a moan, he slipped his tongue between them and plunged to the depths. Then his hands traveled down, caressing her hips, back, and thighs. He found her full, firm breasts again and shifted until he reached them with his mouth. He suckled and nibbled until she moaned aloud in response. He slipped his fingers into her heat and tenderly stroked her swollen nub. "My darling, you're so lovely, so beautiful."

"I don't know where I am, John...lost...floating somewhere...oh God! What are you doing?"

He edged her body beneath his and gently nudged her legs apart. Working his under things off the best he could in the tight quarters they had, he managed to remove hers as well. Cold air crept in at times, but in their mad heat, neither of them felt it. John returned his fingers to the slick moisture of her core and knew she was ready for him. "It might hurt a bit, but not for long, dearest."

He positioned himself over her and eased his fully engorged member into the portal of her warm, writhing body. She gasped and cried out as he thrust inside.

He held her quiet for a moment, comforted her, and whispered his love to her in the darkness. And then, he began a gentle rhythm, going ever deeper until at last she met his ecstasy with her own. Together they fed the burning fires of need, until they descended into the wild, mad spasmodic raptures that accompanied their release.

It ended with a long gasp of wonder from her and a shudder of deepest content from him.

After long moments of holding her tight against his body, he crooned to her, "My God Cherry, you're wonderful!" He raised himself up on an elbow and looked into her eyes, barely outlined in the dimness of the rain-swept cabin. "Are you all right, dearest, darling, girl?"

"I think I am. So this is that great and hidden mystery between a man and a woman. It's unbelievable...I never imagined!" She was quiet for a moment then murmured, nearly purring, "I think it's beyond wonderful, but it hurts some."

"Only at first, my love. As time goes on, a man and woman can discover many wonders in each other, but this first time can be the greatest gift God ever gave to human kind. Or, I should say, it certainly was to me." He hugged her body close again then laid her gently back and stroked her hair. "Cherry, darling, I was the first for you, and God willing, I'll be the last you'll ever need."

"John, nothing will ever be the same for me again, will it?"

"No, my darling, it never will." And he held her, comforting her until the fever took them again.

∽∾∽

The rain continued hammering against the tin roof while lightning flashed against the window panes. But they were warm and cozy. It was a long time before dawn and John had held this lovely woman in his arms for all the hours of darkness. Yet even in the glow of first light, he knew he wanted her again. "Will it ever be enough between us?"

"I don't know. I hope not." She snuggled into his warmth and clung onto him with willing arms.

A smile played about his lips. He would make his life with this girl, but when she'd had a chance to think, would she want to kill him?

CHAPTER 16

Cherry opened her eyes and looked about at the rustic interior of the shack, trying to remember where she was. When she turned her head and saw John lying on his side, looking her in the eye, she gasped, "Oh God! I remember it all!" Thinking of all that had happened between them during the stormy night shook her with guilt and shame. Yet, her body retained the soft fulfilling glow of all the things she had known in this man's arms. It took her some time to set things in focus, but she did at last.

Her cheeks burned with the heat of a furious blush as she tried to turn away from that smiling face and the heated memories of what they had done in the dark of night. She struggled against the wiry encircling arm that held her. "How did this happen?"

"We were caught out in the rain, if you remember." She saw him trying not to grin. "You were kind enough to help me stay warm last night, my dearest Cherry—I truly believe you saved my life."

"How well I remember. And I'm not your dearest anything! I believe you took advantage of me when I was terrified of the lightning and at my very weakest." She tried to move from under his arm, but the bed was so narrow she had no place to go.

"There's nothing weak about you, my dear, I'll have to say that."

"Would you please get out of this bed?" She realized how ridiculous her situation was and that it was far too late to save any vestige of virtue. She faced up to it, as the edges of fear seeped into her mind. *What have I done?*

He chuckled which didn't help Cherry's feelings of guilt. "All right my darling, I'll move out of here, but I have to find what clothes I can. They're scattered somewhere under these sorry blankets—my underclothes, I mean."

Cherry reached under the blankets and fished around for anything he might have lost. Unable to avoid contact with his long legs and big chest, she demanded, "Will you please get out of here so I can look?"

"If I get up, I'm unclothed and you mightn't like what you'll see." She felt him move to the side of the bed and sit up. "You'd best hand me anything you find under there first."

Cherry found a stray bit of cloth and tossed it at him. He caught it and held it out, "I don't believe this'd fit me, but it sure is pretty." She saw her own lacy undergarment waving before her.

She reached out to grab the item of clothing and that action exposed her breasts to full view. He couldn't hold back his delight at the sight of her. "My God, woman, but you're beautiful!"

She drew away from him and pulled the blankets to her chin. At seeing the desire rising in his eyes, she quickly looked away, "Oh! I've got to get out of here!"

She had enough time to think about the situation. Her eyes narrowed and her mouth tightened. "What have I done?" She looked at him, her hands flung out. "There could be a child from this."

"If that happened, I'd be the happiest man on this lovely earth."

She heard the joy and pride in his voice.

"Why...you're a total stranger to me," she huffed. "Really, I don't know how this could have happened!"

John didn't try to answer that unanswerable question as he helped her find the rest of the hidden under garments lost beneath their tangled blankets.

She got a full view of him during the search. Covering her eyes didn't work and in the process of finding the clothing, she'd seen all of him and the man he was. He was beautifully made and she instinctively knew his body complemented hers, each created for their own purposes. She felt the heavy weight of him press the thin mattress down as he sat on the edge of the bunk and remembered everything all over again. The way he had made her feel, the things he had done, and the sweep of desire rose within her at those memories.

He put on his clothes, including the cold, stiff trousers he'd worn in the rain. The shirt and outer jacket had dried some from the small fire they'd had last night. Settling into his soggy clothing, he said, "I'll go out and see if I can find a bit of dry wood somewhere. We'll have a bite to eat before we set out this morning."

Without looking too closely at her newly flushed face, he walked to the door and stepped out into a gleaming, sun-filled morning. The air, clean, fresh, and pine scented, filled his nostrils.

The horses waited for their oats. He dug under the hasty tarp he had thrown over their saddles and tack, dry enough, but no grain. He did find enough dry wood under the tarp where he'd stowed the saddles to make a decent fire and get the shack warmed up a little. He loaded up and went in.

Cherry had donned her clothes.

"Are they dry enough for you?" he asked as he dropped the chunks of semi-dry branches into the empty wood box.

"They'll have to be, won't they?" Sitting on the bunk in her wrinkled, damp clothing, huddled in a blanket, she said nothing more as he coaxed a fire to life in the stove. After it blazed up and warmth spread through the shack, he made biscuits and fixed jerky gravy. He opened a can of peaches he found in the small larder box.

Cherry remained silent. He figured she was worried over what had happened between them in a storm-filled night. Her mind worked in ways a man could never fully understand, but the heat spreading over her cheeks easily gave away her innermost thoughts. He smiled to himself.

"John, what happens to us, now?" He understood her meaning, having given a good bit of thought to that same subject. As she tried to put things in order inside her mind, he knew the flush across her cheeks wasn't from the heat of the stove.

"I reckon marriage might be a good idea." He bent a smile on her. "I hadn't given much thought to marrying before, but after meeting you, I've considered it, quite a lot in fact. That'd be if you're willing."

"How can I marry someone I hardly know? Where would we live? I've lived here all my life and you are certainly no rancher." It sounded more like a business deal to Cherry, and the romance was sadly lacking. The passion she had felt in his arms last night came flooding into her mind, only adding to her confusion. Despite all her worries, a part of her felt it had been right, so very right. The memories of what had happened were vivid enough to set her on edge, partly from desire and partly from fear of what came next.

He handed her a tin plate with half burned food. "I'm not good at this cooking business like Waddie. That lad's a great cook."

"Thanks." She took the plate and balanced it across her knees. She tried seeing John the way he was now, compared to the man who'd set her body aflame and made her bones melt during the night. He'd turned her into a quivering, helpless mass of need, and he'd taken care of that, too. She sighed and put her fork into the gelatinous mess he had fixed for her.

Looking at her plate, she broke into a giggle. "You really aren't much of a cook. This is so *bad*, John." She ate a little of it before she went outside and scraped her plate off on the ground. "I hope you squirrels don't die from this," she muttered at the one she saw in the trees.

"I heard that, missy." John rushed at her, caught her around the waist, swung her around, and lowered his lips onto hers for a good, deep kiss. "At least I got this part right, and don't try telling me I'm wrong. I know all about you, my lovely—I sure as hell do!"

When he finally let her go, the strain between them had lifted, and in relaxed happiness, Cherry worked with John, straightening the shack before saddling their horses.

It was a long ride back but she felt comfortable riding beside him. Her fears and emotions settled for now, she was unable to worry about her future at least for the moment.

☙❧☙

Riding toward the ranch in silence, John was deep in thought. Trouble lay ahead. Men searched for a fortune in some kind of ore, likely gold or silver, on this ranch. He needed to go back to the small village and check for a telegraph message and wondered if the roundup was progressing well enough. He hadn't been much of a ranch foreman. He'd told her up front that he wasn't up on cattle ranching, and had put a lot of trust in young Waddie.

"We're almost there," Cherry said, reluctant to face Margarita's inquiring eyes. The woman was no fool. She would know everything without ever hearing a word from her. Caught out all night with John was a fact she couldn't hide from those wise brown eyes.

"You'll be fine, darling." He smiled at her and would have reached for her, but she put the spurs to Checky and raced for his corral.

After corralling her horse, she made her way to the house. Her steps lagged, thinking of all that had happened to her during the wild and stormy night. Inside herself, everything was different. Would it show? She needed to get a look at herself in her mirror to see.

She opened the door and inside, met Margarita's tear-filled eyes. "Oh, *mija,* you no come back, I think you dead!" She took Cherry in her arms. Then, she held her out to look in her eyes. "Where you been, you are all right?"

"Margarita, I'm fine." She didn't want to tell her more but the woman's innate perception saw the distress on her face.

"Where you stay in big storm, *mija?*" she asked. "Who stay with you?" The suspicion in her dark eyes demanded an explanation.

"Uh—well—Mr. Carmona was out looking at rocks or something when it began to rain. He saw me trying to get home. We were wet and cold and the lightning crashed all around us. I was terrified, Margarita. We had to stay at a line shack to get in from the rain and keep warm. I could have died out in that storm." Cherry knew her defensiveness came as much for her sense of guilt as from justification for spending the night alone with a man she barely knew.

"He make you warm, missy?" Margarita's eyes, so bright with mischief, let Cherry know her secret was out. "He take care you?"

She blushed. "Oh Margarita. Yes, he kept me warm, he did that, too!"

"What you do now? You all right?" Margarita looked into Cherry's eyes and, seeing the distress there, she said once again, "He good man—*mucho* good man, I know this, *hija.*"

"I know it too, but everything is different now. I don't know what to do. I haven't even thought about the roundup or how that's going. What would Dad say if he knew what a sorry rancher I am?"

Her words brought a smile to Margarita's face. She hugged her again. "Ah, *mi hija* is in love. I know this, too."

Cherry flushed at her words and, tearing herself away, ran to her room. After inspecting herself in the mirror, she washed her body vigorously. She then dressed in fresh riding clothes and decided to ride Checky again. It had grown late in the day, but she couldn't stand the inactivity. She hungered to see John.

Donning a jacket, she stepped outside in the cool afternoon air. The ranch yard was empty. Everyone had gone to the roundup valley. "I'd best take a look," she said and laughed at herself. "I'm the owner now and unless I show up once in a while, they might forget who I am."

She took off at a rapid gallop, but after the long ride home from the shack earlier, she felt tired. It had gotten rather late and she decided to turn back. *I can check out the roundup tomorrow.* She turned her horse and headed down the trail toward home.

Hearing the sound of hoof beats, she stopped and waited, hoping it might be John. The rider came up quickly, but it was young Martin Bent. She waved at him. "Howdy, Martin, been at the roundup?"

"I was, Miss Cherry, most of the day, but I decided to come and see how you were doing, or if you needed any help." His cheeks flamed with embarrassment and she realized that, in his boyish way, he was trying to attract her interest. He had tried to be attentive at her father's funeral, and she'd responded politely, agreeing to his offer of service only if the need arose.

"Why, I'm doing just fine, Martin. Does your father know you've left the roundup?" she asked, hoping to deflect the boy's interest in her.

"He's headed back to our place with some of our stock that got mixed in with yours." He flushed again, then, added, "Uh—Miss Cherry, there's somethin' you've got to know about. I ain't supposed to know and I'm a rotten son for telling you about it, but I saw Link and my dad together out on the range, and more than once."

"How does that affect me?"

"Maybe you wouldn't know about it, but my dad's a regular gambler in town and not real good at it either. I heard him say how that man Jeems had cleaned him out too many times. He got in trouble makin' loans and stuff, tryin' to get his money back. It just kept gettin' worse."

He cleared his throat uncomfortably before he went on with his story. "Ma'am, he was takin' some of your red herd and sellin' them to men over on the other side of those mountains." He pointed eastward. "Worse yet, your foreman, Link, he was helpin' my dad with it."

Her anger flared. *Of all the—* Gritting her teeth, she clamped down hard on her temper, knowing it wasn't wise to shoot the messenger. "Well, that's one mystery solved. Thanks for telling me, Martin. I won't say anything to the sheriff about this right now, but if your father keeps on, I certainly will. Rustling is stealing, and I've heard more than once, the man called Jeems was a cheater of the worst kind." Taking a deep breath to steady herself, she patted the young man on the arm. "You're a brave man to tell me these things. If you can't tell your father what you've told me, have him come visit me. I'll scare him into changing his ways. He has a family and I wouldn't want to see the man hang for cattle rustling."

"Oh, Miss Cherry, thank you! I'm glad I told you. You're quite a lady, you are." Obviously relieved, he fidgeted in his saddle. "Would you mind if I came to call on you one day?"

She gave him her best smile. "It would be very nice, Martin, but I'm planning marriage at present, so perhaps it wouldn't be a good idea. But you certainly are a fine young man, kind and thoughtful, and I'm proud to know you."

The news of her engagement both surprised and, from the sagging of his shoulders, disappointed him greatly. He manfully swallowed his damaged pride. "I sure wish you the best, ma'am. Whoever he is, he's a lucky man." He turned his horse. "Well, I'll be headin' on back now," he said and rode away with a decided slump to his body.

Cherry grinned. *Well, Link, there's one you didn't drive away.*

∾ↄᏇↄ

John spent the remaining hours of the day at the roundup, listening to reports. Finally towards evening, Waddie gave him the tally. "We're short on some of the red stock, John. Cattle thieves worked on that herd the most." He shrugged. "Link never seemed to get a handle on where those cattle went. I'm thinkin' he didn't give a damn about 'em. Must'a had his sights set on Miss Cherry, and it's all he ever thought about."

They headed back to the ranch house. "May as well bunk in the bunk house for tonight, Waddie, the boys can keep watch over the cattle." John figured the roundup wouldn't last more than a few days now. Most of the neighboring ranchers had already driven what stock they had back to their own ranges.

He and Waddie put their horses away and washed up for the evening meal. Then he noticed that Checky wasn't in his corral and went to the ranch house to see about Cherry.

Margarita came to the door. "She go riding, no come back! She worry 'bout something."

"Which way'd she go?"

"I don't know Mr. John. She so worry, maybe something bother her?"

He uttered a hasty thanks to the woman and nearly ran towards the corral. As he caught up his buckskin and led him out to be saddled, Cherry rode into the yard.

"Good God, woman, where were you?" he shouted at her. His relief that she was safe was so great he could barely keep his hands off her. He watched her slowly dismount, her chin in the air.

"What are you going on about?" she sniffed. "I was perfectly safe riding about on my own property." She tried to avoid his eyes, but he waited until she faced him.

"Cherry, can we meet in the orchard again tonight?" He didn't plan on taking no for an answer, but he wanted to give her a chance to invite him.

"You might as well join me for dinner then."

He heard the resignation in her voice, but it didn't matter to him as long as he could see her and hold her again. His need had mounted to the point where he would never be able to taste the food at dinner.

"Thank you. I'd be happy to join you, at dinner, or any other time."

His words about his joining her held so much more meaning for her since their rain-filled night together that her legs nearly crumpled beneath her. Getting herself in hand, she walked stiffly past him and into the house, but couldn't help muttering, "Overheated devil!"

John was relieved she was safe at home and contemplated the forthcoming evening in her company. Everything had changed between them, and they had a hell of load of things to work out. He went into the bunk house to await the sound of the dinner bell.

When he heard the dinner bell ringing, he sauntered up to the ranch house, hiding his inner turmoil. He supposed because of her own weakness in giving in to him during their night at the shack, Cherry wanted to despise him. Being a strong woman, she might hate the feeling of being drawn to him and unwillingly made to feel the things she had during that raging storm. But how delightfully he remembered that she'd been more than willing and could never deny it. He approached the house with a smile on his face. He knocked and Margarita opened the door.

"Buenas noches, señor," she purred, and with a mischievous twinkle glowing in her soft, dark eyes, led him into the dining room. He followed her ample figure, keeping an eye out for Cherry.

She came out dressed in white with a red sash knotted about her waist. The neck of her dress lay high against her slender throat, but for him it hid nothing. He remembered very well the soft fullness that lay beneath the dainty batiste of that gown. Her eyes were dark lavender tonight, near into purple, and her hair shone black as a raven's wing. She'd brushed it out and let it fall, waving and curling down her back. He held back an admiring gasp and repeated his thoughts. *She might try to hate me, but she most definitely dresses for me.* It sent his heart soaring.

CHAPTER 17

G ood evening, John." Sounding stiff and formal, she turned and led him to his seat at the table. He sat down and Margarita hustled in with their favorite, a fragrant *albondigas* soup. She said nothing as she served them both, but her eyes expressed enough excitement and a certain softness that he never doubted Margarita's feelings about him. But, would Cherry have him? He was not completely sure about that and it kept him on edge.

"And how is the roundup going, then?" she asked. Her eyes narrowed as she surveyed him. She barely nibbled at her food and continually fiddled with the tableware. "Waddie tells me some of the red herd has been lost," he replied. "Otherwise, he says the count is good. The calves are healthy with only a few lost to varmints."

"Yes, mostly the two-legged kind, I'd say," Cherry said in a low voice. "How well I know. With all that's been going on around this ranch, I suppose we're lucky to have done as well as we have." She gave a sigh then smiled at him with her eyebrows raised. "Rope any calves, then?"

"No, I left that to those who know what they're doing." He returned her smile. "This is a right nice supper, Cherry." He loved saying her name and the newly found familiarity between them made it all that much better. He loved her, had faced it, and had already made room in his life for her. She hadn't confessed her love for him and he suppressed a slight niggling worry over whether she *could* love him after what had happened between them.

The meat was a finely roasted beef and proved to be tender and juicy. He barely noticed while waiting for the invitation to walk in the orchard. He needed his hands on her and ached with the wanting. Did she know it?

After a thick crusty apple pie, served with coffee, he pushed his plate away and looked at her. "Care to take a walk?"

She'd waited through the endless meal in anticipation for his touch once again. *How can I fight this? Can I distance myself from this man? Do I want to?* "I guess so, John—not raining, is it?" With that, she laughed.

That soft, pealing sound broke the tension between them and together they walked out across the patio and under the fragrant trees to the familiar bench beneath the apple tree.

Before sitting, she turned to him. "John, what do we do now? I can't think straight anymore."

He ushered her to the seat and sat close beside her. Then he reached for her and pulled her into his arms. "Cherry, I love you. I don't know your feelings, you haven't said, but I believe we're good together. We need to decide a few things. I'd say we need to sit together and talk to each other."

She had waited to hear what he had to say, dreading, yet praying, for him to say he loved her. He was so strong he frightened her in a dozen ways and it left her trembling with indecision. "I don't know how I feel. This is all so new to me." She looked at him in the dimness of the night. "Being in your arms is the best thing I've ever known and I think of you day and night. Am I in love with you? I think so. I'd like it to be love, but I'm not sure what that is." It wasn't a good answer and she feared he might leave her because of it.

John kissed her deeply and fully. "I wish we were back in that cabin, that's what I wish." He wanted her bare breasts against his chest, and in his mouth, and his legs entangled with hers. He wanted all of her. He wanted to drive her into a moaning frenzy as he had in that lonely shack on a wonderful storm-driven night. She'd bewitched the hell out of him and he couldn't get enough of her.

She clutched onto him and returned his kisses. "Oh John, I know what you're wanting and I want that, too." She could barely speak, nestled against his broad chest. Would he leave her if she refused him? At the thought of what her life would be like without him, her breath caught in her throat. Imagining the loss of him, she realized how closely bound together they were.

She pulled away and looked into his face, thinking of him gone out of her life forever. The thought of never seeing his big body, those gray eyes and hawk-like nose of his was more than Cherry could face. She wanted him—wanted to be loved by him—and faced up to it.

She looked into his eyes, her chin firm, her decision made. "I *am* in love with you! I know it, I am! Wildly, madly, and forever!"

They clung together for a long time and then he eased her slender body away from him and looked into her glowing, purple-shaded eyes. "I want to marry you, Cherry, my love."

Without a moment's hesitation, she exclaimed, "Yes, I'll marry you. I will be your wife." She leapt into his arms. "I'll tell Margarita. She'll be thrilled. That fool woman loved you before I did." She laughed. "I can't believe it. I'll be married to a man from nowhere, a stranger I hardly know!"

"I'm not exactly a total stranger, Cherry, not any more. I don't suppose I could spend the night in your house—in your bed?" He pressed her against his body, tense with wanting.

"No John, you know I can't do that, but the thoughts of you beside me in a big bed! It'll drive me wild all night long thinking about that and the possibilities." She let him kiss her until she couldn't breathe. "Maybe we could ride out and get caught in another storm," she said with a laugh.

They stayed together for several hours and when they finally parted, she asked him to breakfast.

☙❧

Margarita piled a healthy breakfast of eggs, bacon, salsa, and tortillas on John's plate for breakfast, along with several cups of strong black coffee. Cherry joined him and they spent a quiet hour together. Margarita stayed close enough to watch the two of them. He caught her eye and knew she reveled in the love growing between himself and Cherry.

"I sent Waddie to take care of the roundup," he told Cherry. "I must to ride into town and check for messages. I sent a few things off back a while ago and need to catch up on things." He needed more information and had a few ideas how to obtain what he wanted.

"You'll be careful, won't you? Please, John." Worry flashed in her eyes, adding to his feeling that she now belonged to him, and he fell in love with her all over again for her concern.

"Yes, I'll keep an eye out. I may not get back for a day or two. The roundup is near done and Waddie's done a fine job of bossing, even if some of the older hands weren't too happy about him running things. They've razzed the kid unmercifully."

"I owe that young man a lot," she said. "And if he's as good as you say, he's welcome to the job if it isn't what you really want" She hesitated. "I wonder if we're married, where we'll live. Somehow I can't imagine city life. And of course we must have Margarita. She's like a mother to me and has been for years." She thought about it a moment before she admitted, "She has no other home and I really don't know how to cook."

Cherry realized she spent more time wondering about life with this man than taking care of her ranch. *Sorry Dad,*

I'm so bad at taking care of things. Thinking of him, she wished so terribly he were here to share in her joy.

John took her hand. "Lots of time to sort out things like that, girl. Your wishes are of the most importance to me."

Relieved he was open to considering her choice in the matter, she wondered if she should mention what the Bent boy had told her. She would, she decided, but not right now.

John kissed her soundly and held her too long before going out to saddle Muley.

ℰℴℰℴ

The trail ahead was long and John needed to hurry. He traveled at the soft jog-trot he'd worked out with his horse. It covered the miles with a fair amount of comfort in the saddle. As he neared the small town, he entered the hostelry and left Muley in the care of that same garrulous old man.

"Say mister, wasn't you the man in here a while back? I shore do remember that fine lookin' horse of yours." He leaned on a shovel and shuffled his feet in the straw on the floor. "I might have somethin' to tell you later on afore you leave here."

He couched his words in mystery, but John figured it was just his wanting to be noticed and his need to have something important to say.

He gave the man a pat on the back. "Thanks pard, I'll be back in a short while. Sheriff around?"

"Don't know about that, mister. He don't come here much. Keeps his horse near his house other side of town, he does."

He took his leave, before the old man could launch into another long-winded tale, and headed for the telegraph office. At the counter, he asked the young man with the green shade over his eyes, "Any messages for me?" He gave his name and saw the man's eyebrow raise a bit. No movement went unnoticed. John had too much at stake to be careless.

"Yep, right here it is—came a while back." He handed John a yellow sheet of paper, turned away, and went about his business—except that John noticed the man seemed to be waiting for some kind of reaction. This made him question the operator's integrity.

He read the telegraph: *Assayer reports small amount gold present in samples as sent stop strong sample gold mixed element in sample number two stop Moly indicate semi-valuable asset stop.*

John kept his face blank, not wanting to alert the operator. The man had already seen the message and John couldn't help wondering how many others had seen it. What they wouldn't know is where the samples had been taken. He smiled. Whoever they were could look all they want, but the fools wouldn't know what they'd found.

That he had enemies in this town went without saying. He limbered up his right hand before returning to the boardwalk. Deciding to visit the doctor, he walked along until he found the office, and headed up the flight of stairs to the door.

A man answered the door and led him inside. "May I help you, sir?"

John introduced himself as the new ranch foreman at the Bender place and carefully began his questioning. "You saw Charles Bender at the ranch the day he was shot?"

"Yes, I sure did. I told the daughter it was certainly murder. Of course she knew it without my telling her." He shook his head at the loss of a fine man. "Nice girl. Too bad about what happened." The man obviously had more to say on that subject but held off.

"What do you know about the troubles out there?"

"Nothing, but I hear things now and then. There're some pretty dark people in this town, and they're mixed up in things that aren't on the level. "I've often said I ought to leave this place and locate somewhere else."

"Miss Cherry told me you'd said it was murder," John informed him. "I wondered if you knew who or why." He kept his tone even, not wanting to let the doctor know his suspicions. "It's not been solved or any arrests made to my knowledge."

The doctor hesitated. "I work in this location, with these people, and try to stay out of other folk's business. But I sure thought a lot of that family and felt real bad for the young woman."

John kept his voice even, trying not to sound too deeply interested. "She's got some problems, but all in all, it looks to be a right nice place."

The doctor looked at him. "You look to me like a man who can take care of things and I hope you are." He said the words with feeling then turned away as an old woman came hurrying into his office.

Dissatisfied, John left the doctor's place and walked back to the telegraph office. "I'd like to send another message." This time he wrote out a garbled bit that would make no sense to anyone but the governor himself. The operator took it in hand, saying, "Right away, sir." He looked at the garbled message and, with a puzzled look across his face, turned to ask about it.

"I can't make this out. Would you like to rewrite it?"

"No, I wouldn't. Just send it as is." He hoped the man realized his position as an operator could be in jeopardy if it was known he gave out information meant to be private.

The man hastily scrawled something on a bit of paper, shoved it into John's hand, and turned away to send the telegraph message on its way.

Once out of the office, John glanced at the paper. It said: *You are in danger. Be careful. They're hiring a killer named El Tigre*. He tore it into bits and silently thanked the young man. This particular killer was known far and wide for his fiendish cruelty. If what the operator had told him were true, John knew he'd be in for one hell of a fight when they met face to face. This El Tigre was known to use any and all devious methods to achieve his goal of murder. "Damnation! A man like that has no soul!" John muttered.

Thinking of Cherry, he got the icy feeling he needed to hurry back to the ranch and headed for the stables. The old man greeted him then started talking while John saddled his buckskin.

Before he stepped into the saddle, the old man said, "They's some funny business goin' on around here." He shot a wad of tobacco into an old bucket kept for that purpose. "I hear tell a killin' man's bein' brought in. I seen that man once. Had a nice black horse an' wore them long, mean lookin' spurs on his fancy high topped boots." He shook his head. "Gave me the shivers, just to look at 'im." He gave John a look that held a grave warning. "I'm just sayin' now, mind you."

"Thanks, old timer." John rode Muley out on the road toward the ranch for a ways, but then cut off across country. *No need of making myself a target.*

His worry about Cherry made him ride more recklessly than was feasible, but the need to hurry clung to him. He'd heard enough nasty tales of the mysterious *El Tigre.* The man had a special kind of thirst for female flesh. *Bastard lays a hand on my woman, he'll be dead that much quicker.*

Long after the sun had gone down he topped the last rise above the ranch yard. He was greeted by the soft nickering of horses kept close and handy in the bigger corral the cowboys used for their current mounts. He put Muley in a smaller one and shoved a big armful of hay in for him.

Slipping into the bunkhouse, he shucked off his clothes and headed right into his bunk. Waddie came over to him and said, his tone quiet and serious, "You ever plannin' on comin' to the roundup?"

"Why? Any problems you can't handle?"

"No, but I think Harvey Bent's kid might be up to somethin'. I saw him ridin' off towards the ranch house here the other day. Didn't seem right to me and I wondered what he was up to. I was sort of worried about the boss lady. He's a good kid, but I was just thinkin' is all."

"Her horse is in the corral so she's all right, I'd say, but I'll go up to the house and see if she's worrying over anything tonight. Thanks, Waddie."

At his words, the young cowboy let a knowing grin spread across his homely features. "See you in the mornin' then, boss."

John heard his chuckle as he got dressed and headed for the ranch house.

Margarita met him at the door. "Yes?"

"Everything all right with Miss Cherry, ma'am?"

"*Sí*, she sleep now. Why you ask?"

"No reason, just asking. Thanks, Margarita." Satisfied and dying for some sleep himself, he headed back to bed. He guessed the young Bent boy wouldn't be a problem for Cherry. Once in the bunk house, he grabbed onto his pillow and went to sleep. His last thoughts before he drifted off centered on the new menace of the hired killer. *The sneaking bastards want me dead, do they? I believe I'll have something to say about that!*

CHAPTER 18

When John joined Cherry for breakfast, he thought she seemed edgy, like she had something on her mind, waiting for the right moment to bring it up. He was right.

Once they'd finished eating, Cherry cleared her throat. "John, I've learned something. A couple of days ago, I rode out for a little ways and happened to meet young Martin Bent. He was coming to pay a call on me, imagine that." She blushed. "That boy had romantic interests on his mind, of all things! But he also told me something about his father. Wasn't Harvey Bent one of the players in Uncle Omar's last card game?"

"He sure was. Scrawny sort and a big loser if I remember right—darlin'," he added in a whisper.

Cherry blushed. "Stop that!" she warned in hushed tones and then confided her news. "Martin told me Link had helped his father steal from our red herd, and it had gone on for a long time. Said he needed the money for his gambling debts."

"Link, was it?" John nodded, enjoying the flush across her cheeks. "How do you want to handle a thing like that—with him being your neighbor and all?"

"I told Martin I wouldn't report it to our useless sheriff, but I plan to have a discussion with Mr. Bent on my own. He has a nice family he should be taking care of instead of gambling, and as you say, he *is* our neighbor." She glanced at him, obviously seeking approval for her decision, although he knew by the set of her features that she would handle it.

He smiled at her and edged closer, aching to take her in his arms. "You've got a lot of heart, Cherry, to consider the family."

She drew away, smiling. "Don't you start things with me, mister. You know how you are and so do I. Besides, I must check out the roundup today."

She was thrilled by the look of desire she saw on his face, but if she allowed his embrace so early in the day, she wouldn't be able to keep herself from surrendering to him. His power over her was absolute. She didn't know a lot about the man she loved, but she knew that much.

Wild and exciting thoughts and feelings already swirled about in her head and body until she had almost reached the same state she'd fallen into in that pitiful shack in the pouring rain. Fighting her own desires, she whispered to him before she could stop herself, "John, we must go back to that old line shack one day soon. It's out of everything and badly needs re-stocking—and definitely more blankets!"

"You say the word, my darling. I'm ready, oh God, am I ready!" Struggling to keep his distance took all he had. He wanted to hold her. His arms ached for the touch of her.

He sighed, resigned to leaving her for a while. "Well, I'd best get out to the roundup myself. They're most likely saying some pretty gamey things about me." He chuckled. "Some of those boys have a right colorful vocabulary when they get a bit riled." He left her standing there, but it was difficult. He had plenty he needed to do, and it wasn't branding cattle.

Cherry stood there in a pleasant state of shock, constantly amazed at how quickly John could arouse those incredible feelings inside her. They were of such intensity it would take all day to overcome them and going to the line shack suddenly became all important.

Margarita, after watching the exchange between the two, hugged the girl when she came into the room. "He strong, make everything right for you."

"Thanks Margarita." She giggled. "You are right about that, he does make some things right." Then her thoughts turned serious. *At long last I have an answer to one of the things that have happened on this ranch.*

She dressed in her riding clothes, remembering Martin Bent's words against his own father. Shortly after the noon hour, Cherry saddled Checky and headed for the roundup, her pistol buckled around her waist.

It was a sunny day, but with the approach of the fall season, it had become cooler each day, even in full sunshine. The chilly temperatures always invigorated her and she rode her spotted horse with a joy she'd not known for a long while. *It's John that's made me feel this way. It must be him—I've never felt like this before!*

Riding carefully into the busy roundup area, she stayed back from the frenetic activity of bawling calves, upset mother cows, and the smell of burning hair. She didn't want to disrupt the men. Waiting until she spotted Harvey Bent in a good spot, she rode close to him and caught his attention.

"Mr. Bent, if you have a moment, I'd like to speak to you." Wearing her best stern look, she intended to let the man know she meant business and, seeing his face tighten, figured he sensed it.

"Why sure, Miss Cherry, what can I help you with?" He followed her lead away from the hustle, noise, and dust of the work area until she stopped her horse. He rode closer. "You wanted to talk to me?" He couldn't help eyeing her well spotted Appaloosa. "Nice horse you got there."

"Thanks Harvey." She got right to the point. "I've heard something. It's not so good, and I must discuss it with you." Looking at the man's face, she found it hard to continue and regretted what she had to say. But it had to be done.

She took a deep breath, looked him in the eyes, said it right out. "I've recently been informed that you and Link were stealing from our red herd and selling the stock to cover your gambling debts."

"Why, I don't know where you'd hear somethin' like that about me, Miss Cherry," he said defensively. His face had taken on a chalky color. Seeing the sweat on his brow, she didn't need more than that to verify what Martin had told her.

"I had it on good solid authority and we don't need to say another word about it. But, Mr. Bent, if you lay a hand on another of my steers, you'll have me to answer to—and maybe that useless sheriff in Parson's Grove." She kept her voice low and stern. "Being in Yuma prison, you won't be much help to your family, that is, if you escape the hangman's noose."

He looked guilty, cowed, and scared. Disgusted, she wanted to scorn him and laugh in his face, but maintained her solemn demeanor. "You have a nice family and a ranch to run. I don't want harm to come to you or your family, but if you insist on gambling away your family's livelihood that way, you might consider learning how to play poker. Be warned, Mr. Bent." Without further conversation, she left him sitting his horse and began her journey back to the ranch.

She hadn't seen John all day, and while around the cowboys, she'd overheard a few remarks and realized they weren't too happy having a kid like Waddie being their boss.

"Thet new foreman ain't showed his face out here more'n the one time," one of them said.

"Thet new feller's just left the whole dad blamed thing to some kid barely dry behind the ears."

The comments made her wonder about having a man in charge who didn't know the job. She headed back to the ranch, hurrying Checky along in the deepening dusk.

She made it home in deep twilight, tired, hungry, and worried about the character of the man she'd gotten involved with. John's horse was not in the corral this late and she began to worry if he'd run afoul of the person or persons who were out to destroy her. They had to see him as an impediment. She was sure of that. Her worries about his skills as a foreman were quickly forgotten.

She went in to the house to find Margarita. "Have you heard from John, today?"

The Mexican woman turned to her, a puzzled expression across her face. "Where he go, *mi hita*? He no here all day."

"He said he was going to the roundup, but he never showed up there. Not all day, and the men said they hadn't seen him." All her old suspicions raised their ugly heads. *Why did I trust him? Have I been the biggest fool God ever made?*

At the sound of hooves pounding into the ranch yard, she ran to the door flinging it open to see John's tall frame astride the big buckskin. Despite her suspicions, she couldn't stop herself from running out to meet him.

He dismounted, dripping with sweat from his long, hard ride. "Hello, Cherry darling. Having you come greet me like this is more than any man deserves."

"You weren't at the roundup all today. There was talk among the riders about it." He'd never explained himself to her full satisfaction and she'd finally had enough. "John, are you keeping things from me? I don't know where you go or what you do. What am I supposed to think?"

He took his tired horse to water and she followed him. As he took the tack off his horse, she saw the leathern pack he carried behind his saddle. He always carried it. Another mystery about him, she mused, as she waited for an answer.

"Today, I sent off more samples of ore from your ranch and some from your neighbor over to the north. I believe you have a valuable source of a rare mineral on this ranch. Someone is trying to get it from you, but they have the mistaken idea it's gold or silver. Before I happened on that card game that day, where your Uncle Omar was killed, I'd sent some samples in, too." He reached into his pocket and produced the printed telegram he'd received a few days before, "Take a look at this. I'd be happy to explain it in detail if it's hard to understand."

Cherry felt awkward for having forced private information from him, although it *was* her property being discussed, and things *had* been done without her knowledge. She took the paper and read it carefully. "It looks like something of value had been assayed, but I don't know what this ore is or what it means."

"If these last samples prove out, you'll have mining agents here to discuss mineral rights and mining concerns." He waited for her reaction to his information. "It could be as good as any gold or silver mine, and maybe for your friend, Hettie, too."

She watched as he wiped his tired horse down with straw and put him into a corral. "I don't know what to say, John. If something like that is so valuable, why wouldn't they be after that and not gold?"

"It is not much in use yet, but in time it will be and could be very valuable. Most people have never heard of it or its worth." He hesitated then added, "I believe whoever's doing these things to you thinks these samples are gold or possibly silver ores. That's what they're after. I'm positive that's what's been behind a lot of your troubles here."

"Someone knew enough about it to kill my father and try to take this ranch away from us?" She fought her tears. "Link must have been a part of that, too, that low down sneaking skunk!"

She remembered Harvey Bent. "One of our problems had a different cause. I know about it now and I took care of that on my own, John."

"You'll tell me how you did it?" he questioned as he moved closer. He wanted to take hold of her and feel her body again, but she backed away.

"Not until you tell me *everything* about yourself. You've been so secretive, I hardly know how I dare trust you." The heat of a burning blush crept up her neck and face. "And look what's happened between us!"

He reached for her but she stood firm with arms crossed, waiting for him to speak.

His gray eyes darkened with the oncoming night. "After supper, let's go into the orchard again. I'll tell you everything you could possibly want to know about me, where I'm from, and what I do."

Frustrated at having to wait, she took his hand. "Right after supper then. I have to know more about you. You cannot stay a stranger to me any longer."

"I'm no stranger to you, not anymore, my darling girl." He chuckled softly as she turned quickly away from him. "I need to wash up then I'll be right in."

Cherry blushed a flaming crimson, ran from him and darted into the house. He went to the bunkhouse to haul out his last clean shirt.

An hour later, they sat at a table filled with good, solid food that neither of them cared about or tasted. They waited impatiently while they ate. Later they would hold each other in the darkness of the orchard.

As they came to the lone bench beneath the huge old apple tree, he took her in his arms for a good long kiss, deep and searching. "Sweetheart, I've waited forever for this." He drew her down beside him on the bench.

She made no reply, but rather waited to hear all about who he was and why he had come to her ranch.

"Several months ago," he began, "your father wrote the governor stating the problems he'd been having on this ranch and that the local sheriff had given no real help in solving them. He asked for relief. Some of those things were cattle theft, vandalism, and such, but we also had reports from an assayer in Phoenix about certain ore samples sent from this area. They had been sent in over the past few months and when something like Molybdenum comes to light, the governor is always notified."

He paused and gave her a tight, prolonged hug. "I've been sent by him to explore mining possibilities around here in relation to that, as well as to see what I might do to help with the vandalism and theft you have suffered on this ranch. Things other than silver and gold hold a great deal of interest to the government."

He kissed her. "I came here about those interests and what did I find? A woman so beautiful I can't take my eyes off of her. Gold and silver are fine, but nothing compared to you, my darling girl."

"John!" She tried to ignore the endearments and evade his encircling arms. "Why make a big secret out of why you came here then and that kind of mineral you mentioned?"

"Just trying to do my job and stay low. No need to get the people involved in your troubles on my trail before I found out what I needed to know."

"And what have you found out? Anything? I think I certainly have the right to know."

Her tone was cooler than he'd hoped. "There's a good likelihood of there being a lode of Molybdenum on your land and on some others' land around here as well. These locals aren't looking for that. They most likely never heard of it. But in time and under certain circumstances, it's going to be of great value to our government and it's found along with gold or silver, or in many cases it is."

"So all this stealing and vandalism was to get us out of here?" She thought a moment. "That mineral you mentioned, what's it good for? Why so important?"

"It's mostly used in making steel and other sorts of manufacturing back in the East." He hesitated. "It's new and they don't use it much yet, but it'll be very valuable in years to come, more so, in case of a war. The government wants to have a hand in knowing its whereabouts and the control of its use. And with the bit of gold and silver we've mentioned along with it, it makes a right nice find."

"It sounds strange to me, almost bizarre," she said. "But I've seen people poking around on this ranch looking for something, sneaking around, and making a secret of it.

They must have planned to ruin us and take this place away from us, and Link was helping them!"

"Cherry, are you upset with me for not telling everything right out?"

"Yes! I'm trying to understand your thinking but I don't agree with it." Still, she was relieved he had at last laid things out. "I'm so sick of all this trouble. If they know what you're here for, they'll be out to get you, too." Then she changed her line of questioning. "Where do you live? Where do you come from? You haven't mentioned that, either."

"I keep a small place outside of Prescott, run a few head of cattle, and keep about four horses, well at last count, with a mare ready to foal. I have a man who takes care of things. I do travel at times, as I'm doing now." He looked at her, his eyebrows raised. "I have a right nice home there, too. The hacienda was built by the Spanish years ago. It's large and very pretty, so people tell me."

"I thought you didn't know anything about ranching." Her tone was slightly accusing and her eyes narrowed in suspicion, but she smiled.

"Maybe a little, but not on this scale, the way you have it here, no roundup or anything like that."

"Your family, you haven't mentioned anyone."

"You are downright nosey, missy!" He took hold of her shoulders and kissed her deeply. "I've lost all my family one way or another, except for an uncle. I've been a loner all my life, seems like."

"Oh John, I'm sorry to hear that. But the way things have gone lately, I guess that's my story, too. I've lost everyone and I don't even have an uncle anymore." She nodded towards the small cemetery behind the house. "My whole family sleeps out there now with Dad and Uncle Omar gone."

"We'll be two together, Cherry, and start a new family. I'd be happy for that. I didn't expect to find anyone like you—I never did."

He decided to tell her about the threat of *El Tigre*. Though he hated to burden her with additional fears, she needed to know the danger the killer placed them in.

"When I was in the village, I was warned, twice, that someone is hiring some fancy-dude killer to do away with me. I've heard of the man before. He's called *El Tigre*. I've never seen him, but the man's got an evil reputation." He shifted toward her. "Just forewarning you to keep your guard up since they say he has an eye for the ladies. He's a deadly killer, Cherry, of women, too. I wouldn't want to go on living if anything happened to you."

Tears stung her eyes. "John, you frighten me! You've got to be careful yourself. I don't think I could bear to lose you, either. I'd be as alone in this world as you are."

"I won't die that easy, but *he* might."

John's voice, soft and low, gave her the feeling her man was a deadly threat for any gunman. But she felt uneasy at his dire warning. Things could so easily go bad for them.

She clung to him, fearing she would lose him too. "Is he really so evil, John. Do you know enough about this so called *El Tigre,* anything that might help you?"

He hugged her close and stole another kiss, hating this new cloud on their promising horizon. "I've heard a lot of things, darling. But I won't be easy to kill, I promise you that."

CHAPTER 19

Bourdain's heart rate rose when he heard the soft knock at his door. He was alone for this interview. He would rather speak to this visitor on his own and in secret. In no way did he want to be seen publically with this particular person.

He opened the door to admit a slim, black-haired man in his late thirties, Matìn Maldonado, called El Tigre by those who knew of him. The darkly handsome man stood at medium height and wore high quality clothes, well cut, and nicely fitted. Though flashy in a subdued way, they suited his dark, swarthy features. He had the appearance of gentility, but the deadly gleam in the man's eyes belied any softness or gentleness in his nature. Rather, he resembled a deadly sidewinder. Bourdain felt an icy chill creep stealthily over him and he shivered.

"You wish to see me?" El Tigre asked, his voice purring, soft and sinuous, with only the slightest Hispanic accent. "You have something for me?"

Bourdain nodded. "I need some work done and from what I hear, you're the right man for the job."

Looking at this lethal human, Bourdain feared he was about to open a deadlier can of worms than he'd imagined possible. But, with the loss of Link, his options had narrowed. He stifled his feelings of regret.

The man's straight, even teeth flashed white beneath a carefully trimmed, pencil-slim, black moustache. "I can be, *señor.*"

He looked to be somewhat of a dandy. Flashes of red fabric could be seen if he moved at all. A few well-placed silver buttons added to the look. He was known for his long and varied reputation of murder and kidnapping, but it was said that his work on captive women told a far more gruesome story.

Bourdain had heard those stories and he shivered again.

Matin took a chair, sitting on the edge, never relaxing. His right hand held an unlit cheroot. Slick, black, twin-gunned holsters rested on his narrow hips, tied lower down on his legs with fine, black, narrow-cut thongs. He removed his rather small sombrero to reveal black, wavy hair held close to his head by a silken bandana, the tails of which trailed downward.

Bourdain moved close to a table and laid out a crudely-drawn map. "We need to see the last of a big fellow who's taken a job as foreman right about here." He pointed to a spot on the map. "The Bender ranch is set right along here, and at places, across the Tonto River, just there." He gave the particulars as he knew them, including the buckskin horse and the man's size. He then cautioned, "You should know this Carmona gent is faster with a pistol than any man who's ever passed this way. And I don't want the woman touched, not in any way!"

"Woman?" At the mention of female flesh, Matìn's black eyes took on an especially malevolent gleam.

"You're hired to take care of that one person, nothing else, Matìn," Bourdain warned, but he got a sick feeling knowing he'd made no impression on the evil man.

"Tell me about the woman so I will know not to harm her," the bastard purred softly. His voice, filled with quiet, hidden intent, turned Bourdain's blood to ice. "She will no be harmed, *señor*," Matìn reassured him, as a sneer crossed his lips.

When they concluded the meeting, money changed hands with a promise of more when the job was finished. As he departed Matìn, appeared to slither out the door rather than walk. Bourdain watched through his office window as the man mounted a shimmering black horse and rode slowly away.

"In the name of God, I've set wheels in motion that I'm unable to control. That evil bastard rivals Satan himself!"

❧❧❧

Restless, Cherry rode over to visit her friend, Hettie. After the usual greetings, the two of them relaxed in her generously laid out living room. Hettie had furnished it similar to Cherry's, although on a smaller scale.

Cherry heaved a sigh and sat down, feeling more than comfortable with her dearest friend. But with what she had to tell, she was unable to relax. Eager to discuss the recent changes in her life, she hoped for some advice.

Hettie smiled. "My dear, you've never spoken about a man in your life before this one came along. It sounds serious. I must say, I'd darned sure like to meet this fancy dude of yours."

Cherry snorted. "Link made sure I didn't have the chance to meet anyone these past few years, and neither my father or I realized what he was up to. When John came to the ranch, Link met a man he couldn't run off." After passing a few more remarks about those issues, she asked, "Hettie, why not come and spend a couple days at my place?"

Hettie laughed, aglow at the idea. "That sounds wonderful! I'm so lonely for female company. We can ride together and talk for hours. It'd be such fun. How about I come today?"

Hettie hastily got her things together and they rode back to the Bender Ranch, chatting and laughing. Cherry detected a flash of bright metal up in the hills and it gave her an uneasy feeling. She would tell John as soon as she saw him, she decided, but she didn't want to frighten Hettie about the so-called hired killer her hidden enemies had hired.

She didn't know if they had already brought in such a man, but seeing those mysterious flashes, it became far more of a reality. Worried about it, she kept a wary eye out as they rode the trail back to her ranch.

ᖇᖇᖇ

Matin sat his horse on the hillside above the of the ranch house. He sat there, carefully hidden in the thick brush, appraising the surroundings. His gleaming, black horse nipped at the fading grasses while Matin watched the ranch below.

"So very nice, this rancho," he muttered softly, licking his lips in anticipation of meeting this new adversary. "Big man, where do you hide from me?" He breathed the dry, fragrant air of approaching fall as he waited patiently. His guns were well oiled, his small knife honed to razor sharpness, and he was eager and ready.

The wind was soft and warm today. Many leaves had turned to gold and rust, but Matin took no interest in those things as he watched a slim girl, with long black hair in a thick braid down her back, riding on a well-spotted mount. Instantly, his heart rate picked up. This lovely *senorita* was not alone, but rode with another young woman, mounted on a strawberry roan.

His rider's eye took in the Appaloosa and he shook his head in awe. "*Caballo hermoso!*"

The beauty of the girl was evident, even at this distance. His mind envisioned her the way he'd take her— the way he'd subdue her. *Por Dios, mi chica weel fight with me, I like it!* He laughed softly.

She might be off limits, but he paid no attention to any man's warning. He was his own man. His chest swelled with pride and confidence, his chin tilted into the air. *No one tells El Tigre what to do about a woman!*

He followed the women quietly, hidden behind low hills covered with thick brush and the occasional stately Ponderosa as they neared the ranch house. The graveled ground was partially covered with scattered golden leaves of oak scrub, Manzanita, and some of a rust-colored variety. Then his mind focused on the black haired woman, and he took no notice of other things.

❦❦❦

The women reached the ranch yard in the late afternoon and put their mounts away. Cherry led her friend into the ranch house and sought out Margarita. "We'll be having company for a day or two."

The woman bid Hettie welcome, her eyes glowing with excitement, "I make *comida muy excellente por las senoritas.*" She bustled around her kitchen, preparing a bountiful dinner for their guest and, of course, *Señor* John.

Cherry showed Hettie a nicely furnished bedroom. "You can either sleep in here or with me if you want. We could talk all night!" They both cherished the company of someone to talk to that understood the important things of womanhood. She wanted to know about Hettie's love life, too, if she had one. She *had* mentioned a man in Flagstaff.

When dinner was ready, Cherry and Hettie waited eagerly for John to appear. At his knock on the door, Cherry rushed to open it, nearly dragging him inside, and smiling at his puzzled expression.

"What's got you so riled up, my love?" He tried to grab her, but she sidled away and brought him to meet her friend.

She made the introductions. "John, this is my closest friend, and my neighbor, Hettie Jamison. She owns the ranch that adjoins mine to the north."

"Nice to meet any friend of Cherry's, ma'am," he said as he shook her hand. He saw a strong, sturdy self-reliant young woman, qualities he'd seen in many western-born women. Cherry had it too. They had to be strong to survive out here,

He decided Hettie was a fine looker with her tawny, dark-blonde hair and gold-shaded eyes, lined with long, thick lashes. He had the impression she was unmarried and wondered why that was.

During dinner, he learned she had lost her husband and struggled to run her ranch on her own—all the more to recommend the woman. *Some lucky devil would be in for a hellava good ride with that lassie,* he decided with a grin. *And he'd be one happy son of a gun at that.*

After dinner, a walk in the orchard was not in the cards. Instead they played games and Hettie played a few songs on the piano. Despite Hettie's brave front, John detected a deep loneliness about her. He wondered where she'd learned to play so well.

When Hettie tried to get Cherry to play, she declined, laughing. "I haven't touched that piano for two years. I'd be awful on it."

After John left for the bunk house, the two women went into Cherry's room and got ready for bed. "My dear, that is some kind of man," Hettie crowed "You must tell me everything and don't leave anything out." She grinned. "And don't lie to me, either. I know full well what's going on between you two."

Cherry blushed. "John *is* wonderful, isn't he? We're going to be married and I'm asking you to be my maid of honor, or matron, or whatever." Her flush deepened. "And yes, there *is* a lot going on between us, so much I hardly know where to start." She went on to tell her friend about the night she spent in the line shack during the wild rain storm.

Hettie hugged her. "I guess you *had* better give marriage some thought, hadn't you? But after meeting the man, I can't blame you one bit. I know how it can be. I had a good man, too. He was wonderful to me and it'll be hard, if not impossible, to ever find that again." Tears filled her eyes. "We never even had the chance to have a child. Maybe you'll be luckier that way."

"Not too soon, I hope," Cherry confessed. She thought often of the possibility, but never regretted their night in the storm-swept cabin. Those heated memories were with her day and night and the longing to repeat the experience lay heavily on her mind.

∽∾∽

Hettie rode away after a two day visit. They'd gone over a few ideas for Cherry's wedding and had done some planning. Tonight Cherry knew she would meet John in the orchard again and felt the burn clean through her body.

CHAPTER 20

C herry was eager to walk with John in the orchard tonight. It had been too long since they'd been alone. As the day ended, they met again at the dining table and he seemed as impatient as she to head out in the moonlit orchard. And no hired killer was going to stop them.

After the meal, they put on warm coats and walked beneath the trees. It had turned cool, and now that the trees had been stripped of fruit, the rich smell of ripeness was gone. The oncoming fall season was reflected in the moldering odor of decomposed leaves.

They walked to the bench and sat down. Cherry moaned with desire as John reached beneath her coat, took her in his arms, and kissed her deeply.

For a long time they sat close together, enjoying long moments of quiet closeness and the touch of their bodies. He breathed in the scent of her hair and crooned softly in her ear.

Suddenly, he heard the sound of a stone being dislodged and hitting against another. He stiffened and tightened his hold on Cherry. "Someone's out there," he murmured. "It was Link, a while back, but now, it's someone else."

Cherry looked into his face. It was so tense, his jaw clenched tight. Fear sent chills streaking through her body. "Is it that hired killer, John?"

He held her close, listening for a few moments. "I don't know. Act as though nothing is wrong, darling, but you must go inside."

He drew her to her feet, walked beside her to the patio door, and kissed her goodnight. With Cherry safely inside, he headed casually towards the bunk house.

Waddie, Bill Waddell, and Larry were playing cards. The older fellow, Lee, lay in his bunk sleeping off a tough day's work. John shucked off his boots, put his finger to his lips, and slipped out the side door.

"What the hell's got him a goin" now, and in his stockin' feet ta boot?" someone asked.

Another voice chuckled. "Aw, the man's gone plumb loco, lately."

That comment was accompanied by soft snickering. John figured they knew about his involvement with the boss lady.

Once out in the night air, he slipped quietly into the trees across from the ranch yard and circled around. Someone lurked in the shadows next to the house. John stepped silently on the thickly cushioned socks he'd had specially made to soften the fit of his boots. When he heard the whisper of a figure sliding through the trees, he whipped out his gun and growled, "Hold it right there, mister."

Instantly, a shot rang out. He felt the sting and shock of a bullet as it grazed across his left shoulder. He snapped off a return shot at the spot where he'd seen flash of fire from the man's pistol and waited. Listening carefully, he heard nothing for a time, and then from farther away came the ring of a horse's hooves. John touched his burning shoulder. Warm, sticky blood had drenched his sleeve. Feeling slightly woozy, he made it back to the safety of the bunkhouse.

"Boys, that bastard winged me."

He sat on his bunk and allowed the men to treat his wound. Waddie and Bill cut his shirt away and cleaned the shallow gash with whiskey while Booker hurriedly fetched clean rags to bind it with.

John hadn't totally decided about the change in the man's attitude, but Booker wore an expression of concern on his face, and he was glad enough to see it. One less gun at his back was more than welcome.

Cherry appeared at the door. "What's happened? I heard shots." She spotted the blood on his shoulder dressing as it had already soaked through. "My God, John, you've been shot!"

Already pale, she hurried over and studied his face. "That man's here, and he's after you, isn't he?" She took his other arm. "Come to the house. I'll take care of this."

He followed her like a puppy, happy to have her ministrations to his body, anywhere and whatever they might be.

John shot a grin at the cowboys as he left with the black haired beauty. "I'll be back later, boys."

He couldn't help wondering if he might be lucky enough to spend the entire night with the lovely woman after she finished tending his wound, shallow though it was.

But from the stern look on her face, it didn't look that way. Cherry was in a no nonsense mood. He was impressed and proud by the toughness and spirit she displayed. *She's a woman fit enough for any man!*

Once in the house, Cherry settled him into a chair near the kitchen stove. Margarita hustled around, shoving wood into the top, and heating water. "What happen? I hear shot. *Hombre mucho malo* try to get you, *Señor* John?"

"Yes, someone took a shot at him." Cherry's purple eyes narrowed. "Is there more about you I should know? Anything else you've haven't told me, mister? Why do they need to kill *you*, especially?"

She took off the bloodied dressings the cowboys had applied. "Well, it's shallow, thank God, but still bleeding." She asked Margarita for clean cloths. The water was steaming and she poured it into a basin.

He hadn't answered her last question, she noticed, as she busied herself pressing clean fabric onto the wound, which was a shallow groove across the outer aspect of his shoulder. She looked him in the eye. "I mean is there some other reason for someone to shoot you that I don't know about?"

"I guess there's just a mite I haven't mentioned," he admitted.

"So?" she prompted as she wound strips snugly around his shoulders to create a solid barrier and hopefully staunch the bleeding.

"Cherry, in time, I'll tell you everything there is to know. Things will be all right around here. I have a good feeling about it."

Tears threatened to escape from her eyes, but she forced them back. "Maybe *you* do, but I don't. Now that I've found you and with all we have between us, I couldn't bear to lose you, too, John—I just couldn't!" She pulled up another chair. He put his good arm around her and held her tightly against him. "Say, girl, it's worth getting shot to have you sitting by me and all worried over me this way," he said with a laugh and an extra squeeze.

She sniffed. "You could, you know—get killed." It hurt her to say it. He still hadn't told her anything new. "I mean it when I say I love you. I couldn't stand it if anything happened to you, John." She caressed his bandaged shoulder. "Look what happened tonight. That bullet could have been more to the center, and my heart would have been broken forever."

John snorted. "He was damned lucky to get this close. Must be a good shot in the dark, is my guess, or just damned lucky." He hadn't enlightened her further about himself, but she didn't press him about it. Reluctantly, he decided he had best return to the bunkhouse. With his arm out of commission for a few days, some things would have to wait.

After returning to his bed, John slept for a short time. But with then increasing pain and stiffening in his shoulder, he got up and dressed. Seeing a light burning in the kitchen window, he went back to the ranch house and found Cherry sitting alone, her hands clenched in worry. He held her close. "You ought to be getting your sleep, darlin'."

"John, how can I sleep with a monster like that prowling about the place?" She turned to his wound and lifted the dressing to inspect it. "It's stopped bleeding. I don't see signs of infection, but it's early. 'We'll need to watch it closely."

He knew of the creeping death of infection. He had seen it before—more than once. People died easily from a small cut or gash if left untreated. His own family had succumbed one-by-one to poorly treated cuts, fevers, gunshot wounds, and diphtheria. Alone for many years, making his own way, John had had no one but an uncle in his life...until now. He looked forward to living his life with this exciting dark haired beauty and prayed nothing would take that from him, not infection, and certainly not some devil of a gunman.

John traced his finger around a stray curl. "You told me one of your mysteries was solved. How'd that come out?"

She told him how she had handled Harvey Bent and heard him laugh. "I almost feel sorry for the man, having to face you with something like that. You let him off easy and gave him good advice. If I remember correctly, the fool wasn't much at card playing."

They sat together for a long time, until with utter reluctance, he broke away from her and made his way to the bunk house. It was late when he settled into his bed. He did not sleep. His mind ran over several events of the past few days, and with the throbbing ache of his gunshot wound, sleep was hard to come by. Added to his problems, he now had a womanizing killer breathing down his neck. He worried about the safety of the woman he loved so dearly. As for his own hide, despite what had happened this night, he believed he could handle the famed *El Tigre*.

❧❦❧

High above the darkened, sleeping ranch house, a lone figure with a thick, woolen *serape* wrapped about his darkly clad body, sat smoking a long thin cheroot. *Ah, mi chica, I see where you lay your lovely head, sleeping, and waiting for El Tigre to come for you.*

He shut his eyes to rest, but his mind dwelt on dispatching the big hombre, maybe right before her adoring eyes, then making love to the black-haired woman. Her nicely spotted horse had also taken his eye. His fondness for both horse and female flesh had him in a heated sweat of desire. Enjoying his body's response, he imagined in exquisite detail the many and varied fantasies he would carry out on that lovely body sleeping below.

❧❦❧

John got up early and ate with his men. "I'd better show up at the roundup today or the whole country'll want to run me off for being a damned citified greenhorn not fit to sit a horse." The men laughed with him and Waddie's smile was full of warmth. They took him for what he said he was, a passing stranger who would soon be gone, and definitely one who lacked the know-how to be their boss.

Booker's attitude toward him had changed. John often felt the cook's eyes on him. The man certainly had something to say, but he hadn't come forth with it. However, he did bade John a warning. "You'd better keep an eye out. The one that's gunnin' fer you ain't through just yet."

John nodded, welcoming his concern. Booker hadn't spoken about the night Link tried to burn the men he had formerly worked with, and John figured maybe he never would.

They rode out as a tight knit group. Reaching the dwindling herd, John noted how greatly the mass of cattle had shrunk. "Cows have thinned out some, Waddie."

"Yeah, lots of calves have been branded and driven out with their mommas. Better grazin' for the ones we ain't done with yet." He had a look on his face that said a boss ought to know that much, but he didn't voice that opinion.

"Thanks. You've done a grand job of it. I know you've had to take some ribbin', Waddie, but I needed your help."

He ought to let the younger cowboy know more regarding his activities, but it wasn't his nature to spread his business about.

He turned his horse to bring in a few cows and calves, heading them closer to the fires where the irons were heating up for the day. His wound throbbed like hell with the jogging of the horse and he had his mind on way too many things besides ranch work. He wouldn't be much of a boss today in any case. Every cowboy around him knew more than he did about the everyday workings of a big ranch like the Bender spread.

ᘉᘓᘉ

Cherry felt restless. John had told her to be careful since they had a shooter out there somewhere, and she would, but her agitation drove her to action. She decided she ought to put in an appearance at the roundup again.

She dressed carefully, wearing a leather, split riding skirt, a soft white blouse, leather vest, hand-tooled leather boots, and the pistol she was careful to wear these days for certain. As she neared the corral, she heard the soft thudding of horses hooves coming into the ranch yard.

A male voice rang out. "Howdy there, Miss Bender."

She turned to see Harry Bourdain riding into the yard with his sleazy friend, Wilmer Mains. She only knew the men in passing, but despite the chilling sense of uneasiness they gave her, she extended a rancher's hand of welcome to both men.

"Good day gentlemen. How can I help you?"

"We thought to ride out and see how you're handling all the trouble you've had lately," Bourdain said in his best

I'm-here-to-help-you manner. She noted the look of interest in his black eyes as he gazed at her and felt a trace of nausea.

Wilmer Mains was a heavy set man, with a big cud in his cheek, sweating from his long ride. Harry Bourdain was slick and dark with a few lines in his cheeks and around his eyes, but trim of body and neatly dressed. She wondered if he always dressed this way or if it was just to impress her. To her eyes, the man exuded the same oily essence as a snake in some indiscernible way. A chill passed through her.

Mains sat his horse in silence, watching Bourdain work his masculine charms on this tall, lissome girl. He'd heard tales of her beauty, but had never had a real good look at her before today. At the moment, she stood before them in her riding togs, looking like a damned, black-haired, purple-eyed goddess.

Cherry stifled the sharp remark that came to her lips and kept her tone polite. "Why, we're making out just fine around here, Mr. Bourdain. Won't you gentlemen come in and have something cool after your long ride?" She didn't want to seem unfriendly but with the cowboys and John away at the roundup, she felt edgy, though she wasn't sure why.

They dismounted, Bourdain in one slick easy movement and Mains far more ponderously. She took their horses to the watering trough and let them drink, knowing all the while that the two men stood watching her, eyeing her every move.

"I'll just tie them here," she said, indicating the hitching rail near the corrals.

"Thank you, Miss Cherry," Mains said, slyly and by the slight smirk on his face, Cherry got the idea Mains thought his friend was playing the fool if he planned on courting a much younger woman, when he was forty years or more.

She led them to the house, silently applauding Mains for his wisdom. Harry was too old for a young girl like her and Mains saw that even if his friend didn't.

She settled them in the big room in comfortable chairs, and called Margarita. "Do we have something cool to serve these gentlemen after their long ride?"

"*Si*, I make." Her tone very formal, she busied herself in the kitchen, complying with Cherry's request.

As she sat across from the two men, she avoided eye contact with either of them as much as possible, but felt the need to make a bit of conversation.

"We're in the midst of fall roundup just now. We've lost a few head, but had a decent growth of our stock for this year so I'm told." The reason for this visit continued to escape her and she waited to hear it what it was.

"Well, that's mighty good news, considering you've lost your foreman, your uncle, and your father." Bourdain stared at her, and she looked away to avoid the heated message she saw in his eyes. The man had a predatory look about him, and she realized to her utter disbelief that he'd come to pay court to her. *This man is little better than a coyote. He can't be serious, unless it's the ranch and what's on it that he's after*! She smiled, thinking how John would see this visit.

Margarita served Cherry and the men tall glasses of sarsaparilla water. As they sipped the cool drinks, Bourdain finally got around to explaining his reason for the visit.

"Ah...Miss Cherry, there's a dance being held in town in another week. It's to be at the community schoolhouse, and, uh...well, I'd like to escort you if you'd consider it."

The man's face reddened. Obviously, Bourdain wasn't in the habit of asking young women to anything. Cherry surmised he satisfied his need for female companionship at the local saloons.

"Why thank you, Mr. Bourdain," she said politely. "I hadn't heard of a dance being held. How exciting! But I'm afraid must decline your offer. If I do go, it'll most likely be with someone from the ranch." She smiled her prettiest and rose from her chair, hoping they would realize it was time to leave.

They took the hint, and she ushered them out to their horses. After the two men rode off, she heaved a sigh of relief. "Well, I never! First, it's young Bent and now this old gambler, or whatever he is, comes to call. That Harry Bourdain looks like the very devil himself. In no way would I ever be seen with the likes of him!" She laughed. *Link, you kept me isolated all these years, and in this case, I thank you!*

❧❧❧

Mains said nothing for a mile or two then shrugged. "She didn't take to you very well, Harry." He spat a big wad into the bushes. "Maybe you can get a dance or two with her if she shows up and see how that goes."

"You can shut your goddamned yap, Wilmer." Bourdain rode on ahead for a ways, his shoulders stiff and straight.

Mains snickered. "That little gal shore settled your hash, Harry!"

CHAPTER 21

Cherry kept thinking about the upcoming dance. *It'd be wonderful dancing with John. I know he'd be marvelous.* She sighed, remembering their night in the line shack. *He does almost everything so very well, although he's not much of a rancher."*

The idea of being held in his arms while swirling about the floor thrilled her. She agonized over wanting to attend this big community get-together regardless of all the problems they faced at the moment. She was young. It had been far too long since she'd been to town, let alone a dance. She decided to discuss the situation out with John to see if it might be safe to go.

It was too late in the day to visit the roundup, and Cherry decided to stay at the ranch. She set about making a pack of supplies for the next visit to the line shack. Thoughts of what would happen out there kept her riotous imagination working furiously. Her cheeks flushed rosy while she worked.

Margarita watched her charge bustling about, and felt a deep warmth in her heart. "*Mi hita,* she in love. *Mucho.*"

Cherry collected cans from the storage area, bagged extra jerky, a bag of flour, tinned goods, and several fluffy blankets.

After she'd completed packing supplies for the shack, Cherry came to the older woman. "Margarita, there's a dance in town and I want to go if John will take me. Could you help me fix a decent dress?" She held her hands out with a shy smile glowing on her face.

Margarita hadn't seen her smile like that in a long time. "*Por supuesto,* I fix." Together they spent the rest of the day pulling out the few dresses Cherry owned. "Not so many clothes, but you, *mi mucho bonita señorita*...no need." She held out a white dress, softened by age to a color near to ivory. She held it against Cherry's tanned skin. "You like this dress? It was one of your mother's."

Cherry, so long denied social gatherings and dances, was aglow with the idea of twirling about the dance floor held snugly in John's big arms. "Oh, Margarita, I've never seen this dress before, and I think it's beautiful."

She put aside her worries and any thoughts of danger or threats as she prepared for the big event. In her excitement, she readily overlooked John's wounded arm and gave no thought to the deadly killer who lurked to take his life.

When she heard John entering the ranch yard, she ran out, prepared to ask him about going to the dance. On seeing his tired, worn look and the bloody, tattered dressing on his arm, however, the question died on her lips. Alarm raced through her as she hurried to help him off his horse. "John, are you all right?"

She wanted him in the house where she could lavish loving care on him, but his quiet, stern face told her not just yet and she modified her words. "Today was rough for you, I can see that," she said, her voice barely above a whisper.

He dismounted and put his horse away. His movements, though slower than usual, reminded her that he remained independent and solidly capable despite his injury. Deep inside, she marveled at the strength of him.

"I'm all right Cherry—just need the sight of you." He wiped the sweat from his brow, pulled her close with his right arm, and kissed her soundly. His growth of beard scratched and thrilled her at the same time. He smelled of sweat, horses, dust, and smoke from the branding iron fires.

She remembered the pack she'd put together for their trip to the line shack and felt the heat of a blush creep up her neck. "Uh...I've made up a few packs to get ready to visit the shack, when we—"

"When it's safe, we'll go, darling Cherry. I saw flashings of light up in the hills at times today. We'll have to be careful in our movements from now on. That man is out there and I'm his target. If I've been able to see something glinting from the sun, it must be he takes to sporting fancy silver trim on his gear. Can't be all that smart, can he?"

He had that stern set to his jaw she knew so well. She almost felt sorry for the evil *El Tigre*, hiding in the hills, sneaking coward that he was.

She led him to the house, set him in a chair, and went to work on his wound. She gently removed his shirt, casting her eyes across his long, smooth muscled arms and broad chest with that neat mat of black hair in the center. The masculine strength of him made her weak with longing. Wanting to discover more of the mystery they'd found between them kept her in a constant state of frustration. She worked on his wound, soaking it with warm water until the last of the dried, bloody dressing came free. "It looks clean enough, John. I'm surprised at how nicely it's healing. How come it bled so much? What'd you do out there, today?"

He laughed. "Tried roping, but the cow got the better end of it, attempting to save her calf from the branding iron." He chuckled again, remembering, while his whole body trembled at her touch.

"Well, I think we'll need a heavier dressing on this if you plan on wrestling cattle tomorrow." Cherry frowned, pressing her lips firmly together, as she cleaned and rewrapped the narrow slash across his upper left arm.

He watched her with half-closed eyes, while she tended him. Out of the corner of his eye, he noticed Margarita watching them, a conspiratorial twinkle in her dark eyes. Her smile stretched over her entire face and seeing it, John broke into a grin.

"Are you smiling?" Cherry asked. "Isn't this hurting you?"

"I'm feeling no pain at the moment, darlin'." He dodged her faint attempt at hitting him and warned, "Wait till I get you in that orchard, again."

Margarita called them to dinner, a sumptuous repast, in which the woman took justifiable pride. She loved having a man in the house to feed, especially this man who loved her young charge.

Cherry smiled at her. Later, they went to their favorite spot in the orchard and he kissed her so deeply, she nearly fainted. He held her against him and looked into her eyes. "What happened here today, Cherry?"

She looked at him in surprise. "How'd you know something happened?"

"It's on your face and you haven't said anything about it. So, tell me, then."

Cherry told him about the visit from two men from town. "Bourdain asked me to go to a dance in town with him, John." She huffed in remembrance of him and his friend Mains. "He's not only old enough to be my father, he looks like a sneaking coyote as well." She studied him. "How can you possibly read what's on my face?"

"Most honest people have faces that don't try to hide things. I love that about you."

"I've noticed you haven't one of those faces, John."

He laughed and held her quietly, although not one moment passed that his eyes and ears were not tuned for that devil lurking out there, seeking his death. He knew they ought to get inside and the feeling had grown over the past several moments.

"So, you'd like to go to that dance in town, then?" he asked, remembering her invitation from Bourdain.

"Not with that sneaking coyote, but I would with you and only if things weren't so threatening for us right now." She laughed lightly, but it held no humor. None of their troubles were funny.

The nights had grown colder and she wore a wrap around her shoulders against the chill. But still, she shivered. He hugged her to him and ran his hands up and down her arms.

Suddenly, he stiffened. "We'd best get inside."

He said it quietly, and she knew by his voice he'd sensed something or someone. Immediately, visions of the devil-like killer, sprang into her mind.

"Someone's out there?"

"Might be, in fact, I'm damned sure of it. I want you out of here and right quick."

Keeping her shaded beneath the trees, he led her to the stones of the patio. They had nearly reached the safety of solid walls when a sharp report rang out and a bullet slammed into the tree they'd just passed.

"Hurry!" He ran with her across the patio, thrust her inside, and turned to hunt for his would be killer.

Cherry grabbed his arm. "John! What are you planning?"

"Stay inside girl, I won't be long," he growled. He left her and slipped into the darkness. He knew the general area and quietly made his way through the trees. He knew by the flash he'd seen when the shot rang out that the deadly bastard was just outside the edge of the stately row of trees. He hurried toward his nemesis, ready to kill.

Hearing a slight brush of cloth against the tangled growth outside the confines of the orchard, he moved silently that way, his gun drawn. A shadowy figure slipped through the underbrush and he fired at it. He heard the thunk of the bullet hitting solid wood and knew he hadn't hit human flesh. After a time, listening intently, he heard the sound of hooves thudding away, fading into the distance.

He returned to the house to find Cherry. She came to him, eyes wide with concern. "What happened?"

"He got away, but he'll be back. What I'm not sure of is who *they* are." But knowing those men visited the ranch today, and their close ties with the sheriff, visions of Harry Bourdain and his fleshy, overweight partner, Mains, sprang to mind. *That bastard is after this ranch and Cherry, too!*

He settled Cherry in the house and returned to the bunkhouse. When he entered, Waddie waited anxiously for him and again, Booker said nothing, yet John believed the man had something on his mind.

"Shootin' out there? Still gunnin' for you, aren't they?" Waddie's worried face shone pale in the lamp light, "We got to get them bastards, John!"

"I heard in town someone hired a gun hand to take care of me. Looks like it's true enough." He smiled at Waddie. "Nothing I can't handle, son. Don't you worry. This isn't the first time for me."

He settled his big frame in his bunk and pulled up the covers. None of the others had anything to add, other than the comment, "Thet damned fool killer ain't much of a shot, is he?"

CHAPTER 22

Next morning, while John breakfasted with Cherry, he saw the haunted look on her face. "Well, my dear, what's got you tied in knots? Didn't you sleep enough?"

"You know I couldn't, John, when someone's trying to kill you. He's already tried twice and will try again." Her fear for him, apparent in her voice, made him want to take her into his arms to comfort her and convince her not to worry. He knew she'd never stop fretting until the man who stalked him lay dead or in jail.

Cherry then brought up another concern. "I'd love to go to that dance with you. I think about it all the time, but I don't see how we could possibly go with that man out there gunning for you."

"Darlin', if you'd like to go, we'll sure make that dance. No sneaking coward is going to spoil that for us. He patted her hand and rose from the table. "When did you say it was?"

"It's Saturday—in two days. You really think we'll be able to go?" Her eagerness to attend the dance lay in her wide purple eyes. By God, if she wanted to go, he would see that she did and make damn sure she enjoyed every moment of it. No half-assed gunslinger would stop them.

He gave her a confidant smile. "We'll go in a group. The boys need a break from the roundup and you certainly need some time away from this place. Roundup is near done, so Waddie says."

"I'm really excited about it, John. It's been a long time since I've attended anything in town or been off this ranch, not even for goods."

Her worries seemed completely forgotten for the moment. Her face shone with excitement, and he was eager to make this bit of happiness happen for her.

The thought of accompanying so lovely a woman in public made him swell with pride. He'd be pleased as hell to be her escort.

Remembering her desire to revisit the line shack with him, he grinned. "We'll take the supplies out to that crumbling wreck of a line shack one day soon, too."

His sly smile let her know what he planned to do with her when they reached that flimsy pile of boards. She flushed and could feel the heat cover her from neck to hair. Her thoughts rendered her speechless. John kissed her warmly before he went out to saddle his buckskin. He didn't plan to ride to the roundup today. He wasn't much good out there, anyway, and the boys had it well in hand. He turned into the hills where he'd seen the occasional bright metallic flash. John's face grew grim and tight with resolve. *Whoever this El Tigre is, I'd like to meet the sneaky devil face to face. He hadn't ought to be shooting bullets around when a lady's nearby.* He growled into the air. "Mister, it just isn't polite!"

He kept a sharp eye out for signs of the hired killer as he rode and finally caught a flash of light up near the crown of a low rise. He slipped out of his saddle and ground-hitched Muley. He'd come at a whistle to wherever his master was and this had helped John out of a tough spot more than once.

The sun shone weakly through gauzy patches of striated cloud as he cautiously made his way up the hill. The air seemed sharper these days with the odor of fallen leaves moldering into the soil. Fall was on the way for sure. "Damned pretty country hereabouts," he murmured aloud as he often did.

Moving like a wolf on the hunt, he caught the scent of ashes, horse droppings, coffee grounds, stale bacon grease, tortillas, and refuse from the skinning of animals used for camp meat. Elated that he'd found the shooter's digs, he noted it was nicely hidden on a high ridge. *El Tigre* could easily survey the ranch house and outbuildings. *Bastard lays in wait up here until dark and then sneaks down looking for his chance.*

Reaching the camp, he saw no sign of his prey and no horse, only old droppings. He saw scraps of skin and bones, but nothing fresh. He wondered if the Mexican moved his camp every day. It hadn't smelled that way, but it was vacant now. As he turned to make his way back to

Muley, he heard a horse coming his way. He slipped behind a tree, relieved he had approached downwind.

El Tigre crept cautiously into the camp, leading his horse. He carefully scrutinized every detail of the ground, looking for any disturbance. In the crook of his arm, he carried a Winchester repeating rifle, a slender weapon known for deadly accuracy. He also appeared ready to use it in an instant. *Up to snuff on his equipment,* John observed.

El Tigre tied his horse to a tree, seemingly satisfied that he was alone. He made a small fire that gave off little heat and almost no smoke. As he worked, he stopped at intervals to listen and sniff the air and then continued with his food preparations.

"Cautious bastard," John murmured. The slightly built man gave off the essence of death. His movements were smooth and slick as he fed his horse a nosebag of oats and made himself some foul smelling coffee. John sniffed the air for the aroma and guessed the man drank a Chicory mix. Many below the border favored it.

Taking in the fineness of *El Tigre's* horse, John nearly gasped. The shimmering black was a finely molded stallion bred for speed and endurance. By his small dished face, flaring nostrils, and shortened back, John believed him to be an especially fine specimen of Arabian. Recognizing a breed seldom seen in these parts, John delighted in the sight of him. The killer had left his horse saddled and ready for a fast getaway.

The man appeared to relax his guard. He fussed with his bedding, perhaps for the customary afternoon *siesta* so many enjoyed south of the border. John could easily bring up his rifle and kill the man outright, but he wasn't the kind to murder a man in cold blood. He decided to arrest him for attempted murder and stealthily approached the camp, his gun drawn.

He stepped on a dry twig and the snapping sound brought the killer to full alert, but before the man could leap to his feet, John moved out to face him.

"Huntin' for me, are you, mister?" he drawled.

"Ah, my friend, you find me," El Tigre smiled at him. A man who could kill without remorse, he slowly and carefully rose to his feet. White, even teeth shone below his finely drawn black mustache. *El Tigre* made a small bow, accompanied by an oily smile and a delicate flourish of his hand. "Welcome, my friend, *mi casa, su casa.*"

Disgusted at the Mexican's phony civility, John was neither fooled nor disarmed by it. He growled, "Enough of the nonsense, *senor.* I'm placing you under arrest for attempted murder." He moved closer. "I'll take that gun—toss it over here, if you please." He added his own flourish with a wave of his ready pistol.

"Why yes, *mi amigo,* here you are." With those softly uttered words, *El Tigre* whipped out his gun. In the act of tossing it over, his other hand drew a long, slim knife, which he zinged expertly at John's chest.

As John dodged the knife, the killer leaped behind a large tree, grabbed his horse, pulled another gun, and whipped off several shots before he jumped on the horse and rode away, crashing through the underbrush.

John wasn't hit, but he stood there, seething in disgust at himself for the way he'd foolishly underestimated the wily Mexican. His own horse was too far away. He had lost his chance to put an end to the man's deadly career. But there would be another time and he'd sure as hell be ready.

Retracing his steps, he found his horse and decided it would be futile to pursue the man any further today.

Checking out the latest mineral location was next on his list. He had sent a box of ore samples from one site in particular when he'd first hit the area. If there were other locations these unknown miners had found, he hadn't spotted them.

His training in geology led him to seek the minerals according to the configuration of the landscape and the appearance of the ground site. An hour later, nearing the area he sought, he heard men's voices. Wary, he dismounted, and left his horse tied in a small grove of scrub trees. He moved cautiously through the brush and trees until he saw two men part way up the mountainside.

They were digging into rocks and beige-colored earth with a pick and a small hammer. John saw them put a few selected samples into a canvas bag and heard cursing and raucous laughter as he approached.

Recognizing the two men, he walked towards them and called out, "Hello there. Mr. Bourdain, and Mr. Mains, isn't it?"

"What the hell you doin' up this way?" Mains yelled, his face flushing a bright crimson.

"I'm the new ranch foreman for Miss Bender, checking up on some of the illegal activities going on behind her back." He neared the men. "Care to explain what you're lookin' for on her property, and the why of it?"

"None of your damned business, Carmona, we got the right to look about the country some," Bourdain countered, trying to bluff his way out. "It's a free country where mining interests are concerned."

John laughed. "You boys tellin' me you know all about mineral rights and such, do you?" He placed his hand on his holstered gun. "You can leave right now, but those rocks you got there belong on this ranch. Anybody can see you're trying to find something that doesn't belong to you."

Bourdain already knew about John Carmona's agility and lightning speed with a gun. He flung out a hand. "Well, suit yourself. Nothing worth a man's bother around here anyway." He tossed the canvas bag onto the rocks and turned to find his horse. Mains quickly followed suit.

"If you're looking for gold around here, this isn't the place," John told them. "Say, you fellows wouldn't know a fellow called *El Tigre*, would you?" he called after their departing backs. "He's been making trouble at the ranch, but he won't be for long."

The men made no answer as they rode away.

John bent over the canvas bag to look at the contents. *Mmm, same type of ore samples that I sent out. This answers a few more questions as far as I'm concerned.* The sun was lowering in the sky and he decided to head for the ranch. He had a few more things to discuss with Cherry.

✍✍✍

Bourdain and Mains rode away in anger and disgust. "He ain't so damned tough. Actin' like he knows everythin' about rocks and all," Mains volunteered. He rode along, his belly jutting over the saddle horn. He shot a wad of tobacco into a bush to punctuate his comment.

"Now just what the hell would you know about it? He sure as hell ain't no damned cowhand, so what is he, then?"

Bourdain's worried look was not lost on Mains. "I'd say he was here for somethin' besides runnin' the girl's ranch for her." Mains lurched in his saddle as his horse stumbled. He grabbed onto the saddle horn to steady himself. "This damned rent-horse ain't too sure-footed."

"That Carmona won't be around long enough to bother us anyway, so quit your jawin' about him. If he brings the lovely Cherry to the dance, I'll know damned well he's figuring on moving in on her and maybe the ranch."

Bourdain sensed his plans were heading south. It had him plenty worried and he set his jaw so tight it left definite lines along the sides of his face

"Your fancy killer feller ain't come up with anything' yet, has he?"

"Shut the hell up, Wilmer, you dumb son of a bitch, I got worries enough!"

CHAPTER 23

The roundup was over and the cowboys were spread out over the range, except for those going in town for tonight's big dance. The boys had dug out their best duds, got all slicked up to head for town, and most had already left. John had asked a couple of them to wait and ride into Perkins Grove alongside their buggy.

Cherry had done everything she could to prepare herself for the dance. Her head was filled with thoughts of swirling about the dance floor with John and she gave little thought to much else. He would be her escort and protector and she refused to spend precious time worrying about some sneaky killer hiding in the brush or some lecherous old man either.

Between Margarita and her own efforts, she was happy with her dress. It was lacy, and fit snuggly at the top, with a full flowing skirt trimmed about the bottom with small lavender roses entwined with a ribbon of the same color. A few rose buds were delicately embroidered about the top by

Margarita's fine hand. A narrow red satin sash tied around her slim waist completed the outfit.

The cut was a bit low in front, but she looked at herself in the mirror and decided the entire look was very suitable. John hadn't seen it, she'd made sure of that, and he wouldn't until they arrived at the dance. Her white leather slippers were old, but they wouldn't show much below the full skirted dress. She had everything carefully packed away for the journey over rough, dusty roads.

It was early afternoon when John came to the door wearing clean work clothes. He had packed his best duds in a bag as well, after working out the wrinkles as best he could, and was ready to go.

He stared at her. She wore a thick woolen cloak against the cool weather. "You look wonderful, girl. I'd like to put you up at the hotel for the night after the dance. It's cold at night and it'll be a long way back way after dark in your father's old buggy."

"Why, John, I think that's a fine idea." She smiled and edged toward the door, eager to be on their way. "I've never stayed at a hotel." She felt the wild fluttering of her heart, wondering if he planned to stay in that room with her. If he did, she wouldn't say no. The passion they'd shared at the line shack seldom left her mind and flashes of heat passed through her body all too often with the memories.

"The buggy's ready then," John told her. "We'll need a blanket for our legs, being it's pretty cool out there."

He took her bag while she got a warm lap robe and together they entered the well-used conveyance. He had a light team hitched and at a nice trotting gait it should travel well. The *cabriole* was pulled up, as much for warmth as to conceal them inside the buggy. If the killer still lurked, they didn't see any sign of him.

Waddie and Lee rode alongside them and they drove along at a good clip, figuring to make it in plenty of time. Thinking of his assailant, John pondered the amount of time *El Tigre* had spent lurking about in the trees. *He must be low on chuck and getting damned grubby about now.* He chuckled at the thought of the fastidious dandy needing the services of a good hotel room.

His arm had nearly healed. He wore a small, clean dressing beneath his shirt. He felt her nestle against him and with the robe over both laps, they settled in for a nice trip. "Cherry, I'll take a room for myself for appearance, but would you mind a visit in the night from a lonely man? I'd be sure no one saw me."

"You know I wouldn't mind it at all, you devil!" He saw the heat flowing upward, warming her cheeks. "Oh John, I can barely wait, it's been so long."

John gave her a glance that curled her toes, and Cherry felt shameless as the heated ache settled deep within her. His hand touched her frequently beneath the blankets, and she hoped she wouldn't fall out of the buggy as it bounced over the rutted trail.

It was dusk by the time they reached the Rose Hotel. John entered, ordered the rooms and then ushered Cherry to hers. He went to his own room with his pack.

Later, Cherry opened her door to admit him. He was washed and dressed in his best white shirt; tailored, western styled jacket; and long, pinstriped black trousers over slick, shiny boots.

He gasped at the sight of her. "My God, woman, you're more than beautiful!"

He took in the vision before him. She possessed enough grace, poise, beauty, and gentle voice to captivate any man alive. She'd let her long, black hair hang in loose curls, swept back and caught in a velvet ribbon, so the planes of her delicate face were revealed. Her dress clung in all the right places and swung across the floor when she moved. This fine woman could hold her own in any company, anywhere, and his pride in her knew no bounds.

She finally found her voice. "You look absolutely grand yourself, sir, and so handsome!" Being escorted by such a man made her heart pound furiously. She knew every other woman at the dance would envy her having an escort like John. With a sigh, she stepped into his embrace. His scent—leather, soap, and man—set her pulse throbbing.

"You are very powerful, John, in some strange way I can't understand. I can barely wait until after the dance, and yet I'm very proud and excited to be seen with you in public. To dance with a man like you, before all the people in this town, will stir up enough gossip to last them a lifetime. And afterward—oh, John, it's been so long."

His heart swelled with pride and desire. "We'd best get over there right soon, my very fine lady, if not—" He laughed and reached for her. "I heard them tuning up when I was outside a minute ago.'" He helped put on her wrap and together they stepped out and down the wide staircase.

Greedy eyes followed her as she moved out on John's arm. Bourdain watched from the shadows, licking his lips at the sight.

"Won't be hanging on his arm long, my beauty. He wanted this girl, and was already heavily into his cups. "If *El Tigre* ain't getting the job done, by God I'll take care of that big son-of-a-bitch myself," he snarled. He pulled his jacket close before stepping outside to attend the gathering. He'd worn his fanciest and finest for this occasion, feeling sure she would take notice of him. *How could any woman miss seeing what a fine figure of a man he is?*

Wilmer Mains walked up. "Say, pard, did you get a look at that gal? She's damned sure a looker. Ain't any wonder ol' Link kept her corralled out to the ranch—stingy bastard."

He only got a growl from Bourdain. Chuckling at how Link had died trying to hang onto that lovely girl, he followed Bourdain out the door of the Rose hotel. They headed towards the music. It was just beginning.

Cherry and John entered the wide room used by the town for schooling, meetings, courtrooms, and general assemblies, such as these occasional dances.

They found a pair of chairs in a row set up along the sides of the dance floor. Cherry took off her wrap just as a waltz began.

John held out his hand and bowed slightly. "Care to take a spin with me, ma'am?"

His soft, deep voice and deep gray eyes went through her like a firestorm. She tossed her wrap over a chair and took his arm. "Yes sir, I would!"

Smiling, she melted into his arms. He was a strong and skilled dancer. Something in the fine way he moved suggested lessons or training of some kind. Puzzled momentarily, she sighed. She had much more to learn of this man.

Her head was spinning, along with her feet, as they swept across the floor. "John, you're a wonderful dancer. I'm afraid I'm terribly rusty myself. It's been forever since I've danced."

He chuckled and gazed into her glowing eyes. "You're wonderful just like you are, my darlin'." Proud and pleased he could bring her this small bit of joy, he swept her into a deep, graceful dip.

Just then, he felt a hand on his shoulder. "Excuse me, Mr. Carmona, I'd like a turn with your lovely partner, if I may." Bourdain bent his black, shining eyes on Cherry and nodded. "Ma'am?"

He meant to have a dance. It was only polite to accept, and she complied. It was customary. She looked at John. He shrugged then nodded. Cherry moved away in the arms of a man who, she was certain, was behind most of her troubles at the ranch, if not the death of her father. His closeness disgusted her, and she instinctively tried to avoid contact with any part of his body.

"Name's Harry, ma'am, and I'm sure proud to dance with a beauty like you. You step out right fine, I must say."

His touch made her shiver. He held her as close against his darkly speckled, floral satin vest as he dared in public. He was smooth and a fine dancer, but he held her too tightly. She did her best not to struggle against his embrace, not wanting trouble with the man or a nasty scene. "Why, thank you, Mr. Bourdain, you're a very good dancer yourself."

She gazed around the dance floor looking for John and saw him chatting with Waddie, who had a nice looking girl on his arm. Cherry recognized her—Bent's middle daughter, Katie. She had grown quite a bit since Cherry had seen her last. *A budding romance there?* She smiled at the thought of another woman in love.

Bourdain, realizing he'd lost her attention, pulled her tighter against him. "I think you're a right pretty girl, Cherry. If you'd consider it, I'd sure like to see more of you."

"Thank you sir, but you see I'm not interested in seeing anyone just now. Running the ranch takes all my time as you can imagine."

Something about him made her increasingly uncomfortable. She felt his grip tighten.

"Don't pull that talk on me, miss. I've seen how you're all calf-eyes over that big feller, Carmona, and I don't make mistakes when it comes to the ladies."

His dark eyes had grown cold, and she felt his hot breath on her face. The way he leered at her breasts sickened her. Her gown was cut a bit low and they were partially visible under the edge of her neckline. His lascivious gaze at them made her furious and slightly nauseous.

"You can let me go, sir!" she snarled. "I've danced long enough with you, and don't even *think* of asking me again." Flushed with anger, she pulled away from him and darted swiftly across the room to stand beside John.

Her pale face and clenched fists alarmed him. "Cherry, what's wrong?" "Did Bourdain insult you?"

She trembled. "Not exactly, but he makes my hide crawl. I couldn't dance with that man any longer." Not wanting an incident on her account, she kept her voice steady and her hand on his arm. "I just couldn't, John."

Looking across at Harry Bourdain, John disengaged her arm and walked over to the man. He towered over the slickly dressed man. "What did you say to Miss Bender?"

"Asked her if I could come calling, is all." Bourdain kept his voice civil, unwilling to tangle with this fast drawing gent. He'd never live another day if it came to gunplay.

John edged closer. "Weren't satisfied with her answer?"

Bourdain' face reddened with anger. "I did *not* go too far with her, I swear, if that's what's got you all hot and bothered. And what the hell's it got to do with you anyway?"

"It has a lot to do with me. I'm her foreman," John growled. "I watch out for her, and you can take this as a warning. The girl's off limits to you." He believed it was Cherry's business to announce their engagement.

His dark gray eyes, filled with ice, bored into Bourdain. Fear filled Harry's mind, knowing Carmona meant every word of his threat. He faced a gun hand quicker than greased lightning.

Bourdain backed away. "You'll hear from me later," he snarled. His pride was sorely wounded, and he wanted revenge. "*El Tigre*, you worthless scab on the ass of humanity," he muttered into the smoke-filled air. "If you don't get this job done, I'll damned sure have to do it myself!"

Sulking, he downed another glass of whiskey and cast longing eyes on Cherry. He wanted that lovely young woman more than anything he'd ever desired, and he wasn't a man to be refused or denied.

Across the room, Cherry had found her friend, Hettie. "You wouldn't believe how disgusting that Harry Bourdain is!" Seeing John have words with the man, she hoped violence wouldn't follow. "John's speaking to him right now."

Hettie had no interest in discussing scum like Bourdain. "I hope I get to dance with that foreman of yours, Cherry. He's extra handsome tonight!"

Hettie was in a high mood tonight and, through her, Cherry began to see the humor in what had happened. She smothered a giggle. "I guess you're right. No time to worry about a sorry man like that." She saw John walking over. "Here comes my hero."

After John said a warm hello to Hettie, Cherry stretched to her tip toes and whispered in his ear, "Ask her to dance. She's dying to go a few rounds with you."

He complied and politely asked her friend for a dance. A waltz was just beginning as he swept her away. He didn't mind as he had questions for Hettie. Once on the dance floor, he asked, "You're the neighbor north of Cherry, aren't you? I believe that's what I've heard."

"Yes, it's a small outfit, but we make out right fine. My husband bought it before we were married."

She didn't mention her widowhood, but John knew about it—and that she had a tough time making a go of her hardscrabble ranch.

He glanced over to see his boss lady occupied in conversation with young Martin Bent. He smiled down at Hettie and gave her his full attention. It wasn't hard to do. The woman was a beauty in her own right, widow or not.

Across the room, Martin's face flamed red. "Mind havin' a dance with me, Miss Cherry?"

"Why certainly, I'd love to." She went into his arms and they moved across the floor. He was rather good if a bit stiff and awkward. She hoped she didn't make him too nervous.

From the corner of her eye, she saw Bourdain fuming along the sidelines watching her every move. *I feel like some sort of prey. What am I—a nice meal for a sneaking coyote?* She averted her gaze and paid attention to her partner. He'd relaxed by now and she enjoyed the dance.

"I'm thinkin' on maybe getting married, Miss Cherry," he said, his face flaming red again.

"Oh Martin, I think that's just fine. Is it anyone I'd know?"

"No ma'am, I don't think so. She lives in town here. Name's Jennie. Her daddy, Lonnie Helms, keeps the general store."

"Why, good for you, Martin. I think that's a good idea if you both agree on it. Will you live at the ranch then?"

"If—if she wants to—to, I guess," he stuttered. "Whatever she says. Her daddy might need a hand with the store, too." The dance had ended and he escorted her back to her chair, grinning. "Thank you, ma'am." With a slight bow, he left her.

John claimed her and held her extra close for the next dance. "You're not getting away from me again, my darlin'. We've got a long night ahead of us, and this is only the beginning."

She felt faint at his suggestive words and sank against him, thinking of the night ahead, entangled in his arms. The fun of dancing had lost some of its earlier luster and excitement as her wildly racing thoughts dwelt on what lay in store for the remainder of her night. She imagined how he would take her and all the things he'd do to make her into someone she'd never thought possible. Those wild thoughts claimed her mind until she barely knew what the dance was or what steps were called for.

They took a break from the activities and sat talking, surveying the other couples. Hettie danced in the arms of a tall cowboy, and Cherry wondered if he might be the man her friend longed for. She heard John murmur, "If I hadn't met you first, darling girl, I believe I'd be shaggin' after that golden-eyed temptress out there on the dance floor."

She glared at him. "Would you now?"

"Look for yourself, my dear, she's one hell of a package."

CHAPTER 24

Cherry felt a tinge of jealousy and wanted to hit him, but she had to agree with his assessment of Hettie. She was a beauty.

Cherry looked for Bent's daughter, Katie. Waddie was nowhere around and the girl was deep in conversation with a small, worn-out-appearing, shabbily-dressed woman with her graying hair pulled into a knot on the top of her head. Cherry recognized the woman as Mrs. Bent, the girl's mother. Again, Cherry was glad she'd given Bent the option of going straight from his cattle thieving. His family needed him. She didn't see any more of Bourdain and heaved a sigh of relief.

The Bents came over and Cherry introduced them to John. "This is Mrs. Elvira Bent and her daughter Katie. They're our closest neighbors on the Tonto. You may have met her husband at the roundup."

John nodded. "Believe I did. Nice to meet you, ma'am." He extended his hand and took her small, thin one in greeting. "Enjoying the dance, are you?"

She smiled. "Not so much myself, but Katie seems to be having a fine time." She wore a pleased look on her tired features as Waddie appeared and claimed Katie for another dance. He gave Cherry and John a sly wink as he led the girl off.

Cherry decided having her daughter married might relieve some of Mrs. Bent's burdens at home. She nudged John and shot him a conspiratorial smile. "Looks like our Waddie's found himself a girl." She had nearly forgotten her dust-up with Bourdain in the wonder of a budding romance.

"Looks like." John held out an arm to Cherry and they moved across the floor in a high stepping Schottische. Cherry wasn't too sure of the steps. But her man was a good leader, and she quickly got into the spins and turns. "Oh, this is so much fun!"

Flushed with pleasure and fatigue from the dance, Cherry fanned herself as John escorted her off the floor. He led her to a chair near the side of the wide room filled with sweating, shuffling people. Most of their cowhands had found willing girls and made the most of it.

Across the room, a fight broke out and they heard a man yelling, "Ah did not insult yer wife," to the meaty sound of a fist crashing against flesh.

John chuckled. "Sounds like things are progressing normally at this party."

Cherry's feet were tired by the time the dance wound down. She'd seen Hettie leave earlier and was ready to go to the hotel herself. Her heart beat hard and fast as they put on their outer clothing. John took her arm and, after a few hasty goodbyes to folks she knew but rarely saw, they left.

Icy air struck them as they emerged from the warmth of the school room-dance hall and headed for the hotel. She shivered, her nerves tightly strung with anticipation and wonder for the night ahead.

Arm in arm, they made their way down an uneven boardwalk, laid many years ago in front of the major town buildings to keep mud and muck out of the stores. The passion and reverie between her and John was broken when a piercing voice rang out.

"Hold on there, a minute, Mr. Carmona, you interfering bastard," Bourdain yelled, his tone more than ugly. "You won't be getting in my way again."

Bourdain reeled against a store front, deep in his cups. He weaved in front of them to block their path and held up a hand. In the lamp-lit glow from the store front alongside of them, his glittering eyes shone with madness.

"Harry, Harry, calm down," John, called out, hoping to settle the infuriated man. "You don't want to do this."

He sensed Bourdain had gone too deep into his private stock of fine malt whiskey. In his enraged state, Bourdain had become a danger to everyone on the boardwalk.

Putting away a slimy character like Bourdain didn't bother John so much, but he did want to avoid an ugly scene in front of Cherry. Blood and guns stood a good chance of befouling the fine evening they'd just enjoyed and, certainly, the night that lay ahead.

"Aw, the hell you say!" Bourdain screamed. "You've got in my way one time too many, you son-of-a-bitch! I'm not letting the likes of you get ahead of me again! Reach, you interfering bastard!" His hand darted for the fancy little Derringer he always carried in his vest pocket.

John drew and shot in one slick movement. Cherry never even saw his hand move, but she did see Bourdain crumple onto the sidewalk. She clung to John's arm, shaking and stiff at what she had just witnessed.

"Sorry, girl, but he didn't give me a choice. Man wouldn't listen to reason." John placed his smoking gun back in the holster and told a man nearby to go for the sheriff.

The man complied, rushing away towards the dance hall.

In short order, Sheriff Monte Delavan arrived, pushing his way through the gathering crowd. "What's going on here?" He saw it was Cherry and recognized her escort. "It's you again, is it?" The sheriff had an unfriendly look on his face, but John knew a good part of his attitude related to the loss of another of his close associates.

"Care to fill me in on this," the sheriff demanded.

John explained the details. Cherry verified it, as did several others who'd happened along, including Harvey Bent, his wife, and daughter.

They stood together, taking in the scene of violent death, their faces white. "I seen it all, Sheriff. He tried to kill this man here." Bent waved a hand at John. "The man acted crazy, all riled up over somethin'. John here tried to reason with him, but he just went loco."

"Well, you folks go your way then," the sheriff said, dismissing the onlookers. The small crowd that had gathered began to disperse. "Don't leave town," Devlan said to John. "I might like a statement from you in the mornin'."

"We'll be goin' in then," John told him. "We've taken rooms at the hotel for the night, and if you want to see me in the morning, I'll be around."

Cherry looked stricken, and she trembled with shock. John took her by the arm and led her away. He would take her to her room and call it a night after what had just happened. Filled with disappointment at losing the night with her, he muttered softly, "Damn you, Bourdain, you sick bastard!"

At the hotel, he took Cherry to her room and went in with her. "I'm sorry for what happened, but I had to defend myself, as well as you." He eased her into a chair. "Will you be all right if I leave you here? I suppose it wouldn't be right to stay." Pulling her into his arms, he kissed her forehead. No longer soft and filled with desire, her body was stiff and unyielding.

John silently cursed Bourdain once more. He turned toward the door, but before he could leave, Cherry stirred.

"I don't know if I'll be all right, John, but I appreciate your consideration in the light of what's happened." She sat there, frozen, longing for the comforting presence of Margarita, her thoughts in a turmoil. Who was this stranger she loved so much? She wondered again. Trouble followed him everywhere. *People shoot at him, his mission here is doubtful, and I'm totally caught up in it!*

He was also her protector and comforter, she reminded herself, as well as this mysterious stranger she'd agree to marry. She knew she couldn't face being alone for the rest of the night, not after the horror of seeing a man die in the streets.

"Could you stay with me and maybe just hold me tonight? I'm only asking you to hold me in your arms, nothing more. I don't think I'll ever get to sleep if you aren't here to keep me from seeing it happening, over and over again."

He looked at her standing there, pale, and shaking. "Yes, darlin', I'll stay. You bet I will." He sat in a chair and took off his boots and outer clothing—as much as decency allowed. At her earnest request, he slipped between those pristine sheets and into the waiting bed.

Cherry washed up and dressed for sleep. She climbed into the bed and into his waiting arms. "Oh John, please hold me like this forever."

Sleep never came, but her tears did. He held her close as the wet drops cleansed her mind of the horror she'd seen. A man had been shot dead, and her man had done the shooting. It hurt her, even though she understood and accepted it. He'd had to protect himself. It was the way of things—it always had been.

He held her snug against his chest until a comforting warmth from their physical and emotional closeness crept steadily into their bodies. In the wide, commodious bed, he kissed her wet cheeks and declared his love.

"Cherry darling, for as long as I live, I'll hold you in my arms. I love you beyond thinking and I always will."

The heat stirring within his loins made him heavy with desire. He carefully held himself away from her, trying his best to honor his commitment to only embrace her.

Cherry's shock and horror, along with her tears, slowly drained away from her heart and mind. As those things left her, the nearness of his body went deeply into her soul, and she turned in his arms. "I love you with all my heart, too. I don't ever want to spend another night away from you, John, not ever." She pressed herself against him and felt that part of him that told her how much he desired her.

Feeling that his loving had the power to heal the terrible things that had happened, she gave into her passion and kissed him, opening her lips to his probing tongue. "Make love to me, John."

He needed no further invitation. In the lamplight, he stripped off his remaining clothes.

She watched him in utter fascination. "Our bodies are so different." Her eyes filled with wonder. "You are beautiful, John."

"We're just the way God created us, Cherry. He made a man and a woman for each other." He slipped into bed beside her and began his gentle assault on her body.

She felt his hands moving, caressing, and touching. She marveled at how quickly his kisses took her into a firestorm of heat. It wasn't long until she nearly begged him to take her. She writhed beneath him, feeling his long, hardened flesh pressing into her stomach. He kept her waiting until she was nearly mad with desire. Finally, he plunged inside her.

The strange and wonderful things he did to her gave her a sense of completion. She could spend the rest of her life wrapped in the feel and the taste of him and never get enough.

When, at last, they lay gasping together in the wide bed, he whispered softly in her ear, "I love you, my darling, I always will."

"And I love you," she returned. "I can't wait until we can live together and have this wondrous closeness between us every moment of the day and night." She snuggled closer, reveling in his scent and the feel of his body against hers. "It's like everything is right with the world, isn't it?" she purred.

The dreadful death in the streets, and the horror she'd felt, had drained away. For now, she was safe in his arms, wonderfully content.

He hugged her tight. "Everything *is* right with the world when we're like this because it's meant to be. I can't remember anything else when I'm lying beside you, holding you, and having you. It's magic, that's what it is."

John felt a new and soaring happiness, something nearly unknown for most of his lonely life. "I think we'd best get this wedding in the works, dear girl. But first, we've a little more healing to do..." he murmured as his mouth found her breast.

❧❦❧

Sheriff Delavan sat with Wilmer Mains, who grumbled his worries aloud.

"Everything is falling apart, Monte. I don't know where to turn now. Harry always had a handle on things, but he never told me everything or what other irons he had in the fire."

"We'd best lay low," Delavan replied. "This Carmona feller isn't who we thought he was. I'd bet the ranch on that."

"Harry hired a killer," Mains continued. "I know about that, but he's not had any luck there." He sighed then suddenly blinked. "By God, I ain't payin' that evil bastard. I hope Bourdain gave him enough or he'll be gunnin' for me, and maybe you."

Delavan began to sweat. "Good God! Are you talking about the one that blathering old coot at the stable was goin' on about? El Tigre? If things go on like they have been, El Tigre had better oil up his guns and work on his draw. Whoever the hell he is, he ain't much at killin' is he?" His harsh chuckle held not the slightest trace of humor. "That Carmona feller's still around and he's got a helluva fast draw. Ol' El Tigre might just better watch out fer his own ass with that gent around."

"Ain't heard nothin' on them ore samples, neither." Mains couldn't keep disillusionment from his voice. Everything was slipping from his grasp and going to hell without Bourdain around to run things.

CHAPTER 25

John awakened after a long night of loving the beautiful woman who lay beside him. She had roused enough to raise her head and push her elbow against the bedding. He knew she was looking at him through a slit in her eyelids. He kept his own eyes closed as near as possible and listened to her soft breath.

"He's beautiful even in his sleep," she murmured softly.

"I heard that, woman." He opened his eyes with a deep sense of satisfaction and saw Cherry leaning on her arm, watching him. Finding this beautiful woman had made big changes in his life. He was in love and everything was right with the world. But the next steps puzzled him some. Having a woman and taking care of her was new to him. But he'd find his way and he welcomed the journey.

"Woman, is it?" She laughed. "What are you thinking, John?"

"That I am one damned lucky man, darlin', that's what I'm thinking. I'm lying here beside the most beautiful woman God ever made, and she's mine, or she'd damned well better be."

"This wonderful, beautiful woman is starving and wants her breakfast." She laughed again and then ducked the pillow he tossed at her.

He moved to the edge of the bed. "I'll just toss on a few clothes and sneak down to my room. That's where I left everything." He pulled on his pants, boots, and jacket. With the rest tucked beneath his arm, and a sly wink in her direction, he left her.

It was new and strange for Cherry to awaken in the morning next to him—not only to have slept in the same bed with him, but to see him softened. He looked younger with his thick black hair tousled and his long black lashes shadowed against his cheeks. She shook her head. "What a night!" she murmured. And she wasn't referring to Bourdain.

She quickly washed herself, dressing for breakfast and the long trip home. She felt complete this morning, in some new way, and content, but she didn't bother trying to understand it.

After a time, she answered the soft knock on her door. John stood there, dressed in traveling clothes, and carrying his pack. "Let's have a good, solid feed before we start for the ranch. I expect I'll need to see the sheriff a minute, too."

He was obviously trying to sound as if he hadn't seen her at all last night. The devilish twinkle in his eye only made her laugh at his attempts to cover up what they had shared in the dark of night, lest some nosey person happened to overhear.

But his mention of the sheriff made her hesitate for a moment. She had no faith or trust in that man. "Yes, I suppose you must see him after what happened last night. But in any case, I'm starved enough for a real good breakfast." She looked him in the eye. "I'll be all right now, I will. It always takes me a while to get things straight in my head." Her chin rose as she straightened her shoulders. "Thanks for last night, John."

"Bad things happen in life, Cherry, and we have to face up to them. But I'm sorry as hell it had to be last night." He gave her a sardonic smile, dark and full of meaning, his thoughts on the past many hours spent in each other's arms while Bourdain lay somewhere in death, cold and alone.

She didn't miss his message. "I'm sorry for what happened, too." she said, though she felt no lingering sadness. "But not for everything."

She smiled as he took her bag. They walked together down the winding staircase and took seats in the dining room.

While sharing a quiet meal with little conversation, Cherry looked at the man across from her, wondering about him, again, and what her future with a man like him would entail. She'd crossed the line of intimacy between them and her life was in his hands from now on. She shrugged happily and kept eating, knowing she'd manage.

He ate with impeccable table manners, something that still puzzled her, but he kept his own council and said little.

He did occasionally look about, as if checking to see if some friend of Bourdain would chance a shot at him.

The sheriff came in for his breakfast, and nodding to John, came over to their table. "I won't be needing any more from you on the shooting, son. Looks straight enough to me, the way it happened."

Since he didn't discuss the shooting any further, nor did he offer any other conversation, Cherry decided if he was mixed up with Bourdain, he'd probably lost too much already.

Since no one else from their ranch appeared to be present, Cherry surmised they had made the long ride home, in the dark after the dance, or had camped out as many folks did at these affairs.

"Wait right here and I'll bring the buggy around," John said when they'd finished breakfast.

Watching his tall figure walk out the door of the hotel, Cherry felt as if the light had left the room. Without a doubt, she loved him truly, but for some reason she had yet to grasp, he remained enough of a stranger to confuse her. *I wish Dad were here. I need him so much, especially now.*

John brought the carriage around and, with her things stowed aboard, they headed out of the village. Cherry sat close to him, taking in his warmth and strength. From now on, she would trust him, despite the troubles that constantly dogged his footsteps. But then, John seemed more than able to handle anything that came along—she'd seen enough to be sure of that.

Watching the hills and trees that surrounded them on their way, she saw the occasional flash of light reflected off something bright and shiny, perhaps a silver *concho* or a bit of trim off a man's fancy leather trappings. "He's still out there, isn't he?"

John nodded. "'Fraid so. El Tigre will dog my trail until one of us is dead. That'll be the next thing and it's coming close."

Suddenly chilled, Cherry shivered.

It was early afternoon by the time they reached the ranch house. Cherry flung herself into Margarita's welcoming arms. "The dance was wonderful but afterward—it was so horrible!" She told Margarita about the shooting but carefully omitted the events of the rest of the night

"Your man, he take care you, he save you, mmm?" She patted Cherry's head. "It will be good again, *mi pobrecita*, you see." She let the girl go to her room and smiled again at the thought of such a fine husband for her young charge. "He much man."

Cherry felt tired and very relaxed. "Trouble's not over yet," she told herself.

But once she laid her head on her own pillow, sleep claimed her. Dreams of a stalking killer haunted her and she thrashed about. When she woke, the sun had gone down and night shadows crept over the land. She looked at her tangled bed linens. "I must have had some crazy dreams."

Margarita prepared a small supper for her and John. Cherry looked forward to seeing his face again and wondered would everything be the same? She had to find out and, in her nervousness, his knock on the door startled her. With pounding pulse, she hurried to open it. "Come in, John," she said, hating the formal way she sounded.

"Good evening, Cherry," he responded in like tone, but she saw the mischievous twinkle in his eye.

It brought a flush to her cheeks as she led him to the table. Could she even eat? They sat across from each other and dined on the fragrant, spicy dishes Margarita placed before them. Cherry felt the tension rising by the moment. She tasted the food, and found it delicious, but was eager to finish with the meal and go into the orchard with him where he would take her in his arms and make this unsettled feeling go away.

Finally, he rose from the table and held out an arm. "How about we check out the orchard tonight, my dear? Might need a wrap with the weather getting so much cooler," he added with a sly grin.

"All right, I suppose we could." She stood, as if in a dream, and moved to pick up her wrap that was thrown haphazardly across a chair. Drawing it around her shoulders, she walked outside to the bench.

He followed her closely, taking in the scent of her body and long black hair.

The trees were rapidly losing their leaves and the smell of the orchard had become more of decaying refuse which made the odor, sharper and more pungent.

"This all right?" she asked.

In the softness of the early night, she turned to face him, her eyes full of longing and uncertainty.

"Oh, John, I..." Her words faltered.

He caught her close against him, muffling any further talk, and sought her lips, kissing her deeply, slowly edging her lips open until she met him half-way. They clung together for a long time, locked in a tight embrace, saying nothing. Her legs were so weakened, she would have fallen if his arms hadn't held her up.

"It hasn't been that long, but I could barely wait to get you out here," he gasped as she drew away for a bit.

"It's the same for me, John. I can't stay away from you and I don't want to!" She wrapped her arms around his neck and pressed her face against his chest. "You scare me sometimes, and I'm not really sure about a lot of things. I know you've told me a lot about yourself, but what a man of mystery you are."

"Cherry, I need to have you again." He eased her back and looked deeply into her purple-hued eyes. "We must plan a way. I can't believe this has happened to me. I'm generally a very sane person, I really am, not some silly young boy." He pulled her close again and kissed her. "Don't worry about who I am. I did tell you all that's worth knowing. You can believe me when I say I have only your best interests at heart."

"I do believe you, John. But when I see men trying to kill you and the way something happens everywhere you turn, I'm fearful. Nothing is for certain, is it? I'm caught up in something, and I don't know what's going on."

"It'll be all right. Things are coming clearer every day. I believe Bourdain had a lot to do with what's been happening on your ranch. Link, too. You've taken care of the cattle rustling yourself."

And the last samples he'd sent would clear things up even more, but he left off mentioning that.

She accepted his words on the workings of the ranch and gave more thought to their personal situation. "We must find a way to get together more often. We'd best get the preacher out here, but for now, that line shack certainly needs stocking." She nearly giggled. "I'd like a proper wedding, though, and that needs a bit of time."

He laughed and grabbed her in a tight embrace. "I guess it's the line shack again, then."

She clung to him, returning kiss after kiss. "John, will it always be like this?" She giggled. "Imagine us having at one another night and day."

"If it's that way for us, I'd say we were more than lucky, but my knowledge of such things is thin at best."

She finally sat down on the bench beneath the apple tree with John close beside her. Wary, he kept watch for the hired killer, but lately he'd begun to wonder if the man was simply inept. His reputation had to have its basis at least partly in fact, but how much fiction had been thrown in?

A tiny cracking of a twig, a brush of clothing against shrubbery, put John on full alert. "We must go in," he whispered. He drew her from the bench, under the safety of trees, onto the patio, and into the house. Saying good night, he slipped out the patio door and into the deeper shadows.

She let him go, fearing for his safety. Inside, behind thick walls of her house, she sat close to Margarita and listened for the sounds of gunfire. "I hope he gets that killer," she cried in anguish. "Why do we have to put up with a man like that?"

She gave thought to going out with her own gun drawn, but decided against it.

"John get him—you see." Margarita hugged Cherry and headed to her bed. "Good night, *mi hija.*"

After waiting for a long while, Cherry sought the comfort of her own bed. "I'm tired, even though I slept for several hours this afternoon—I'm just worn out with so much on my mind."

She lay awake for a long while, lost in romantic fantasies and hoping no insidious evil managed to destroy them.

೧೫೧

Earlier, in a fireless camp, El Tigre sat huddled in thick woven blankets to ward off the cold of encroaching night. A fire, or the drifting smoke of one, could alert someone to his presence. He only needed another day or two, if he was quick, and his work would be done. He had seen the lovers in the orchard several times, and his jealousy burned hotly.

His mind dwelt on the lovely young female he'd seen riding on a spotted horse. *She will be mine. No one tells El Tigre what to do about a woman.* He nestled deeper into his blankets and dozed off. His sleek black horse stood tied to a tree with no grass in reach. He stamped his hooves impatiently and tossed his head.

In the deep of the night he saddled his horse, planning to encroach upon the ranch while the occupants were asleep. "I must see once again where the beautiful *senorita* sleeps." Having had the one encounter with Carmona, he wasn't eager to repeat it. He'd heard the big man was dangerous but more, he felt it in his bones. He didn't plan to take the chance of facing the cowboy's guns again.

Waiting until all lights were out in the ranch house and everything was quiet, he approached carefully, gliding alongside the outer wall and around the back. He found a window, peered in, but saw nothing. Edging along to another and then another, he finally saw his prize, lying asleep, the soft glow of moonlight highlighting her face.

He watched her with utter fascination—saw the soft mounds of her hips and breasts beneath her sheets. He'd dreamed of what he would do to that beautiful body and how she would scream his name as he marked her lovely curves with his tiny, sharp knife. How well she would know the fine art of his love making as she gasped her final breath beneath him.

Terribly aroused at the sight of her sleeping body, he pressed his face to the window and stared at her lovely form. In his eagerness, El Tigre pressed his hand to the window, barely noticing that his fingers made a slight scratching sound on the glass.

℃ℑℂℑ

Cherry woke with a start, turned her head toward the sound, and saw that dark face at the window. It made her want to scream with fear, but she quickly stifled the impulse. The face quickly disappeared. Not wanting to waken the household, she reached for her pistol and cocked it. She always kept her gun close by at night. Her father had insisted upon it.

Outside her window, El Tigre ran to his horse, hoping to ride away before the big *hombre* came hunting him.

Cherry could hardly believe she'd seen El Tigre at her window. He was dark with a slim mustache above a set of thin lips, his eyes black as they stared at her in the dim moonlight. Seeing that shadowed face, with the moonlight behind him, had left her shaken, afraid, and very angry. If he peeked in again, he'd feel the blast of her pistol right between those smirking eyes.

"Come on, you devil, I'm ready for you!" She crept to the window and peered out. It was secure, locked from the inside. Though she stared intently, she saw nothing but the darkness outside.

Though she was furious, as well as terrified, she decided to wait until morning to tell John. She could shoot as well as most men and would take care of herself.

"I'll not sleep any more this night, not after that!"

She sat in her bed, watching her window for the remainder of the long, dark hours of the night, with her gun drawn and her anger at the boiling point. But El Tigre didn't reappear.

CHAPTER 26

Fidgeting and tense, Cherry, waited for John to come in for breakfast. As soon as he did, she rushed to his arms.

"That awful man peeked into my window last night. I pulled my gun, but he disappeared. I stayed up the rest of the night waiting for a chance at him, but he never came back."

"You what?" He stared at her. "Cherry!" His heart had grown cold at the man's boldness. He felt an icy chill, knowing that black-hearted devil was after Cherry. "I've got to get that bastard before he..." He couldn't go on for a moment. "He'll see hell before he lays a hand on my woman," he growled. Though he feared for her, he also took great pride in her fighting spirit. Cherry had to have a western woman's strength to take the stand she had.

She laughed, but it sounded hollow to him and the purple shadows beneath her eyes from lack of sleep, made him wince.

"Maybe we can trap him," she offered. "You can use me as bait."

"Don't talk like that!" He followed her to the breakfast table. "I won't have you being reckless."

Still nervous from last night, she couldn't relax. "Eat something, John." she said. "I made up a pack of supplies for the line shack a few days ago. Maybe we could take care of that before the next calamity befalls us."

"Better eat something yourself, girl, you're pacing like a wildcat." He grinned and nudged her into a seat. "Come, sit down."

They enjoyed hot biscuits and thin slices of ham with a small pile of scrambled eggs. Cherry poured his coffee and some for herself while sending sly glances at him from beneath her half closed lids.

"I do believe you're flirting with me—you are, aren't you?" His desire rising, he felt nervous as a wildcat himself. He really should take her away from here. With El Tigre out there, he'd never feel safe for either of them.

"Only a little flirting, John." She giggled softly as she finished as much breakfast as she could. "If we're going today, I'll get my riding clothes on."

"You wait till I get you up to that line shack."

His threat made her blush furiously. He watched her walk away to change and called after her, "It might be little dicey going out there with that slimy devil lurking about, waiting his chance to jump me." He sighed. "Or you. He's a sneaky sort, a monster full of tricks, but I'd prefer to meet him on the up and up."

But the chance of that was most likely nonexistent. The man liked his cover. John had the healing scar on his shoulder to prove it. Shooting from an ambush was more to El Tigre's liking than an honest fight.

While he waited for Cherry, John went to the corral and saddled Muley, got a burro from another corral, and put the pack saddle on him. The cowboys were gone, lined out for their days work already. He had taken care of that first thing before breakfast. His gaze swept the surrounding area for signs of El Tigre but he saw nothing. He hadn't expected to. "Bastard must be more careful these days." He snorted. "Sure as hell oughta be."

Cherry came swinging out in her riding clothes with a tense little smile on her face. "Everything's ready in the store room." She pointed towards the thickly sided building where most of the supplies were stored.

John hauled out the canvas packs and began loading them onto the pack saddle. He secured the supplies with a tarp, fastened on by a neat, diamond hitch. He led the burro back to Cherry who had Checky saddled and was ready to ride.

"Nice hitch there."

Her compliment made him smile. She knew the pride most riders took in throwing a neat diamond. She mounted and waited for him, her thoughts heavily on what would happen at the line shack. She frequently worried she shouldn't feel this way about a man she wasn't married to, but she did. She'd learned his hands on her body were magic and she craved more of it.

Before they could set out on the trail to the shack, the sound of pounding hooves made them turn about. Larry Price, the cowboy John had shot with the scatter gun, rode into the yard, his horse lathered and blowing. John saw trouble clearly written on his face.

He hurried to the distraught rider. "Why' you ridin' in here, hell for leather that way, what's wrong?"

"Waddie's got hurt! I think he's got a broke leg an' I come for the wagon. Gotta bring him in."

The young man leaped off his horse and started for the pair of light draft horses kept for harness use. John and Cherry rushed to help him, and in short order they had the team and wagon ready, piled with straw and blankets. Booker came to see what was wrong, and John sent him for the doctor.

"I've got to check on Waddie," John told Cherry. "Sorry, girl, we'll go another time." He leaped onto Muley and followed Larry, who drove the wagon team off at a dead run.

Cherry watched them leave the ranch, readily understanding and approving that John would take care of his ranch hand. Ashamed of feeling selfish and disappointed at not being able to lie with him again, she decided to unpack the burro.

As she worked, she daydreamed, wanting to relive the passion between them even though they had just spent a night together in the Rose Hotel. It never seemed to be enough. Would it ever?

As she started to remove the packs from the saddle and put them back in the storage shed, she stopped and reconsidered. Everything was packed and ready. *I'll take the supplies to the shack. I'm armed. I can take care of myself. If I get everything put away, we won't need to bother with it when we do have the chance to go.*

Satisfied with her plan, she grabbed the lead rope of the furry, long-eared burro, patiently waiting with the huge pack tied onto the wooden frame pack saddle he wore. "I hope Waddie will be all right," she murmured. She climbed on her horse and started up the trail leading the burro.

By now, the sun was high in the heavens and a much earlier start would have been wiser. As it was, she would either have to ride back in the dark or spend a long night alone at the line shack. Maybe John would come and find her. She grew excited thinking about meeting him in that isolated place. *He'll be mad as hell at me for coming out here alone.* She planned how she would take the fire out of his anger and blushed at the errant ideas that thought engendered. Shaking her head, she laughed. "Shame on me, I'm all alone and I'm blushing!"

For this late in the year, it was a rather hot day, and it was late afternoon by the time Cherry reached the shack. Hot and tired, she worked quickly to off load the packs and put them inside. She thought about stowing everything in their proper places, but decided it would take too much time. She needed to start back immediately.

John hadn't come and that meant Waddie was more seriously injured than Larry figured. That worried her and made her feel a load of guilt to have ridden way out here in what she now regarded as a silly romantic haze.

She hadn't unsaddled her horse. He'd grazed in the corral along with the burro, while she had stowed the supplies. Tired and ready to leave, she left the line shack to get Checky then gasped to see a slim, dark man standing in her path. Cherry's heart leapt into her throat. She'd been an utter fool to come out here alone—she knew that now.

She held her stance and faced him. "Who are you and what are you doing on my ranch?" she demanded in her most indignant voice. Her heart beat so rapidly she could scarcely breathe. The exotically-dressed man before her seeped evil from his very pores. She knew instantly he was the infamous El Tigre.

Cherry fought her wildly rising panic, waiting for the man to say something. *What a cruel, simpering dandy you are. I'd laugh in your face if you weren't out to kill me.*

His smile reminded her of a poisonous snake. A forked tongue would have suited him well. "*Hola, mi chica,* at last we meet. I look for you, *Chica.* I find you."

As he looked at the beautiful girl with her raven hair and those mysterious purple eyes, he knew he'd never seen anything to equal her. His eyes raked her figure, which was slender and shapely. She nearly reached his height. Pleased she was alone and in his power, he caressed her with his voice.

"I am Matìn Maldonado. There are those who call me, El Tigre, but for you, my beauty, I am only Matín, a man who loves you already." He snaked out his gloved hand and caught her arm.

She moved quickly to slap it away, but his hands, though slim and finely shaped, held her in a vice-like grip and pushed her toward the shack. "You come with me, *mi chica,* we talk."

She heard his amused chuckle and her blood ran cold. But her mind stayed clear. Her hand crept to the pistol she had strapped around her hips.

El Tigre moved smoothly with his other hand to draw his own pistol and level it at her midsection. "No, no, my beautiful one, I take thees gun from you."

She noted his speech had slipped into the more Spanish way of speaking as he stepped close and whipped the gun from her holster.

He tossed her gun into the bushes and Cherry felt the sickness of fear overwhelming her senses. This terrifying man threatened far more than her life. She was sure of that as he whipped his gun in the direction of the shack.

"Come inside weeth me, my lady, I talk weeth you."

His poisonous laugh chilled her bones as she moved slowly and unwillingly toward the shack. *If I go in there, he'll destroy my life. John won't want me after this fiend gets through with me. I'd rather be dead than go through that. I probably will be when he gets done with me.*"

In seeming compliance, Cherry walked ahead of him. Nearing the decrepit door, she threw her body backward against him, hoping to knock him off his feet and get hold of his gun. It was worth any attempt, since being dead was better than what this man had in mind. He fell backward, but quickly recovered his balance.

"*I—ee, carumba! Por Dios!*" It sounded like the scream of a puma and, evading her grasping hand, he aimed a solid kick into her stomach. "Ah, you fight me like thee wildcat. I like—*que mucho!*"

Cherry lay crumpled in pain on the ground, gasping for breath as he grasped her arm. Dragging her towards the shack, he kicked open the door and pulled her limp form inside. She didn't know exactly what he would do, but it would be evil and soul shattering—she knew that much. She tried to think as a thick darkness came over her, clouding her senses.

She awoke to find herself thrown onto that same narrow bunk where she and John had discovered so much about each other that magical rainy night. Terrified and angry with herself for coming out here alone, she faced her deadly fate.

Fighting for the courage she needed to face what lay ahead, she told herself, *I asked for trouble and now I've got it. I may not win, but I'll fight this devil to the end of my life.* And she lay there quietly preparing to do just that.

"Now, *mi amore,* I must see you."

His glittering eyes reflected his rising desire as he moved close to her, grasped her thin, white blouse in his hand, and ripped it off her in one strong pull. His gloating expression at the sight of her bare, heaving breasts sickened her. She gasped in anger, as well as horror, only to see it further excited him.

"*Por dios!*" His low chuckling laugh turned her blood to ice. "You are marvelous and so very beautiful!" He gazed hungrily at her exposed flesh and then grasped her riding skirt, tearing it off her twisting, writhing body. The buttons went flying across the shack.

His visibly rising response to her nakedness made her nauseous. If she died for it, she had to render him helpless. Death would be better than what this slimy creature had in mind.

He flung her riding skirt away, but she got in a few good kicks as he tore the last of her underclothes away. Her boots, decked with short, roweled spurs, were yanked off before she could use those metal points against him.

The cold air against her naked skin underscored her total exposure to this monstrous creature. She heard him gloating at the sight of her female flesh and the glow in his eyes and the lascivious leer in his eyes foretold of what lay ahead.

He removed his jacket and, keeping his other clothes on, pulled a tiny, thin knife and kissed it before her staring eyes. "And now, my lovely one, I kiss you."

He pressed the knife against the skin of her abdomen. A drop of blood sprang out. She screamed.

To her utter disgust, saliva nearly escaped his lips and his erection seemed to explode. "Ah, *sangre rojo!*"

Stung by the horror that he planned to use that tiny knife on her, Cherry gathered all the strength she could manage and kicked him in his disgustingly bulging groin. She got in another good kick and watched him crumple onto the floor in a groaning heap. His moaning and vicious cursing gave her added courage.

As she rose from the bunk to escape, his arm flashed out blindly, attempting to sink his knife into her. "Beetch!" he screamed as she evaded his thrust, pulled herself away from his crumpled form, and made it to the door.

She bolted outside and gasped at the icy night air. She ran to the corral, found her horse, scrambled into the saddle, and headed out. Behind her, a shot rang out and the wind of a bullet whistled past her ear. She kicked her heels into Checky's spotted hide and, riding low in the saddle, raced away into the night.

Out of the dimness, she saw John ride past her at a furious clip. He did not stop at the sight of her or pause to attend her in spite of her nakedness. Seeing him charge back to face El Tigre, she pulled her horse up and turned around.

John had seen her naked body astride the horse in the cold night air and knew she'd met trouble. Nearing the shack, he dismounted, turned Muley away, and crept close, his gun in hand.

The shadow of a slim figure slipped behind a tree. John snapped off a shot at him. In return, he heard the sharp staccato of return fire. The slamming impact as a bullet entered his chest, told him El Tigre had hit his mark. Feeling himself go down, he squeezed off a shot at the furtive figure advancing in the gloom, laughing and gloating.

His sight dimmed as he hit the ground and his last fading thought was that the devil had been victorious after all.

Cherry kicked her bare heels into her horse's flanks, tearing back to find John. After hearing the shots, she knew a dreadful, icy fear. With stunning relief, she saw the dim outline of El Tigre lying on the ground several feet away, no longer a threat. She flung herself off the horse and hunted about for John until she found where he'd fallen. Feeling the warmth of him she searched him for signs of life. She shook him gently, but got no response to her cries. "Oh, God, John, no!"

He uttered a soft moan. With a sudden burst of hope and relief, she struggled with his big body, enough to turn him on his back. But it had grown too dark to see.

"I've got to have some light!" she cried.

She left him and ran into the cabin where she donned her torn clothes and jacket as best she could. She lit the lantern with trembling fingers and grabbed several blankets.

Running outside, she found John and quickly covered him with the blankets. By lantern light, she opened his jacket and shirt enough to see the bullet wound. It was in his right shoulder and far enough from his lungs and heart that he could survive. "I've got to get help for you." But right now, she needed to get him inside or he'd die of the cold from lying on the ground.

Cherry heard a soft groan and, turning toward the form of El Tigre, realized the man wasn't dead. "You evil bastard, I won't help you," she snarled. "I don't care how badly you're wounded!"

The blood had soaked through John's shirt. The warm, sticky ooze flowing from his chest looked so like her father's fatal wound, it frightened her even more. "John, do you hear me?"

He moaned a warning, "Careful, Cherry, that devil's here somewhere." He looked up at her and then his sight faded as he slipped into unconsciousness.

"I think he might be dying, John," she said, but he didn't hear her. She opened his shirt and inspected the wound. It looked clean, but she had to stop the bleeding and quickly. She left him to run back to the shack for the worn sheeting kept to wrap beef when they did some unplanned butchering. She found it, tore it into strips, grabbed another blanket, and ran back to where he lay. She bunched up the clean fabric and pressed it into his wound, working at it until she was satisfied it was the best she could do.

She needed help but hated to leave him. Shivering with cold, she covered him with all the blankets she found and headed for the shack, carrying the lantern.

As she neared it, an arm reached out to encircle her body and a hand covered her mouth. "El Tigre, he no dead, chica my love, but you, you little beetch, soon will be—very soon. I make you promise of that. You will beg for it, my lovely, you will beg for death to take you!"

After the way she'd kicked his manhood, Cherry knew he'd be filled with a deep abiding hatred of her. She was amazed at the depth of his cruelty and wondered what terrible things in his past had driven the man to commit the evil things she'd heard that he'd done.

He pulled her into the shack. "You make light for me—now!" His words dripped with fury. "I wish to see you die, my lovely."

She shivered in horror. John lay wounded outside in the cold, dying, and she would meet her death in some hideous, sadistic way here in a lonely line shack with a sick, destroying monster.

CHAPTER 27

Cherry turned up the wick of the lantern and the flare of light further illuminated the shack's dingy interior. Though El Tigre had taken a bullet, she feared he had the strength to carry out his evil promises. When she saw blood drip from his fingertips onto the floor, she felt a surge of hope. Maybe the evil soul would weaken and die before he succeeded in his plans.

She would pretend to comply with him for a while. Her goal was to keep him away from John, should he moan out loud. Any sound from him would draw the killer to where he lay wounded and bleeding. She prayed she'd done enough to stop his bleeding and keep his wounded body warm enough to survive the night.

"Come, *mi amore*, I wish to look once more upon your wondrous beauty before I destroy it—oh so very slowly." El Tigre gestured at the lantern, and Cherry raised it high enough to satisfy the man. Partially clad now, she played for time, desperately seeking any small chance against this fiendish devil.

Keeping herself busy also held his attention at bay. She set a fire in the small stove to ward off the chills creeping over her. El Tigre watched her, but made no move to stop her.

She believed he wanted her, but seemed to be afraid of her. She saw the wariness in his eyes and in the way he watched her every move. Her mind worked frantically, seeking some way to help John and fend off the enraged killer.

Apparently, he fancied himself very refined and skilled, but to Cherry, this egotistical monster was nothing more than another face of evil. To El Tigre, human life merely meant money earned as he snuffed out someone's existence.

He moved closer to her. Head up, chin out, she stood her ground, waiting. "What are you doing out here in this area? It's our ranch and off limits to strangers." Those words sounded utterly ridiculous, even to her.

"Nothing is off limits to me, *Chica,* nothing—*nada!*" He spit out the words, reached for her, and pulled her into his arms, though she held herself stiff and unyielding.

"Let go of me, you sick bastard!" Then she tried a different tack. "If you go away now, I will say nothing, I promise you." She tried to sound convincing, but her voice was filled with the ice she felt in her veins. It matched her hatred for this man. Though she'd never shot a man in her life, if she could find a way, she'd kill this hideous creature without a backward glance.

She changed her tactics again, deciding to play the helpless female. It was only a small chance. Matín was no fool, but in her desperation, she had to try.

Forcing herself to change and soften in his arms, she let him hold her tight against his erection. Vomit rising into her throat, she spied the man's blood draining onto her skin and torn clothes. His ragged breathing, as his lips nuzzled down into her tattered blouse, gave her a small bit of hope. His passion had risen to a high degree once again and she saw her opportunity.

She let her body slump helplessly against him, while twisting herself enough to get her hand on the deadly little pistol she'd seen in the back of his waistband. Struggling, she reached it, shoved it against his side and pulled the trigger. She felt his body stiffen and heard his deep, gurgling scream.

"Ayee! You beetch!" He crumpled to the floor. Somehow, he found enough strength to grab his other sidearm and raise it toward her, eager to pump a bullet into her body.

As Cherry stood, staring at the raised gun and waiting for her end, El Tigre bent his finger around the trigger and a loud blast filled the shack.

Puzzled and shocked when no bullet entered her flesh, she felt light headed and wanted to collapse in a dead faint. But El Tigre had changed, his eyes closed, his body flaccid. She turned to see John, haggard and pale, weaving just inside the door, his gun smoking.

He had managed to drag himself that far and shoot the devil, just as he was about to kill her. She cried at the sight of him. "Oh John, thank God, you're alive. You've saved me!" In the dimness of the lantern light, he was pale as moonlight and weaving. She worked her way around the form of the killer and rushed to him. "Are you all right?"

"I don't know, darlin'."

She helped him step over the curled, limp form of the wounded Mexican, who lay gasping on the floor. John sat on the bunk, barely able to remain upright. Fresh blood had soaked through his clothes, but she kept him there long enough to clean and bind his wound once again. Then she laid him down on the bunk.

"I'd best go find those blankets." She hesitated, not wanting to leave him, and glanced over at El Tigre. "Looks like he's dead or dying. Can't say I'm sorry about it."

Shivering at the sight of the dead man, she felt much of her anger dissipate, seeing that John still lived. She ran her hands through his hair, smoothing it back from his face, and fought against her unshed tears. There was no time for that. "You came in time to save my life."

"You saved mine, too."

After he passed out again, she ran outside to find the blankets and bring them inside. Damp from the cold, she held them to the stove for a while before putting them over John. She then threw more wood on the fire and felt the lifesaving heat fill the little shack.

El Tigre lay still and pale. She was sure he had died and wanted to drag his body outside. But she worried he would come to life, reach up, and grab her leg. She ought to bash his head in with a chunk of fire wood just to be sure he was dead. But now that her fight was over, a heavy feeling of exhaustion crept over her.

It would have been easy to faint dead away after all that had happened, but she didn't have that luxury. A long night lay before them, but because she had made the foolish decision to bring supplies up here, they now had plenty of food, enough wood for the fire, and kerosene for the lantern. With a rueful shrug of her shoulders, she tended John as best she could and kept the fire burning for warmth.

He slept and Cherry settled into a chair to wait out a long and terrifying night. She would ride for help in the morning.

But El Tigre was not dead. He lay quietly on the cold floor, knowing his life slowly ebbed away. He didn't wish to die alone and his mind plotted some vicious way to take these two with him to the hell that lay beyond. His mind spun with ways to kill them both and it lent him strength, kept him alive.

His gun lay where he'd dropped it. *Stupid woman—never pick it up. Maybe good I never make love with her. She no deserve fine man like me. I gut shoot her, take many days die—bitch suffer, big man, too.* He moved his hand carefully, making no sound.

Sitting in the chair, exhausted and half asleep Cherry saw nothing and heard nothing. She only listened for John's voice in the night.

Matin's fingers closed around the cold metal of the gun, comforting him. His vision, limited and fading, saw the woman slumped in the chair with her eyes closed. He heard the ragged breathing of the big man on the bunk and believed him unconscious. *He no stop me now.*

El Tigre scarcely had enough breath anymore. His end was near, but the hatred within his mind gave him enough strength to kill those two, just as they had killed him. He raised his gun towards the sleeping woman, aiming for her stomach. He cocked it and heard the metallic click. *Did she hear it? No, she sleeps on.* He smiled as he curled his finger around the trigger. A loud blast was the last thing he ever heard.

Hearing the cocking of the gun, John jolted awake. His heart raced as he saw what El Tigre had in mind. With all the strength he could muster, he found his gun and pulled the trigger, praying he had one more bullet in the chamber. He saw Cherry scream and leap to her feet before he blacked out again.

"John? What happened?" She looked at the fresh blood oozing from El Tigre's chest and understood. "Oh God, he wasn't dead." The light from the lantern had faded, dying for lack of kerosene, but she saw the body lying on the floor. Shivering in distaste, she checked his neck for a pulse, cringing at having to touch him. "He is now. Thank God he is!" She looked over at John lying back on the bunk. "You're a tough one you are."

"I couldn't let him get you, my darlin'," he whispered, wanting to hold her and comfort her, but he fell back on the bunk. His wound burned like fire, and he had lost a lot of blood.

"I should have pulled him outside before, but I felt so weak," Cherry said. "You can bet I'll drag his rotten carcass out of here right now, if it's the last thing I ever do. That sick monster will not befoul this shack another moment."

She grabbed his fancy tooled boots and dragged the man toward the door. He was not a large man, but heavy enough. She reached the door, opened it, hauled his limp corpse outside onto the gravel and dirt, and left it there.

She returned to the shack and closed the door. Still fearful of the man lying on the gravel outside, Cherry shoved a chair under the handle. She built up the fire and refilled the lantern before looking down at John with tears in her eyes. "Please, John, tell me you'll make it?" she begged him "I couldn't stand to lose you.""

"If you've got any whiskey in that stuff you packed, get it and pour it into my wounds," he said, though they both knew it would burn like hell.

She dug around and came up with a half bottle of the vile stuff John and Waddie had enjoyed on their first trip to this shack. She removed the bloodied dressings and looked at the wound in the light of the lantern. "I guess it looks clean enough, and if the bullet went on through, you should be all right." She turned him and found an exit wound, a ragged hole, far up on the back his shoulder. "Yes it did, thank you, God."

Pouring the whiskey into the hole in the front of his chest, she wanted to cry at the pain it caused him. "Sorry John!"

"Keep on. You're doing just fine." He gritted his teeth at the hot, flaming pain the rot-gut whiskey made as it burned its way into the bullet wound. After a while, she turned him enough to pour some of it into the hole in his back. He held his breath again at the fire of the stinging, burning, cleansing alcohol. After that, she gave him a hefty slug to swallow.

"Damn, this stuff isn't fit to clean a wound," he muttered.

Cherry was able to laugh a bit while she tore more strips off the cloths she'd found to cover the injury, binding them with fresh strips from the clean beef wrappers. He was pale and dripping with sweat when she finished. With tears in her eyes at his suffering, she prayed she had done enough.

"You've done a fine job, Cherry." He sank back on the bunk and let himself go into unconsciousness or sleep, she didn't know which. In the morning, she would get the boys and a wagon to bring him home.

After putting more wood in the little stove, she made a pot of coffee. It had to be morning soon. She looked out the window, but saw no lightning of the eastern sky. Settling back in her chair, she rested.

CHAPTER 28

Daylight came slowly, and John still slept. Cherry ate a little and drank some coffee before she went out and found her still-saddled horse. She regretted that he had spent the night that way, but she hadn't been able to tend to him.

She woke John. "I'm going for help."

Before she left him, she removed the soiled, bloody dressings she had placed over his wound in the night, cleaned it front and back with more of the rot-gut alcohol, and redressed it. She added what small bits of wood remained to the little stove, set water beside him, and laid on enough blankets to keep him warm.

"You are something, Cherry," he rasped. The tears she saw lurking in his eyes said more than his words.

It would be a long time before she got back and they both knew it. After throwing a tarp over the dead killer, she rode away with great misgivings. She hated to leave John alone, but it couldn't be helped.

ᏨᏒᏨᏒ

It was early afternoon when she reached the ranch. She found Booker, the only one available. She explained everything to him and then ran to the house to tell Margarita what she needed. The woman, shocked at the sight of Cherry's torn, disheveled clothing, hurried to help. After learning what had happened, she uttered a prayer for Señor John.

Decently clad again, Cherry met Booker by the bunkhouse. He said he would ride for the doctor and had sent young Manny out for the boys. "Waddie's in the bunkhouse," he added. "The doctor was out to set his leg, said he'll be all right in a few weeks."

Cherry entered the bunkhouse to find the young cowboy lying in his bunk, his leg tied with slim rods of wood and wrapped heavily with cloth strips to hold it all in place.

She went to him. "How are you, Waddie?"

"I'm fine ma'am, sorry for bein' so clumsy. It just happened when I wasn't lookin'." His face flushed red as he looked up at her. "I heard you sayin' out there that John's been shot. I hope he makes it, Miss Cherry, we'll all be pullin' for him. He's a right good man."

"El Tigre shot him, and he almost killed me, too. John's got a chance and I'm praying he makes it." She turned to go. "I have to go back to him now. Might be two of you laid up in here." Then she felt a cold smile twist her lips. "We got that killer and he's gone for good."

She left the bunk house and hurried over to Booker. "We need to hitch a team to the wagon, and I'll drive it back to John. Keep the doc here and tell Manny to send the boys to the first line shack, will you?"

"Yes, I will ma'am, and when there's time, I've got something to say."

"Later then," she said and ran to catch up two horses used for harness.

Booker helped her get them hitched to the wagon. Margarita brought out a pile of blankets to throw over the big pile of straw they'd put in for padding against the rough ride back with the wounded man.

She stood, crying and wringing her hands. "*Por Dios,* I pray for him!"

"Thanks Margarita, I love him so!" She slapped the reins over the team and sent them off at a rapid trot.

God, she was tired. She hadn't slept for so long, she couldn't even remember it. But she kept going on raw nerves and fear for John's life. He filled her heart. She loved him, and feared she would lose him as she'd lost everyone else. Toughening her spine, she urged the team to a faster pace over the rough ground, determined to save him.

಼಼಼

It was late afternoon, edging on toward evening, when she reached the shack. Praying she'd find him alive, she shoved open the door and dashed inside. She saw nothing in the dim interior and needed to let her eyes adjust. At first it was eerily silent, then a soft chuckle reached her ears. Her heart leaped with relief.

"Hey darlin', I'm right here waiting for you."

He was propped up sitting on the bunk.

She rushed to his side. "How'd you get sitting up like that?"

He shot her a grin. "I'm bad off, my darling, but not dead. I had to move a bit for comfort. I think that rot-gut whiskey you poured in the wounds helped a little—when it quit burning me alive like ten devils, that is."

Her major worry was of infection. His wound had bled out clean before the whiskey went in, but his eyes had a certain brightness that the dimness of the shack couldn't hide. Alarm struck clear through her, although she did her best to hide it.

"The boys are on the way here to bring you back to the house, and Booker's gone for the doctor. I brought the wagon." She studied him intently, praying she would not find signs of a deadly infection setting in. "Let me see your wound. I must clean it before you have to ride in that wagon. It has a lot of straw and blankets to make it softer, but it'll be tough on you."

She removed his soiled dressings and used the whiskey to clean his wound once again. It hurt him, she knew, but it just might save his life.

After a time, she heard the pounding of hooves and ran to the door as her crew rode up. "Oh, thank God, you're here!"

They quickly dismounted, threw their reins to the ground, and followed her into the shack.

"How's the boss doin?" Larry asked. His worried face told her of his respect for the man who had become his foreman and let him keep his job.

"He's awake and moving himself around, but I'm worried his wound is going bad." She rushed back to John's side before turning to face the men that entered. "I cleaned his wound a while ago, but again wouldn't hurt. Maybe a couple of you could help me."

Larry helped her move John and turned pale as the man grimaced and cursed beneath his breath when she poured the last of the whiskey into his wound. After another good wrap, the cowboys got him to his feet and half dragged him out to the wagon. His face was gray with pain and drenched with sweat from the effort, but they never stopped until he lay on blankets, nestled in deep straw. Cherry climbed in beside him and the wagon started moving.

Larry drove, hurrying, yet careful to avoid the roughest spots as best he could in the moonlit darkness. Cherry believed her man unconscious. Fresh blood seeped from his wound as they traveled over the untamed landscape. There was no trail or road to this particular line shack since it was usually reached on horseback.

Facing the loss of this man she had come to love, she felt her tired, worn body betray her and she broke into tears. She lay down next to John, sobbing and hoping he didn't hear it. A couple of the boys had stayed behind to bury the outlaw and bring in his fine black stallion, John's horse, Muley, all the tack, and the burro.

They reached the ranch long after dark. Cherry was gratified to see Doctor Coogan's horse tied to the hitching rail, standing patiently. She uttered a silent prayer that the man could bring John through this gunshot wound. Nearing exhaustion, she crawled out of the wagon and ran unsteadily to the house to find him.

Dr. Coogan met her at the door and they hurried to John's side. After a precursory look, the doctor instructed the cowboys to bring him in and be careful about it. He and Margarita had a bed prepared right in the front room and it struck Cherry eerily that it was the same one her father had died in.

Larry took charge, directing the men as they lifted the wounded foreman gently on a blanket and brought him into the house. The doctor went to work immediately while Cherry hovered over him offering assistance.

He glanced over at her. "Young woman, you are on your last legs. Get her to bed before she collapses," he told Margarita. "Or I'll have two patients here, and one's enough."

He gave some comfort to Cherry before Margarita took her away. "This man is very strong. Try not to worry. I'll do my best for him and you'll help him more by being strong and rested after I leave. He's going to need a lot of care for the next few weeks."

She nodded, went to her bed, and collapsed on it. Margarita came in later and covered her, tenderly crooning, *"Mi Pobrecita,"* before she left to help the doctor.

Coogan worked over the injury, cleaned it, and shook his head at the ragged exit wound in John's back. "Thank

God the bullet went on through and missed the major blood vessels."

Margarita listened but didn't understand the bulk of his murmurings. Wringing her hands, she brought fresh linens for him to tear into dressings. Larry refused to leave. He sat in the big room, hoping to find a way to help the man who had been a friend when he'd needed one.

Long after midnight Cherry awoke and came to John's bedside, a long robe wrapped about her body. She searched the doctor's eyes for the answer to her unspoken question. *Will he live?* She couldn't keep the fear and doubt from her eyes.

He nodded. "We'll know in another day or two. He has some fever and a small amount of infection in the wound. We must watch for septicemia. It'll be a fight to save him. Gunshot wounds are particularly nasty, but he's a strong one." He held out hope without empty promises, which left her encouraged, but with considerable anxiety.

"Thank you, Doctor," she whispered, remembering that he had said he would need to stay another day. To her that meant John was in for a hellish fight to live. "You can use my father's bed if you need some sleep. I'll keep watch over him."

ᥱᎧᥱᎧ

She never went far from John's bedside.

"You awake, John?" She looked down at him, desperate to see the steely gray of those eyes once again, but he slept on, his face flushed with fever. Frequent, incoherent, and disconnected bits of speech escaped his lips, but she didn't understand a word.

In the brightness of the morning, he awakened. His face red and flushed, he looked at her with glazed eyes and didn't know her. He uttered fevered words again and again, "Aw, Gov, why send me so far, my horse is due to foal and I won't be..."

The gibberish meant nothing to her, but spoke of a part of his life unknown to her. Hearing his slurred muttering, she screamed for Coogan. "Doctor, he's out of his head!"

"Not surprising, Cherry, give him another day. I believe he'll come out of it." He patted her on the head as if she were a child. "I see how you regard the man. Looks like you've found someone, and you're not ready to lose him, too."

She nodded. Her tears began to flow though she tried to stop them. "Yes, I love him dearly. We plan to be married."

"That's wonderful. We need good people like this man in our community." He placed his hand on John's forehead. "He's still burning with fever, but that sometimes helps the healing." He removed most of the coverings and shrugged, having done all he knew to do. "We'll have to wait it out."

Margarita kept food ready and fed everyone who came to call. The Bents came to see John, but Katie went directly to the bunkhouse to visit Waddie. Cherry noticed Mrs. Bent nodding her head and smiling at Katie's action.

Booker sidled up to her. "I'd like to tell you somethin', Miss. Shoulda said it long ago, but I'm sayin' it now."

She tried to give him her attention. "Yes Booker, what is it,"

He drew her away from listening ears. "I knew what happened that day your father was killed." He hung his head, his face flushed. "I was in the bunkhouse fixin' vittles for later when I heard yellin', an' noise. Right soon, I heard a shot comin' from inside the barn and in a bit, I saw Link come roarin' out and take off on his horse. I was always sure he's the one that done it, Miss Cherry."

"Why didn't you tell me sooner?" her voice rose with frustration while she fought her anger at his secrecy.

"I don't rightly know—Link was always real good to me and give me this job. It wasn't right of me, and I'm real sorry for holdin' back on it." He shuffled his feet. "Sorry about the boss there, too. He did right by all of us when Link was set to burn us out that a way."

"Thanks Booker. I suppose it doesn't make any difference now that Link's gone." She patted him on the shoulder, too tired to worry about his keeping her father's killing a secret. "It's all right. It won't change anything, but I'm glad to know the truth, and I thank you for it."

Cherry didn't spend time worrying over what Link had done. It was too late for that, but she would think about it later, hoping John could help her decide what to do, if anything.

Hettie came to call and stayed to help. "He looks real bad, but he's tougher than a leather boot. I'm sure he'll make it." The way she flashed her gold-shaded eyes, hoping she'd believe that, made Cherry smile.

Neighbors came by to visit and finally after three days of semi-consciousness, John awoke.

The doctor smiled. "His fever's down. He'll recover with good nursing care and you'll need to see to that part."

Cherry went wild with joy. She'd kissed John's pale face over and over with tears running down her cheeks.

Hettie scoffed. "You're making a big baby out of that man!"

They laughed together and Margarita hugged them both. Waddie had improved enough to come into the house, his leg heavily wrapped, hobbling rather well on rudely made crutches, to see John.

"We're a fine bunch of cripples," he said. He and John had a good laugh before he limped his way back to the bunkhouse.

CHAPTER 29

A few days later, Cherry heard the sound of horses trotting into the ranch yard. Looking out the window, she saw a fine, large carriage with trim that looked like silver.

It was drawn by a matched set of fine, glossy bays, very grand in their silver mounted harness. She stood with Hettie, looking out the window, amazed at seeing something so fine pull into her ranch yard.

"Well, what do you suppose this is all about?"

An older gentleman descended from the conveyance. He was a well-dressed man with a graying handlebar moustache and a wide gray felt hat. He looked very impressive indeed and gave off an air of importance as he headed to her door. A nicely dressed younger gentleman, with a fine, thin moustache accompanied the older gent. He carried a leather briefcase that bulged at the sides.

Cherry opened her door and stood waiting as the men approached. The older man, tall and sharp-eyed with sandy, gray-streaked hair, walked with a purposeful stride as he mounted the steps to meet her. "Good day ma'am, I've come to see my nephew, John Carmona. I understand he's been wounded and is recovering here at your ranch."

He stared as if appraising her and Cherry decided, by the faint smile on his lips, that the man liked what he saw.

Cherry held the door open for both men. "Yes sir, he was and is. He's right inside. Won't you come in?"

The older man took her hand as he entered. "I'm Nathan Murphy, ma'am, and this is my assistant, Timothy Haynes. May I see the man in question?"

"Nice to meet you both. Yes, certainly." She led him to the bedside and gave John a quizzical look, her eyebrows raised. "John dear, there's someone here to see you."

John looked up in surprise. A wide smile spread across his pale features. "Uncle! How'd you know about this?"

His uncle sat in the chair Cherry placed beside the bed. Mr. Haynes took a chair farther back, ready to be of assistance.

"I'm privy to a few things that happen in this territory." Nathan shook John's hand as he took in the wide white dressings. "You look to be on the mend, son." He gestured at his heavy leather briefcase. "I brought a few things with me. With the telegraph situation being what it is, I thought it best this way."

John had more important things on his mind. "Uncle, please meet my bride to be, Miss Cherry Bender." He turned to face her. "Dear, I'd like you to meet my uncle, Nathan Murphy, currently our Territorial Governor."

Frozen in shock at finding John had yet another secret about himself that he hadn't managed to tell her, Cherry stammered a reply. "Y—yes, ah—pleased to meet you, sir." She gave John a look that said plenty and extended her hand to his uncle, but couldn't find further words at the moment. '

She brought Hettie forth. "This is my neighbor, Hettie Jamison."

The governor took her hand in his and looked her in the eye. "Pleased to meet you too, ma'am. Actually, I'm glad you're here, Mrs. Jamison, I have something to say to both you ladies but it can wait a bit until I see how my nephew is doing." He looked back at John and shook his head. "You never fail to surprise me, son. Congratulations to you both on your forthcoming marriage." He shook his nephew's hand again and kissed Cherry's cheek.

Then he settled back and turned to the women. "I have rather good news for both you young ladies. John sent several ore samples from your properties to confirm what we had already learned from other samples sent from this area. They had previously been sent to the assayer by a gentleman from this area, a man named Harry Bourdain.

"We also had a letter of complaint from your father, stating his suspicions of illegal mining interests on your land. That was in addition to his complaints of cattle rustling and vandalism, Miss Bender.

"When we learned what had been found, we took notice. There'll likely be some silver or gold on these claims, but the mineral, Molybdenum, in particular, drew our interest. You see it's in the national interest to keep close track of this particular element.

"It's new to manufacturing, but will be of extreme importance in years to come, and we are required to monitor the locations as well as the mining of it."

"How does that affect us?" Cherry asked, needing answers. At long last she was about to learn the truth about why their ranch had been under siege.

"John has found deposits on both ranches. Mrs. Jamison's is the larger mine, while yours, Miss Bender, is somewhat smaller, but also valuable. In a few weeks, men will come here to discuss the mining and mineral rights with both you young ladies." He smiled broadly, always pleased to bear welcome news. "I hasten to add it will be nicely profitable for each of you."

Hettie said little, but things had been tough for her since her husband's death.

"It's a Godsend, huh?" Cherry said as she hugged her friend.

The young woman nodded and fought her tears. She took the governor's hand and said, "Thank you sir, for this news."

Cherry did the same.

Margarita called them for dinner and they all enjoyed a fine repast of roasted beef with garlic laced potatoes, a great array of vegetables, and *boletas* with flan and apple pie for dessert. The governor and his aide praised her skills, and with a flushed face she muttered, "*muchas gracias, señores.*"

❧❧❧

The governor left the next day, as did Hettie. Cherry had patiently waited for a moment alone with John.

She wanted answers and gave no quarter for his injury. "So, mister, why have you kept so much from me? Why do that?"

"Darling, I'm not much for talk or laying out my personal life, and I never thought that who my uncle might be should make a difference," he said, although he knew full well it did, but had failed to mention it anyway.

"Sometimes I wonder if I'll ever know everything about you."

He brushed a straying curl from her face. "You'll know more than most, my darling."

A giggle escaped her. "When we can be together again is another question and I don't know the answer to that either."

"Well, I'm better every day, every hour, and I'm pretty near ready for that, too." He tried to grab her, but she shied away. "When are we getting married, then?"

"As soon as possible. Could we live at your hacienda? Waddie can manage this ranch and if he marries Katie, they could live right here," she added. "I've lived in this same place all my life, John. I'd like to travel, maybe see things, something or someplace different."

"As soon as I can stand up as your husband, we'll do whatever you'd like. I have money enough and some time coming."

"I'll get it put together with Hettie. I can't wait."

"Anything else, dearest Cherry?"

"Does that wonderful hacienda of yours have a big, wide bed?"

The End

About the Author

Ramona Forrest is a retired RN. She keeps busy writing novels—and traveling whenever possible. Forrest has resided in the back country of Arizona, assisted in round-ups, worked in Saudi Arabia, and has had the pleasure of traveling extensively. She now resides in Phoenix and spends much time in gardening, writing, entertaining friends, and family.